TIGHT SPOT

NASHVILLE STEEL BOOK THREE

STACEY LYNN

Tight Spot

Nashville Steel Series

Book Three

Stacey Lynn

Content Editing: My Brother's Editor

Proofreading: Virginia Tesi Carey, TK Rapp

Cover Design: Shanoff Designs

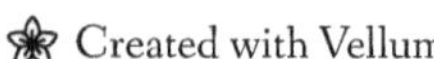

PROLOGUE

DAWSON

FEW PEOPLE HAD the code to my house and the ability to get through security at the front of my neighborhood in Brentwood. Considering I lived in a neighborhood with several of my teammates, the doorbell ringing as I got out of the shower made me think it could have been one of them.

Except I hadn't invited anyone over, and everyone knew never to show up unannounced.

I bought a ridiculous eight thousand square foot home when I only needed a tenth of the space to live in because I liked being alone, and space gave me peace. It wasn't even the house, but the two acres of land that gave me privacy and room to not feel enclosed.

I wrapped the towel around my body, tucked it in at my hip, and was heading down the stairs when my phone buzzed in my hand and the doorbell ringing turned to a furious pounding. Fucking hell. They'd shatter the glass at this point.

My sister's name flashed on my phone with an incoming call. Mystery solved.

"Damn it."

The day I gave her the code and the go-ahead with security at the front gate to always be allowed entrance was only one of my mistakes when it came to her. I made a mental note to fix that as soon as I could kick her out this time.

"I'm coming, damn it!" I shouted loud enough so she'd hear outside.

The call ended, and the pounding stopped.

My hair was dripping. Water was rolling down my back and chest. I white-knuckled my grip on my towel.

If Crystal was here, shit was about to get ugly, and I did not need this, or her antics, in my life right before my team was headed out of town for one of our most important games of the season.

She came with baggage, both the literal and figurative type.

She was visible through the glass door, a set of Gucci luggage piled around her.

I dropped my chin to my chest, stared at the marble flooring, and braced myself.

Gucci luggage was an upgrade which meant she'd blown through whatever money I already gave her and any sugar daddy dumb enough to trust her.

Awesome.

"What are you doing here?" I was blocking the doorway, leaning against the frame with my fisted hand at my towel and holding the door open.

She shoved right into me. I was forced to reach for her to steady myself or step back if I didn't want the towel to fall and have my sister see all of me.

"Happy New Year to you, too, Dawsy." She lifted her sunglasses off her eyes and gave me a quick scan. "You should probably get dressed before you answer the door. Can you get my luggage? They're kind of heavy." She was halfway to the kitchen as she asked.

"Can I get dressed first?" I muttered and closed the door.

She didn't answer.

Re-securing my towel, I found her exactly where I figured she'd be. In the wine fridge, perusing the bottles and wrinkling her nose at each one.

"Do you have anything nicer?"

I drank red wine on occasion but never needed anything more than a fifty-dollar bottle of wine to be satisfied.

My sister, somehow, believed anything under a hundred was beneath her.

"No, Crystal. I don't have nicer wine on hand in case you show up on my doorstep with enough luggage for a month. What are you doing here?"

She scrunched up her nose at a bottle of chardonnay, but it must have been good enough for the moment because she grabbed the electric opener on the counter. "Lorenzo kicked me out of my apartment."

The apartment he probably paid for until his wife found out he had some mistress and lost her shit on both her husband and Crystal. It wasn't the first time.

"Am I going to have to pay off another scorned wife?"

When it came to Crystal, she had no morals, no values, no concept of respecting anyone's marriage, and hadn't worked a job outside pretending she was a social media influencer since she failed out of college.

She'd become the spitting image of our mother, and I detested her very presence as much as I still hoped she would change.

"Probably not." She shrugged and poured her first glass. She'd have two bottles gone before I had to get to the practice field. "You didn't bring my stuff in."

"I'll get it."

Because I'd give her anything. Even if it killed me.

An hour later, I'd brought all of Crystal's luggage in and moved it to the main floor guest bedroom. I was dressed to get to the practice field where I played for the Nashville Steel. We had an away game tomorrow in Raleigh, and today's practice would be light before I would need to come back, grab something to eat and change for the flight out.

Shame.

I could have used a heavy workout day to unload the stress Crystal's unannounced presence brought.

After a quick search, I found her outside, tanning in the sun despite the fact it was January in Tennessee, and it was only sixty degrees outside. It wasn't normal weather, and it certainly wasn't hot, but there she was, sipping her wine, bottle in a chiller next to her, wearing a string bikini, and holding her phone away from her face and snapping selfies.

My sister was gorgeous. Grabbed attention from every male as soon as she walked into a room or bar or club. Since she was only two years younger than me, all my friends had wanted her.

In both high school and college.

It was too bad her beauty didn't go beyond skin deep. Any good things on the inside shriveled and died as soon as our mom had an affair, ditched not only our dad and the house we'd grown up in our entire lives, but her children as well.

But long before that happened, I'd made a promise to my dad to always take care of her, and I wasn't a man who went back on his word, painful as it was to keep it.

He'd been a pilot, gone a lot more than he was home, but he wasn't absent. We grew up with daily phone calls and nightly games of finding where he was on maps he'd set up all over his home office. We'd put push pins in them every time he flew somewhere new and we'd play countdown games until he came back home. When he was home, we had him. All of his attention, whether it was my football or hockey games, Crystal's dance or cheer competitions. Laughter over dinners. Board game nights. He'd mow the lawn and sit one of us on his lap on the riding mower and always, always, freely and openly gave our mom affection.

Until that fateful day he caught his wife sleeping with the neighbor. After that, all fond memories of time with my dad were just that. Memories. He might as well have left us that day as well for as little as we saw him after.

After Crystal drained three credit cards he opened for her, totaling sixty thousand dollars in debt, and then ghosted him for a year, he was done with her, but I still couldn't let the promise I gave him when I was a little boy go.

I opened the sliding door and peeked my head outside. "Hey."

She smiled into her phone and took a picture. "Yes?" She stared at her screen, treating me more like the help than the one person in our life who hadn't abandoned her.

I was used to it.

"I have an away game this weekend."

"Have fun."

"Want to come?" There was a time she never missed one. Sure, I covered the flights and the tickets and the hotel rooms, but she'd always been there.

"I'm good here." She laid her head back on the lounger and from here, I could see her skin covered in goose bumps from the cold. She'd do anything to get a follow, even freeze. "I've just been so stressed lately. I need the rest."

Sure she did. Ruining marriages was a full-time job for her.

Lucrative considering she usually walked away with some hush money.

"Fine. I'll be back after practice."

She was back to staring at her phone. I gave her time to respond.

Wasn't surprised when I didn't get one.

New Year's Eve.

My team was at The Honky Tonk, a popular country bar on Nashville's Broadway Street. The single guys like to go there after we won games, usually to sit and be seen in the VIP section, take home women or make out with them there or wherever.

I rarely joined them.

Country music wasn't my scene. Most game nights I was too damn sore to do much other than sit in my sauna and watch a movie with an ice pack on whatever body part had been pummeled the worst during the game.

Tonight was no exception. We'd flown to Raleigh on Friday night. Saturday, we did a quick walk-through on their field before having a team dinner, watched film in the hotel's conference room and then lights out by ten. We woke up, ate, played the game, and went straight from their field to the airport.

The sun was already setting by the time I turned down the street that would take me to my neighborhood and my sauna was calling my name.

My phone rang, and I glanced at the CarPlay screen on my Tahoe.

Security. Fantastic.

"Hello?"

"Hello, Mr. Butler. This is Shannon calling from the security station."

"What's up?"

"We received a noise complaint from your neighbors this evening and I know it's New Year's Eve, so that's to be expected, but two of our other security guards thought you were out of town tonight. Need us to go check on the place?"

Would have been nice if they would have checked the place before calling. What was I going to do on a normal day?

Except this wasn't a normal day or night.

This was Crystal.

"I'm pulling into the front security post right now and have family in town. I'll be home in a few minutes and will shut it down. Please tell my neighbors I've taken care of it."

"Will do, Mr. Butler. Thank you."

"Yep." I stabbed at the End Call button on the screen and fisted the steering wheel.

Goddamn, Crystal. Two acres of land, granted it was because my yard was deep and not overly wide, but what in the hell was she pulling where I was getting noise complaints at seven o'clock at night?

Question answered as soon as I turned onto my street.

"Fucking hell." A party. She was having a goddamn party.

There were so many cars parked in my driveway and on the street out front, I had to drive through my own front yard to get close enough to the garage. Lamborghinis. Ferraris. A McLaren and two G-Wagons took up a few of the spaces. It could have been my team's parking garage for as wealthy as the cars were, but how in the hell had she found the richest people of Tennessee already?

"Jesus fuck." I slammed my driver's door and jogged up to the front door. It was unlocked, not a surprise, and I soon found myself in a crush of people decked in cowboy boots, Wrangler jeans, and my ears bleeding from the country music blasting through my home stereo. Gold and black decorations hung from the ceiling and every piece of available furniture and oh...she had to be kidding me...

There was a girl, legs spread, one thrown over the back of my tan leather couch. All I saw was leather and flesh and a guy still wearing a black shirt on top of her.

"Hey." I grabbed the guy on the couch by the back of his T-shirt and tore him off the girl he was actually fucking on my couch. "Get the fuck out of here."

His dick, wet, smacked against his stomach. Oh god. I was going to puke.

"Hey!" the girl cried out, covering her tits with his cowboy hat. "What was that for?"

"Get out of my goddamn house. Now."

I was ready to tear them apart limb by limb. My face must have shown it because they both scrambled up, grabbing clothes and covering naked body parts faster than I snatched the football out of thin air.

Fucking kill me.

I cupped my hands around my mouth and lost my absolute shit. "Crystal!"

She had to be kidding me.

Of course she wasn't.

Crystal was on the hot mess express train, and until I grew a pair of balls and did what my parents had done years ago, I was along for the ride.

For better or for worse.

Yee-freaking-haw.

CHAPTER 1
DAWSON

SIX WEEKS. She'd been here for less than two months and this time, I was done. D.O.N.E. Done with my sister.

Giving her money was one thing. Taking an unknown amount of ibuprofen to deal with the headaches she caused was workable.

Spending a night in county jail because my sister was a batshit crazy freaking lunatic?

Unacceptable.

I slammed my front door behind me. I needed a shower. Wash away the stench from the bar the night before. I hadn't been able to congratulate my teammate, Davis, or his girlfriend Maggie on a killer first showing on stage singing live music because my sister had, once again, caused a scene to make the night all about her.

I stunk like stale beer, piss, and vomit, thanks to the drunken assholes that had been hauled in at two o'clock in the morning.

And as I walked into my kitchen, Crystal was there, showered, made up, sipping what was most likely a mimosa, and smiled. Right before her nose scrunched up as she took in my wrinkled clothes.

"You're late. You said you'd take me shopping today, and we need to get going."

I dropped my keys to the counter and stared at her. "Are you serious?"

"Stores open soon."

She was kidding. Had to be absolutely joking. I'd laugh, but the look on her face told me she was one hundred percent serious.

"I spent the night in jail over your bullshit last night, Crystal."

"I know. That's why I said you need to shower."

She was right. I needed a shower. I needed a damn minute to calm down before I picked up my own sister by her skinny ass and chucked her straight through my glass front door.

"You're a fucking piece of work," I mumbled, but she was back to staring at her phone screen, ignoring me.

I headed up the stairs toward my bedroom, and my phone rang in my hand.

"Damn it." This day kept getting worse, and I wasn't sure that could happen after being arrested less than twenty-four hours ago. "Hey, Dad."

"Tell me what I'm seeing on the news is false. An over exaggeration. Something. Anything, Dawson."

"I haven't seen the news."

I'd barely seen my own face until I walked into the bathroom and caught my reflection. A night in county jail apparently made you look five years older. Great.

"What happened?" He bit it out and then sighed. "And are you okay? That's most important, I should have started with that."

Harrison Butler had been the best man in the entire world when I was growing up. At least, that was until my parents divorced, and he threw himself into work to avoid coming back to an empty home. That home was eventually sold, and Crystal and I barely saw him outside birthdays and holidays after Mom moved us into boyfriend's one, two, three, four, and five's houses while she went through the rich men of Tennessee, working to find someone to treat her right which for my mom meant, opening up his bank account.

I hadn't heard from Dad since our first preseason game.

"I'm fine. Just got home and I'm not really sure what's going on."

"News is saying you'll have to be suspended."

"Probably."

"Shit, Dawson. Why?" He cussed and then muttered something I didn't quite catch. "Crystal," he finally guessed. "She's there."

Awesome and smart.

"Yeah." I shoved my hair back off my forehead and flinched. It was greasy and smelled, for some reason, like cigarette smoke. I was in desperate need of a shower. "Listen, I need to shower and call my agent and probably my coach. Hell, maybe our GM. Can I call you back once I know more?"

"Cut her loose, son. She won't learn if you're always there to pick her back up. Hate to say it, she's my daughter, but just like you had to fight for your future, she has to learn someday. All these handouts you give her..."

I quit listening and turned on the shower.

"Gotta go. Bye, Dad."

He might have been able to turn his back on her, but I had never been able to break that damn promise he had me make. He didn't know the pain we went through. The fighting over us. Our mom telling Crystal she didn't want her. That shit had to hit a teenage girl right in the prefrontal cortex. Imagine not having your brain fully developed and being reminded how unwanted and unlovable you were.

Back when Crystal and I were twelve and fourteen, we thought we had the perfect life. Not nearly as rich as I lived now, but it'd been perfect for us. That all changed the day Dad came home from work and caught our mom fucking the neighbor. His best friend. Who made twice as much money as Dad did.

Trent and his wife got divorced, and Mom moved us in with him before the ink was dry.

Dad sold the home and moved across town. We lived with Trent for a year before he kicked us out because he caught Mom cheating on him. That started the rest of the hell my mom put us through, and my dad avoided.

Crystal was never the same after that. Neither was I. I learned early on that love didn't mean shit when those who were supposed to love you the most abandoned you as soon as shit got hard.

So yeah, I didn't really like my sister, but for years, she was all I had.

She was my sister. The only one who understood what we went through. If I turned my back on her, she'd have no one.

But that was before her choices and shitty decisions threatened to ruin everything I'd built for myself.

My phone rang again. Looked like my shower might have to wait.

An hour later, I left Crystal pouting on my couch. Showered and shaved, I was dressed in dress pants and a gray T-shirt as I walked into Rick Marchand's office.

Our general manager was a decent guy, a kind one, but we weren't his friends or his buddies. We were his employees, and it was his job to bring in as much money to keep lining not only his pockets, but those of the owners and everyone who worked for the entire Steel organization. From the owner to the custodians, the team's success determined the success of everyone else.

And right now? Right now, I was the walking red flag. The blemish.

I was the problem he had to fix. If it hadn't been clear enough from the tone in his voice when he demanded I get my ass into management's offices as soon as possible, it was definitely obvious in the way he glared at me as I entered.

"It was an accident," I told him immediately.

I'd take my hits where I earned them, and last night might have started out as Crystal's fault, but the shit that happened after wasn't intentional.

"Reports say you assaulted a man inside the bar on Broadway, slammed his face into the bar. Unprovoked by him, you attacked him without cause and smashed not only his nose but his right cheekbone."

"The floor was wet, and he slipped."

"Is this funny to you, Dawson?"

Not a damn thing about this was funny.

"No sir." I shook my head and took a seat I hadn't been invited to take across from him at his desk. "I'm not trying to be funny. My sister told me he wasn't leaving her alone. She screamed. I went to protect her. Guy said he hadn't done anything, but by then, he and his friends were worked up, and I was pissed. Shoving happened, and I grabbed his shirt, but I didn't throw him into the bar or slam his face into it. We were both shoved. He slipped. I was yanked back, and his head slammed into the bar, but I didn't do it. Not on purpose."

"So our press statement should just read, 'Oops. My bad. Didn't mean it?'"

I hated politics. Hated the marketing and the promotion, and I was shit at it. I was paid to do a job, and I did it well. Yeah, we were public figures. I knew that, too, but the focus on players should be on their job, not their lives. Every damn secret or mistake shouldn't be swept across the internet for keyboard warriors to dissect when they knew jack shit, and the media should keep their mouths shut until the entire story was out. Before that, it was gossip and conjecture, and I hated that bullshit.

I'd leave the press release to him. If I had it my way, it'd say fuck off, and that'd only make things worse.

"How much trouble am I in?"

"Owners want you gone. You know that last year an online poll was done and you're one of the top five most disliked players in the entire professional football organization?"

I'd seen that BuzzFeed poll that moved to Instagram and Twitter and all across social platforms. Cole had given me shit for it, too. We'd laughed it off.

Marchand was not laughing.

"I also score more touchdowns than any other tight end and some wide receivers." Perhaps pointing out my usefulness doing the actual job would help.

"That's why they're not demanding you're immediately let go. But there will be changes."

"Like what? Smile for a toothpaste ad?" I gave him a fake, winning smile.

Had to hand it to the guy, he cracked a little. A barely there hint of a chuckle came before he went all serious again.

Then he laid out my future.

I was fucked in the worst ways.

Stay with the team. Settle down or ship out after next season.

How in the hell was I going to do that when I'd sworn a vow to myself at the age of fifteen I would never let a woman get close enough to my heart to destroy it like Mom had done to Dad?

By the time I returned home, Crystal had given up her need to go shopping. She was napping.

I took the time to pack up her shit. Given that she didn't wake up or so much as twitch while I did it, I figured she wasn't napping but passed out from too many mimosas. A peek at my kitchen counter told me she'd also switched to wine at some point.

She was a disaster. I should probably haul her ass off to a treatment facility. Somewhere in the Bahamas or some shit. Maybe that'd keep her out of my hair.

It was hours later that she woke up. I'd had to miss practice to deal with Marchand, but since I was suspended for a game during playoffs, for fuck's sake, it wasn't like I had to be there. I should have been. Definitely. Coach Bowles had already called and yelled at me, but Crystal took precedence.

Instead, while she slammed cabinets and doors in the guest bedroom, looking for her shit, I called her an Uber.

When she finally stepped foot into the living room, her face was blank of all emotion.

"Your shit is outside the door. Your Uber ride to the airport is coming now. Be here any minute. You're leaving. I've transferred a million dollars into your account, and I want to see you again... never. You understand me?"

Her face went from blank to a wicked sneer in a blink. "You're kicking me out? Just like Dad and Mom. Fuck you, Dawson."

We'd been through this before. Many times. She cried. I caved. Round and round we went.

Not this time.

"I mean it, Crystal. I want nothing to do with you ever again. That shit from last night almost cost me my career today. My dream. You're not worth it. Thought you were, tried to get you help, but now I know you won't help yourself and I can't force you into it."

"I don't need help. I need someone to give a shit about me."

"Then maybe you should start by giving a shit about yourself and being a decent human being."

Steam poured out of her, so damn angry I could feel it from across the room right before her chin started shaking. "Why does no one love me?"

"Because you don't love yourself and never bothered trying. Get out, and if you're not out on the stoop and in your Uber when it pulls up, I won't be shoving you into it, I'll be calling the cops and have you arrested for trespassing."

CHAPTER 2
HAILEY

"NO. ABSOLUTELY NOT. NO WAY."

"Yes."

I stared down at my best friend, Meredith, who was running a straightener through her red hair and groaned. "I'm not ready."

She ran the most successful romantic dating match service in the Southeast. I'd been dumped at the altar two months ago. Not even dumped. Darrick didn't have the courtesy to let me know he wasn't showing up for our wedding I'd spent a year planning. He ghosted me, didn't bother showing up at all, unless you count the parking lot of the country club. But that was only because he needed to pick up my bridesmaid who slipped into his car and disappeared right along with him.

Destination? Our honeymoon to Greece and Italy and the rest of the Mediterranean.

Which I knew because they had no problems flaunting their vacation on their Instagram accounts. Overnight, they'd both wiped off any pictures of me on their social media accounts. Not that I was forced to check their profiles daily, sometimes multiple times, but I was an addict.

A heartbroken one.

The man who insisted we wait until we were married to do

anything without clothes on had run off with one of my friends. How long had they been having sex?

My stomach still rolled at the thought. Two months later, with zero answers to my unasked questions, and I was still obsessed. Hurting.

Also, pathetic.

"It's the best way for you to get back out there again, and you know it." Her sky-blue eyes watched me from her mirror's reflection where we were currently getting dressed to meet our other two friends out for drinks on a Thursday night.

Something I'd never done while engaged to Darrick.

But screw him and Bianca, my old college roommate, who I knew, always knew, had a crush on Darrick.

Joke was on me. Along with the deposits and fees from the wedding, I was still paying off on payment plans. They were worse than my student loan debt and at this point, my children's grandchildren would still be paying off my debt.

I collapsed onto her fluffy white comforter. "I don't think a new long-term relationship is the right thing for me."

"And a Tinder hook-up is?"

"I hate you," I grumbled. "Maybe?"

She chuckled. "You haven't passed third base, Hailey. Tinder guys would eat you alive."

"Well, maybe I want to be eaten."

She turned and flung a hair clip at me. I barely dodged the plastic thing from smacking me in the face. "Hey!"

"Get real. Trust me. This is my gift."

She'd started matchmaking people in college and every single couple, as unlikely or likely as they could be, were still married. Her Instagram feed was picture after picture of all the happy couples she'd successfully brought together. To say she had a gift was downplaying it. I long ago started believing Meredith could sniff out perfectly complementary pheromones on soulmates.

There was no other explanation. That she'd never fully believed

Darrick and I were meant to be together should have been my first red flag and the only one I needed.

But I wasn't ready for her to go sniffing around for a man for me.

I wanted freedom. I'd been with the same man for six years, never been able to explore my sexuality or any experience sex fully outside of Darrick's fingers.

I wanted to take time to make sure my heart was healed and in the right place before I started another relationship. More so, I needed to make sure I knew what I liked and needed—both in bed and out of it.

"I'll think about it," I finally sighed. It was a carrot dangled in front of her, one I figured she'd run with but whatever.

It gave me time and got me out of this conversation.

For now, at least. Pretty sure happy hour was going to be a different story.

"Okay. How about this?" Misty flung back her blonde hair and tipped her wineglass in my direction. "Let Meredith go through the men she has in her files. Maybe she'll find someone in it who can give you the D."

"That's not what I do," Meredith grumbled.

I slumped down in the booth on the rooftop bar area at Vecchio Mondo Vino and rested my head on Sloane's shoulder. "Can we please stop talking about this?"

Mission: Get Hailey to have hot sex, commenced as soon as Sloane, the last of our party of four, joined us and poured herself a drink from the bottle of Montalcino we'd started with.

The table was filled with a variety of tapas, including my personal favorite, bruschetta.

Sloane patted the top of my head. "There, there. It'll be okay."

I huffed a laugh and sat back up. "Why can't we focus on Sloane or Misty? They're single, too."

"Yeah, but I'm dating," Misty said. "And I'm perfectly happy with my situationship."

Situationship. I didn't even know what that stupid term meant. Friends with benefits? Fuck buddies? Seemed like that's what it was supposed to be, but Misty's situationship bought her flowers and had soup delivered to her when she was sick and took her out on real dates. Seemed an awful like dating to me, especially after four months, but both claimed they didn't want a relationship. Except, wasn't that exactly what they were doing? Sometimes the dating world made my head spin.

"Sloane isn't."

"Don't bring me into this." She bumped her shoulder into mine, and I lifted the glass of wine over the table, thankfully not spilling any of it. "I'm in my post-divorce healing era."

So she had a pass. At least my relationship ended before I'd changed my name, moved in together, built a life and mixed finances, and then had it all blow up.

Small mercies. I grabbed a piece of bruschetta and bit into it, moaning at the flavorful burst of tomato, basil, and fresh mozzarella. Vecchio not only made the cheese on site, but grew the basil and tomatoes on the rooftop gardens on the other side of the deck from us.

"How about this, then?" Meredith sipped her wine and tilted her head to the side. "I won't force you to listen to me, again, by the way, because I think I already tried..."

She arched a brow.

I rolled my eyes. "Can you please stop telling me I told you so?"

"Sure. Happily." She grinned like a maniac. "If you agree that if I find someone who fits exactly what you think you're looking for, you'll consider it for twenty-four hours before telling me no."

Think? I knew what I wanted. Someone who was the complete opposite of Darrick in every single way I could imagine.

If the tall, lean, tennis-playing, country club blond, blue-eyed boy who looked like the sweetest boy in the world could screw me over this epically, my next guy would be his exact opposite.

"Exactly what I'm looking for?"

She reached into her Burberry bag and pulled out her old-school paper planner, flipping to the notebook at the back. "Let's make a list. Shall we?"

She clicked the tip of her pen and put it to paper.

I'd play this game. And make it completely impossible for Meredith to deliver. Then I'd never have to be the target of her matchmaking again.

Drop-dead sexy.

A little bit rough looking.

Tattoos because Darrick said they were skanky and classless, even if I'd always wanted one.

A body that showed confidence and his ability to please a woman.

Maybe a piercing somewhere. Anywhere.

He had to be strong.

Most importantly, he needed to be a little possessive and a whole lot protective even if he wasn't looking for forever.

The forever part was what was going to get me out of this.

No man went to Meredith if they were looking for a good time and not a long time.

I sat back in my booth when we were done, grinning behind my wineglass at Meredith's scowl.

Checkmate to me.

CHAPTER 3
DAWSON

JUST OVER FOUR MONTHS AGO, I was celebrating Christmas alone, exactly how I liked it. I ended the year on a high note. My football team smashed our regular season and our eyes were on planning for the postseason. I had everything I wanted, exactly how I wanted it.

Then Crystal showed up and started wreaking havoc. She might as well have shown up at my house that day with a wrecking ball in tow for as much damage as she caused.

Six weeks after I finally kicked her ass out with a check for a million dollars and telling her it was the last penny she'd ever receive from me, I was still paying for her visit.

Not with money, but with an ultimatum.

"Fans don't like you, Dawson. They might like the touchdowns you score, but in this day and age where everyone and everything is on social media, your off-the-field attitude matters as much, if not more, than your on-the-field performance."

"What are you getting at?"

I'd been called to his office the day after my arrest. Fortunately, the man whose face I almost broke in two—by accident, mostly—wasn't pressing charges if I paid the medical bills.

Fine. Happy to.

I had no doubt they'd be minimal compared to what Rick Marchand, our team's general manager, had in store for me.

"Your contract is up after next season. You'll be a free agent. I need a reason to convince the rest of the organization to keep you. Frankly, I don't give a shit about your personality, or lack of one, but if you want to see the field this season, and stay beyond..."

He waited for me to respond.

"I do." I absolutely did.

I started my career in Nashville and wanted to end it here. I didn't have that many more years left. Getting bounced to a new team now, especially with us on the cusp of going to the Super Bowl was not how I wanted to go out.

"Good. Then you need to play for me right now."

"What exactly does that mean?"

He danced around the topic for several more minutes before finally singing.

Find a girlfriend. A suitable one. Plaster my happy little relationship all over social media. Take the non-required interviews that were now required for me. Meet with our social media manager to get me all over the internet proving what a stable, kind guy I was.

If I wanted to stay in Nashville, I was Rick's new puppet. A marionette, really, because he basically shoved his fist up my ass and owned me.

Four months later and I had the Super Bowl Championship, an empty, quiet house, and I was no closer to figuring out how to fulfill the deal I'd made with Rick than I was the day I agreed to it.

Time was ticking down though, and I was out of options.

I needed help, and for the first time in my life, I was going to have to ask for it.

"Shit," I grumbled and hauled myself out of my pool where I'd been swimming laps to try to clear my mind.

How in the hell did one go on finding a girlfriend, someone Rick and our team's management would find acceptable? I found women at bars and clubs, occasionally on the road. I'd used the dating app for celebrities, but I wasn't going there again.

Too many narcissist drama queens who were better at gaslighting than any man I'd ever met.

I needed someone simple. Quiet. Believable. I needed her to want the exact same things I did so there were no complications once I fulfilled my end of the deal and we went our separate ways.

I grabbed a towel and dried my hair and gave my body a quick wipe-down before heading to the shower.

If I needed help, I needed my brothers. My teammates.

The ones I could trust to keep this quiet and who could actually give me decent advice were slim pickings, though.

Davis, who'd grown a lot since finding out he got a girl pregnant on a one-night stand and who was now planning their wedding in a few weeks, was at least trying to take this seriously. Mason Yeets, on the other hand, was looking like a kid in a candy shop at the prospect of finding me a girlfriend.

I called Davis because he was the only person who I'd mentioned this to and that was moments before we took the field for the Super Bowl. Not the right time but getting it off my chest then had allowed me to focus on helping our team win the game.

I didn't have brothers growing up, only teammates, but I imagined the look on Davis's face would be one a brother would make when they were trying to keep from laughing their asses off.

Cole Buchanan, my saving grace, was inside grabbing us all beers while the other two lunatics and myself were hanging out on the covered patio of my backyard, overlooking acres of land, my pool, and a putting green.

"I can't believe you haven't found someone yet," Davis said. "It's been months."

"It's not like chicks who make management happy come in a

catalog."

Mason hid his laughter, poorly, behind his fist. "Catalog. Wouldn't that be awesome? Didn't they used to do that way back when? Mail-order bride or some shit? Maybe do that, bruh. Put out a wanted ad online."

If he was closer to me, I'd punch him. He probably took the seat across the table from me so he could be this big of a jackass and stay out of my reach.

"Right. That's what Rick meant when he told me to be someone respected. A billboard in Times Square was just what he was thinking."

"Why not just go to the clubs? Find someone you're attracted to, and that's the end of it."

"Because I won't know anything about them or if I can trust them. And the last thing I want is to be attracted to a woman who's playing the part of my girlfriend."

"Yeah, that'd suck." Mason laughed. "Being attracted to someone you have to spend months with." He shivered.

I grabbed the bottle cap from the table and flicked it at his face. "I'm paying them, idiot. A fuckton of money so they keep their mouths shut. I don't need to be tortured by someone I want to fuck, and I'm not hiring a goddamn prostitute."

"Might be easier," Davis said.

"What would be easier?" Cole asked and set down a bucket in the center of the table.

It was filled with ice and more beer than I usually drank in a month, and I only used the metal tin when I had parties. How in the hell he found it in my butler's pantry in a matter of minutes was anyone's guess.

Mason lost his hold of his laughter. "Hiring a prostitute."

Davis chuckled, laughed louder, and soon enough, both men were doubled over laughing their asses off.

At me. I hated being laughed at.

Cole gave me a wide-eyed look and I shook my head. No, I was not hiring a hooker.

"Should have known not to invite the kids to the adult party."

"Live and learn," he said and took a seat next to me.

"Noted," I agreed and drained the rest of my beer. I'd ordered pizza after I got a hold of them, but we'd already demolished the five pies while I was telling them all the bullshit that went down.

"So, if you don't trust meeting someone at a club, how can we help? I mean, Eden's made some friends in Marysville. I think Nora and Sarah are both available. They have pretty normal lives. I could talk to them."

Nora was a vet, and Sarah owned a local dog rescue. Talk about perfect professions for me to be associated with. I'd met them both when I spent time with Cole in the small town he and his new wife lived in. They'd hauled off right after the Super Bowl and been married in the Caribbean with only their families in attendance.

Not a step I ever saw myself taking, ever wanted to, but more power to Eden and him because they were happy and together after years of being apart.

As far as Nora and Sarah? They weren't right. Not for what I wanted. Not for the time I needed. If I was actually desperate enough to pull something like this off, it needed to be believable.

Besides, when this was over, I would see them again.

"No. Not them, but that's the problem. I don't know what Rick expects from me and how in the hell do I find it without potentially hurting someone?"

"I've got it," Davis said, head down in his phone.

Mason leaned over and his black brows rose right before his tan lips curled. "Oh, yes." He punched Davis in the shoulder. "Perfect. Yo, check this out."

He grabbed the phone from Davis and handed it to me.

"What the hell is it?" I really hoped it wasn't porn. We weren't that close.

Cole leaned toward me, and I tilted the screen so we could both see it at the same time.

Meredith's Matchmaking. The Most Successful Matchmaker in

the Southeast.

"Is this a joke?" Had to be. What woman could claim she was successful at setting people up?

I read the website in between taking turns to scowl at Davis. "You're joking. I'm not looking for long-term love, you idiot."

I went to hand the phone back to him, but Mason practically jumped over the table and snagged it first.

"No. Yo, it's serious. Check this out." He came around the table and shoved the phone in my face. "She'll be able to help. Check out her Instagram."

Two thousand happily married couples and counting...

That was her Instagram bio. As I scrolled, there was picture after picture with the caption of their wedding date and how long they dated before getting married.

All right, so maybe this woman had a good business going for her.

She still wasn't selling what I needed.

"Could be worth a shot," Cole muttered and shrugged. "Better than a random at some club, you know? Never know."

"I don't want long-term."

"Maybe whatever you're offering to pay would help someone change their mind in the short-term. Besides, wouldn't it help them in the long-term? Connected to you after you break up?"

"We wouldn't break up because we wouldn't actually be together."

Cole sighed. Davis chuckled.

"Fine," Davis said. "I'm just sayin', the women who go to this Meredith are looking for something. There has to be something you can give them more than money, maybe the status of dating an athlete would help. And when your business deal comes to its mutual, contractual end...everyone walks away satisfied."

Mutual, contractual end.

At least he was getting it. That was vastly different from a breakup.

"What do you have to lose?" Cole asked and reached for a fresh beer.

"My dignity?"

"That was gone the moment you agreed to Rick's asinine deal."

He had a point there.

It was a week before I could get in for an appointment with Meredith Skyye. In which time, I did a vast amount of research on the woman. The last thing I needed was to be scammed by some con artist. Turned out, Meredith Skyye was legit.

At least, as a person. She was married to Tuevo Skyye, a Finnish hockey player for Tennessee's professional hockey team, the Avengers, and after making a few phone calls to players on the team I knew, they assured me her business was legit. Not only had Meredith successfully matched two other players on the team, she'd started it as a side gig in college, hooking up her sorority sisters with fraternity guys for formal events and when those couples started dating and gave all the thanks to Meredith, her future was sealed.

Still, I didn't quite know what to expect when I found her office building, a suite on the third floor of a four-story building near downtown. Based on her pink-flowered, black-glittered website, I expected her suite to be decked out in shades of pink and sprinkle confetti from the ceiling.

Instead, it was all black leather and chrome with clear glass desks. Modern, with abstract art on the walls, there was only one woman in the open reception area.

She peered at me from behind her plastic, red-framed glasses. With her graying hair pulled up in a bun and the age lines around her eyes, the woman looked more like a mother or grandmother than mine had ever looked.

"Hello. May I help you?"

I stepped toward her, and damn if my palms weren't getting clammier by the second. Professional football player used to breaking tackles by men and shoving others out of the way to help my team score, and I was reduced to a nervous pre-teen all over again.

Fucking Rick.

"Yeah." I cleared my throat and cringed. Dry as the Sahara. "I'm Dawson, Dawson Butler? Here to see—"

"Mr. Butler."

I spun on my heels at the sound of the new voice and nodded. "Yes, ma'am. You must be Mrs. Skyye?"

"Please." She came to me with her arm extended, her smile pleasant and welcoming. Too bad I was a second away from declaring this a bad idea and bolting. "Call me Meredith. I hear you've done some checking up on me."

I shook her hand and didn't bother apologizing. "I'm in a unique situation."

"Understood. Come back to my office?" She turned and started walking.

Might as well have been in stocks, walking to a public execution for all the excitement in my steps as I followed her.

As soon as we reached her office, my hesitation worsened. Unlike the front office, hers was homey with a light wood desk and bookshelves covering one wall. A round, same light wood table that looked more fit for a breakfast nook in a kitchen with cream cushions on the chairs. Two small, tan leather couches not unlike my own were in another corner with a cream fur rug in the middle and a coffee table set up as a seating area.

It was meant to bring comfort.

It only further hijacked my nerves.

What the hell was I doing? Was I supposed to open up to this woman like she was a therapist or my best friend? Spill all my secrets, my deepest desires?

A shiver rolled down my spine at the thought, and I curled my hands into fists, my toes into my Doc Marten boots to fight the urge to flee.

I left a modern office area and stepped into my own personal hell.

Clearing my throat, I glanced at Meredith who wore an expectant look on her face.

"Yes?"

She was still smiling. Pleasantly. "I said Tuevo says hello and congratulations on the win."

"Oh." Damn. Missed that. "Thanks. So...what now?"

"Considering the couch made you look like you were about to pass out, how about we sit at my desk and talk for a bit?"

I could do the sitting. It was the talking that made me want to swallow a cup full of glass shards.

I went straight to the leather-backed chair opposite her desk and collapsed into it. Not a moment too soon. It was possible my legs wouldn't have held me up much longer. The desk was better anyway, kept everything more professional.

As she slid into the chair across the desk from me, she grabbed some kind of band and did a quick flip with her red hair. In seconds it was up and off her shoulders in some twist thing.

The move to be casual helped me slightly.

"So, I know we spoke on the phone last week, but maybe you should tell me a little bit more about what you're looking for."

I went through the exact spiel I told her on the phone, the mild threat from our GM I hadn't shared before. Since she was married to a professional athlete, I figured she'd understand that this time. After, we went through a list of questions. What kind of woman I was usually attracted to, what I wanted this girlfriend to look like. Height. Hair color. Eye color. Body shape. Career. For me, the only preference I had was the taller, the better. I was six-four. Anyone shorter than five-six felt too small next to me. I didn't need to bend in half to give someone a kiss or a hug. The rest, I couldn't give two shits about. Curvy, thin, athletic, blue-eyed, brown-eyed, I had never narrowed down my type of woman to one small niche. Didn't need to, considering I wouldn't be spending much time with any one woman ever.

When I was done, she tapped her pink pen on her desk. "You have to realize this puts me in a difficult position. I've made a name for myself finding long-term relationships for people that have often ended in marriage. If anyone finds out I had a hand in this ruse, and it failed... well, there goes my reputation."

"I'll ensure that doesn't happen. Outside my three teammates, I have no plans on telling anyone else I've been here. No offense."

"Very little taken." She smirked and grabbed a binder from the bookshelf behind her desk. Filled with relationship books and a few that mentioned personality assessments. The rest of the shelves were filled with framed wedding photos.

The binder landed in between us on her desk with a heavy thump.

What was this? Buy-a-Bride?

I didn't want a bride. I needed to get our GM off my ass so I could play next season.

End of. I shoved it back toward her.

"I understand the position you're in." I did. No one wanted a reputation they'd worked hard for to be ruined. But this was mutually beneficial because we both wanted to keep this private. "But I promise you, I don't want long-term. I need someone willing to fake it."

She quirked a brow and grinned. "I think that's the first time I've heard a man wanting that from a woman."

Oh, the ginger had jokes. Funny.

"Not orgasms," I all but growled and as I did, her eyes flared. "I can make any woman come as many times as I want. That's not my issue. What I don't want is an actual relationship. Can you help me or not? Because I'm willing to pay a boatload of money for this, but if you can't help me, I don't want either of us to waste more of each other's time."

This was what I'd been reduced to. Begging. Desperation. Crystal and Rick were going to give me a heart attack before I was thirty.

"Hmmm." Her pink pen tapped the binder. Of course the matchmaker used a pink freaking pen. Probably doodled hearts in her sleep. "I might have someone, at least, if what you're saying about the orgasms is true."

"They're not on the table. I need a fake girlfriend, not a prostitute." What kind of business was this?

I never should have trusted Davis or Mason's Google abilities.

Yeah, they were my teammates, but they were idiots. I'd always suspected. Now it was confirmed.

Assholes. All of them.

If I played defense, I'd lay their asses out for this. Maybe I could invest Carr's help. But that'd involve talking. Explaining. And being grateful for the help.

No thanks.

That pink pen kept tap, tap, tapping.

I was about ready to rip it out of her slim, long fingers and snap it in two.

"Okay. No orgasms. Disappointing. For her, I mean. But I still think I have someone."

"Great." I curled my hands around the edge of the armrests and went to stand.

"You'll need to text her by Monday. I'll send you her contact info via email shortly, and I'll let her know to expect you. If this doesn't work out, let me know, but I think you'll like her."

I didn't need to like her. I needed her to do a job. If Meredith didn't make that clear to her, I would our first night.

"Fine. Great."

I turned to leave, and Meredith's voice halted me in my tracks. "Do you at least want to see a picture of her?"

Would probably be smart, but frankly, she was all I had, and her looks didn't matter as long as she looked wholesome. Dateable. Maybe a little sassy with a few tattoos. No one would believe I fell for the preschool teacher. But it didn't matter. Because this was fake, and she'd be getting a shit ton of money to pretend to like me back until Rick was off my ass and my penalty for not purposely breaking an asshole's face open was fulfilled.

"No."

Smarter that way. Better. If I didn't find her good enough, I'd have to start over.

And if I did find her attractive, well, that'd be an equal pain in my ass.

CHAPTER 4
HAILEY

"I HAVE SOMEONE FOR YOU."

The mimosa I took a sip of spewed out of my mouth and went flying across the table. "What?"

When Meredith suggested we meet for brunch before I had to open my store that afternoon, I had no idea this would be the topic of conversation.

"You're kidding me."

She had to be. I was so incredibly specific with the details there was no way she'd found a man who fit every criterion I listed last week.

Meredith picked up the white napkin and patted her cheeks, completely unfazed. That was Meredith. Her husband Tuevo was an uptight prick to everyone but her, but everything rolled off Meredith's back. I used to tease her that she had to be a faux redhead because of it. It's not like they were known for their patience.

"Tell me."

"He's supposed to text you by tomorrow, so I'm assuming he hasn't."

"Nope." That meant he met with her yesterday and she'd waited a full day to let me know. And he hadn't called. Great. Now I could be a nervous wreck for the rest of the weekend. Fun times. I knew the rules. Forty-eight hours to initiate contact once Meredith chose someone for the seeker. Laugh all you want, but she was a genius. She started matchmaking when we were in college, and the vast majority of relationships she paired up were now married, most with multiple children. It was at a brunch similar to this where we were laughing about another success, this time to strangers in a bar—to both each other and Meredith—when I suggested she start her own business.

Now, she made as much, if not more money than Tuevo Skyye, her Finnish husband who played professional hockey for the Tennessee Avengers. All because she had a gift of making happily ever afters work.

It was wild.

It was perfect for her.

And until last week's happy hour, I'd always sworn I'd never let her work her magic on me. Although, up until February, I'd always had Darrick, so I never thought I'd need it.

"It's tricky, and you're my best friend, so you need to know the details, but I swear to you, you stick with this guy regardless of the bullshit he spews your way, and he's your one."

Um. Red flag. "Bullshit?"

She rolled her eyes and took a bite of her spinach and mushroom crêpe. "I can't tell. But you'll be in for a wild ride, so strap yourself in now. Got it?"

With that kind of cryptic warning, where did I sign up? "You're forgetting one tiny little thing."

"What's that?"

"I was pretty sure I told you I wanted someone who didn't want forever."

"I know." She shot me a sassy little grin. "And I know you thought that'd make it harder for me, but I'm telling you, that's what makes him perfect for you."

That didn't make sense. Meredith's only clients were always someone looking for a forever kind of love. It was a requirement. One of the very few she insisted on when she first started turning this into a career. She ran a matchmaking service, not a hook-up or escort service, and she was adamant about it. If she broke her steadfast rule for me...

"You took on a client who is only looking for something short-term?"

"I prefer to call the timing kismet."

Kismet, my ass. There had to be something else going on with this, some kind of trick.

"Trust me, Hails. You'll understand when he reaches out."

I trusted Meredith with my life, my heart, my soul, the lives of, hopefully, my future children, and every single one of my belongings.

I trusted her, but that didn't mean I had to like it. "Fine."

"That's the spirit." She grinned. "Now, tell me how Suzanne and Ken are."

My parents were wonderful, super people. A daughter to a former firefighter captain and middle school math teacher, I'd grown up having the perfect, suburban all-American upbringing. All they ever wanted for their children were to be happy and find their own brand of success. Tate did that by becoming a plastic surgeon currently living out in San Diego. Charlie went to school for art and graphic design and was now working at a tattoo shop in Portland. My sister, Holly, and my closest sibling in age, was the only married sibling. She and her husband lived in New York and were both lawyers.

I was born six years later, at a time when my parents thought they were done having children. I didn't have two parents, but five, and now that they were all off doing incredible things, I was still very much looked down upon as still a child, still trying to "find myself." None of my siblings understood I liked the quiet little life I'd created outside of Nashville in our small hometown of Friendswood, Tennessee, where I ran a refurbished furniture business in our town's small downtown. I scoured Facebook and garage and estate sales to snag incredible deals on vintage pieces, and then I refinished them. For me, it was perfect.

For everyone else in my family, it was supposed to be a hobby. It'd started out that way in high school, when I bought a nightstand for five dollars at a garage sale. From there, it grew. Now, I not only owned my own store, but it was successful. My siblings still kept wondering when I'd go back to college and get a business degree so I could manage it "better."

"Suzanne is still out hunting for the perfect sword to run through Darrick," I admitted, and Meredith laughed.

To say my mom was a Mama Bear was far too mild. She was a dragon, and she was pissed the hell off at Darrick for embarrassing me. Not quite so upset I didn't marry him, though. She'd always tolerated him at a surface level.

Probably should have been my second red flag. The two women who knew me best didn't quite like him. Sometimes, when I was alone in my small bungalow house, I almost wondered if the only reason I insisted he was perfect was to finally have something to make my siblings proud of me for doing. Get married. Be an adult. Check.

Holly, had called me almost every day since the wedding didn't happen to check in on me. Two months later, though, her calls were now starting to include the suggestive, "You know what you should do now..." tone, and those things included going back to school.

No thank you. I barely survived college the first time around.

"I can't wait until your mom gets a hold of him."

"I'd prefer if we could all go on like he doesn't exist."

In a perfect world, I never would have met Darrick. Actually, in a perfect world, Darrick would have actually been the man I naively believed him to be.

"Enough about him." I didn't need to go to work with him on my mind.

"You're right. Subject change. Help me do some shopping for our upcoming trip."

Tuevo was taking Meredith to Puerto Vallarta next week.

She didn't need shopping help. She had everything money could buy and everything money couldn't.

"You're leaving me now? When this guy is supposed to call me on Monday?"

"You're right. I'll text Tuevo right now and tell him we have to cancel the plans he spent months making all because you might be going on a date with some new guy. My bad." She grabbed her phone and swiped her thumb on the screen to unlock it.

"Shut up. You know what I mean. You have to be able to tell me something about him."

"I can do better than that, but you have to swear you won't tell a soul. Not even Sloane or Misty until you meet him."

"Cross my heart." I made the sign of an X over my chest.

"Here." She flipped her phone around, and on the screen was the guy.

The very guy I'd suggested last week. She wrote down my exact parameters and requirements and then had to go find someone who fit every single description.

Tanned skin. Hair at his shoulders. Muscles everywhere.

"Who is that?" I peered closer, so close I could practically inhale what would have to be an incredibly masculine scent.

He even had a nose ring. Not the kind of piercing I'd expected and yet with that square-cut jaw, minimal scruff, he totally worked it. He worked everything. A tattoo was barely visible on his forearm, and that hair...long, thick, and with a slight wave to it and strips of a lighter caramel through it.

He was perfection. Absolutely, manly perfection.

"This is your guy."

Oh, she had to be freaking kidding me.

Voted one of America's favorite Main Street districts, my store was busy from open to close every Friday night, Saturday and Sunday, especially during the spring and fall when Tennessee was alive with tourists. Most weekends had festivals, and every Saturday morning there was a farmers' market that brought people from hours away to explore.

I'd splurged two years ago, taking a massive risk when there was an open building. The cost had been outside my budget, and I'd eaten so much ramen and Campbell's chicken noodle soup that first year to make ends meet the smell of chicken broth now made me nauseous. Fortunately with the help of loans for women-owned businesses, my savings I'd been diligent in growing since my first babysitting job when I was twelve, and a little bit of help from my parents, I was able to swing it.

The gamble paid off in ways larger than I could have predicted. I received rent income from the upstairs apartment, currently rented to Isaac. Isaac was a single guy in his early twenties and had two Siamese cats. I was pretty certain Peanut Butter and Jelly the Cat—and Isaac did not like when you shortened it—peered straight into my soul with those eyes of theirs every time I saw Isaac walking them on the street.

Yes, he took his cats for walks.

He was a character, but he was quiet, paid his rent on time, and made it a point to stop into my store at least once a week to see how things were going. I returned the favor by ensuring I ended my workdays by eight at night so the sounds of sanders and other tools I used in the workshop at the back of the building didn't bother him when he got home from work.

Isaac paid a third of the total mortgage on the building, making it easier for me to make ends meet and since I took the risk to open my own store instead of only seeing items I refinished on Facebook or through my own website and advertising, my income had quadrupled. Once Isaac moved in, I was also able to buy my own home, a small bungalow a five-minute walk away from my store and the same home Darrick was supposed to move into once we got married.

Regardless, today, neither Isaac's company nor the sight of Peanut Butter and Jelly the Cat on a leash in my store or the constant activity in and out of it could erase the vision of the man on the phone screen from brunch.

"Is this new?" Isaac held up a small handheld vintage mirror. I'd had to refinish the silver polish on it and now it shone as bright as the many overhead chandeliers.

"Finished it last week."

He set it back down as gentle as could be and nodded. "My mom would like something like that."

"You know the rule," I sang.

"Don't need your friends and family discount."

I didn't quite know what Isaac did for a living, but outside his cats with the goofy names and the penchant for taking them both on walks, he traveled frequently during the fall and winter. This spring, he purchased a Maserati he had no problems keeping parked out back in the private lot. Never even seemed concerned it would get stolen. Occasionally, I bumped into a female guest leaving his apartment when I showed up to work early, but even that wasn't often. He was a mystery to me, but a good renter and I enjoyed his occasional company.

"Miss Parillo?"

"Yes, Grace?"

One of my high school employees, my favorite one, came to me and smiled at Isaac. "Excuse me for interrupting."

"No problem, Grace. Gotta get Peanut Butter and Jelly the Cat back home anyway. See you two around."

"Bye, Isaac."

We both waited until he left the store and Grace turned to me, giggling like the sixteen-year-old she was. "He's so weird, but so cute."

He was definitely a different one.

"What'd you need?"

"Oh. Right. You have a phone call."

The prickling sensation slipping down my spine that had been there since lunch returned in full force.

"Did they say who it was?"

"I think it's your brother? But he didn't really say."

"Great. You've got the store?"

"On it, boss."

I hurried to the register at the back of the store where my phones were. I had one for work and a personal one, and it wasn't uncommon for my employees to grab my personal phone by accident.

"Hello?"

"Is this Hailey Parillo?"

Oh dear. The rumble of the man's voice shot straight to my knees and made them wobble.

"This is."

But this was most definitely not my brother.

CHAPTER 5
DAWSON

I SHOULD HAVE LOOKED at the picture when Meredith offered it to me.

I definitely should have tried to Google the name Hailey Parillo before I picked up the phone and called her.

Sexy librarian came to my mind at the sound of her voice. That one-word hello sent a flare of arousal to my balls, tightening them, and in a flash, I imagined her. Tall, lean, but with a perfect handful of tits. Hips made to hold, and legs created to wrap around my waist. She'd wear glasses but would hide it and she probably had her share of cardigans she'd always carry with her in case she got cold in restaurants.

The hello turned to a strangled, husky sound as she cleared her throat, and fuck me. That sound.

I should have gone to the club last night, found a woman for the night to get rid of any urge. Instead, I'd stayed home and worn a hole in my wood floors trying to figure out what in the hell I'd say to this woman.

I hadn't at all expected such a visceral reaction to the sound of her voice.

"This is. You must be Dawson?"

"Yeah. Meredith Skyye told you to expect my call?"

There was the sound of light, nervous laughter. "She did. This is weird, isn't it?"

Thank god she was the one to break the ice. Instead of trying to figure out how to start, I now had a million questions I was trying to hold back. Why did she go to Meredith? What did she do? Who was she?

My own laughter was brief. "Did she explain anything about why I went to see her?"

"Um. No? Not really."

Damn.

"I mean, well, she told me you weren't looking for something permanent? And she may have shown me your picture."

If I wasn't mistaken, there were nerves making her throat shake. "That okay with you?"

"The picture?"

"The short-term thing."

"Oh." Another nervous giggle. Should have asked about her thoughts on the picture. I never had problems picking women up, and God hadn't only gifted me with quick feet and fast, ready hands. I knew I looked good.

But never had I wanted to hear a woman tell me that until now.

Shit. This wasn't good. Not at all.

"Yes, actually, short-term is perfect for me."

"Really?" If she'd seen my picture, I assumed she knew who I was. Meredith hadn't taken mine, and I sure as hell hadn't sent her any, so that meant the only way she found a picture of me was online. There was no shortage of them there.

"Um. Yeah, so I'm guessing Meredith didn't tell you a lot about me either?"

"Nothing."

And now I was thankful for it. It worried me yesterday, but based on the sound of her voice alone, I wanted to be the only one to discover her. Learn from her.

"How about we change that?"

"Okay. That sounds good. Sometime later this week, maybe? Meet for dinner or something?"

"What about tonight. You all right coming to my house?"

"Tonight?" Her voice went high-pitched.

Shit. It was Saturday. Of course she'd be busy. Probably had plans.

"If you can. But to be honest, I really need to talk to you about what I need, and I don't really have the time to put it off anymore."

Silence hit the phone, heavy and thick, so much I checked the screen to make sure I hadn't lost her.

"Um. I don't...I mean, tonight works, but I need to close my store..."

What store? Where? She had to be close. My pulse raced. So many questions. Such a surprising and very much unwanted response.

"Okay," she finally said. "Yeah, tonight. That's fine with me, but... your place?"

I couldn't blame her. What stranger invited a woman to his house for a first meeting? But I needed somewhere private...

Damn. I could think of something.

"How about I see if I can make reservations for a restaurant. Are you okay wth coming into Brentwood?"

Hell, I didn't even know where she lived.

"Brentwood's great, actually. I could be there around seven? Seven-thirty."

"Seven thirty it is." I'd never had a *date* sound so much like a business deal.

Which was exactly what this was. Shit. I needed to remember that.

"I'll text once I make the reservation. That okay?"

"Sounds good." There was a smile in her voice now. And damn... I *really* wished I'd asked Meredith for that picture. "See you later?"

"You will. Bye, Hailey."

As soon as the call ended, I tossed my phone onto the couch and scrubbed my hands through my hair. They ripped through my hair band, and I yanked it out of my hair, redid my ponytail, and shoved off the couch.

My house was clean because I was a clean freak and hired cleaners in addition to picking up after myself.

My fridge was stocked with meals for the week, delivered earlier that day to keep me fit both during the season and off. I'd considered having a professional chef come in and cook meals for me in my kitchen, but that lasted two weeks before the mess drove me crazy, along with the clattering noise of pots and pans. Now I had them delivered.

No mess. No fuss. And no stranger in my home once a week.

Basically, I had shit to do except consider another workout and wait.

Seven thirty. Four and a half hours away. Too damn far away and much too close.

"Shit," I muttered.

Workout it was because I needed something to burn off the adrenaline a simple phone call created. No way I was using my hand. Not before I met her.

Reservation made, and another shower taken, I was fifteen minutes early for my meeting with Hailey at an upscale Italian restaurant in Brentwood. Dressed in charcoal dress pants and a light blue T-shirt, I'd taken the time to clean up my beard and sideburns, but left my hair down. My staple black hair band was on my wrist, right next to my old-school Seiko black watch. I'd been able to reserve a private party room at the back of Valentina's Italiana but as I leaned back in my chair, I had a straight shot view of the hostess stand through the small restaurant.

Which meant I knew the exact second Hailey walked in. She'd paused outside the restaurant's front window, peered in. Stepped through the door and glanced down at her phone. Right on time, but it wouldn't surprise me if she waited a few minutes.

She didn't though. A few seconds later and the door to the restaurant opened and she swept in, shoulders back, and strolled to the hostess as if she owned the place.

Long, tan legs were visible until they disappeared beneath a mid-thigh floral skirt and white tank top where the hem brushed along the waistband of her skirt.

If she moved, I'd see a sliver of skin across her stomach, and she wasn't only cute but dangerous.

Her blonde hair was platinum, highlighted, and it swayed back and forth behind her shoulders as she followed the hostess toward the room.

I was on my feet, next to the table, when Elisia, the same woman I'd spoken with earlier and the one who showed me to our table guided her into the room.

"Hailey?"

She turned to face me and sucked the breath straight from my chest. Holy fucking shit, she was perfect. Cute, yes. Too damn cute for me, but the rest of her made my blood sing with excitement.

She was everything I would have listed if I had gone to Meredith to find someone I actually wanted and not needed.

Her smile trembled. "That's me."

A cute little shoulder shrug and my earlier thought was correct. That sliver of skin appeared and vanished, revealing my worst nightmares.

Tanned, toned skin. I was slow to raise my eyes from the flash of flesh to meet Hailey's eyes, and when I finally managed, a deep pink color darkened her cheeks.

"Dawson." I finally managed to remember my name and that I did have actual access to a vocabulary. "Thanks for being willing to meet me tonight." I gestured toward the table already set for us. "Sit?"

She hesitated before entering the room, but once she breached the doorway, her steps elongated, turned more confident. I pulled out a chair for her across from me.

"Thank you," she whispered as she fell into it and adjusted it so she was comfortable.

Now all I needed was to keep sweat from beading at my temples and my palms from going clammy again.

This was awkward. Everything about sitting across the table from a woman who I was immediately attracted to and actually didn't want to be was why I was here.

"Would you like something to drink?"

There was a carafe of ice water on the table, along with both a bottle of red wine and a bottle of white in an ice bucket.

Hailey scanned the room, darkened, but not overly so, and let out a nervous chuckle. "I can't believe you reserved an entire room for this."

I would have rented the entire restaurant if I could have. "I thought privacy would be better."

Her fingers drummed on the edge of the table. "Why?"

She tilted her head to one side, and her shimmering curtain of platinum hair fell over her shoulder.

"Why privacy?"

"Yeah." She started to reach for the water, but I beat her to it.

"Let me." Her hands fell back to the edge of the table, and I poured the water, careful not to spill. "You saw my pictures online? You said Meredith showed them to you."

"I did."

"So you know who I am?"

It was supposed to be a statement but came out more of a question. I would have figured my career was the first thing Meredith would have mentioned.

"Um. No?" Her hand trembled as she reached for her glass of water. I'd tried to make her more comfortable by meeting somewhere public, not private, but if this was going to terrify her, we could move.

It wasn't like I was recognized all the time, but it did happen. I could deal with it if I had to.

"Should I?"

My turn to laugh. I took a sip of my own water and scraped my upper lip between my teeth. Leaning forward, I rested my forearms on the table. "I play tight end for the Nashville Steel, Hailey."

"The who...oh, that's a sports team, right?"

She grinned then, glacial-blue eyes lighting up like she was proud of herself for guessing right.

A small amount of pressure released. At least she wasn't here for my name or status like Mason and Davis suggested I find. That hadn't sat well with me.

"Football," I filled in for her, and she leaned back in her chair.

"Huh. That's cool. You like it?"

Did I like being one of the best athletes in the entire country? Absolutely, but her nonchalance was refreshing.

"Yeah, Hailey, I like my job. I take it you're not into sports?"

"My parents were more brains over brawn." As soon as she said the words, her mouth formed a perfect O. "I'm sorry. That probably sounded really mean, and I didn't mean to imply you weren't smart... gosh, how horrible of me. I just meant my parents didn't really let me or my siblings play sports. We always had to be focused on academics and clubs like that."

"I know the stereotype."

"Still, not nice of me to say."

"I have a degree in mechanical engineering and a minor in sports medicine, so rest assured, Hailey. I'm not some dumb jock."

Having someone assume I had no brains because I liked smashing skulls together and playing a game for a living wasn't a new thing.

What was new was my desire to defend myself over it.

CHAPTER 6
HAILEY

WELL, hello. Let me open my mouth and shove my gladiator sandal right into it. Pretty sure my common sense brain cells scrambled on sight as soon as I stepped into the doorway to the private room at Valentina's. The restaurant was crowded and there'd been a large group of people waiting in their entryway. It'd been years since I stepped foot into a restaurant this nice. Self-consciousness only increased my nerves as I followed the hostess through the restaurant in my casual summer skirt and tank top, but that had eased when I finally saw Dawson.

His casual clothing, gray dress pants and a casual shirt was the only thing that had me relaxing.

He was so much larger in person than I'd anticipated seeing his picture online. His nose ring caught the light of the wall sconces, and his hair edged his shoulders. His biceps were larger than my thighs, and the rest of him was chiseled perfection, easily viewable beneath the fabric bulging at the seams and the way those pants had fit his hips. His thighs.

Of course he was an athlete. That was oh so obvious on sight, but my faux pas at basically calling him an idiot made me want to puke into my water glass.

"I'm sorry," I said again in a rush. This wasn't like me, but I guess, maybe it was?

I had never dated anyone besides Darrick, not in any serious way. And back then, it'd been in high school and college where nerves were a requirement.

"It's all right. And yes, I play professional football, but I did want a degree in case my dreams never came true."

Fortunately, he didn't seem upset and was willing to move on.

I, on the other hand, glanced at the chilled bottle of white wine. Might settle my nerves. Might make my word vomit worse.

Better not to chance it.

"So." I unrolled the silverware from the white, thick napkin and settled it in my lap to give my hands something to do. "I assume the privacy is because you didn't want people recognizing you?"

Or seeing him with me, at least before he did?

The self-consciousness rose back in a gentle tide.

"I figure, yes, what we need to discuss should be in private."

"Right." He'd mentioned something cryptic over the phone, and Meredith had been equally stonewalling me. Not responding to my texts this afternoon left me more scattered.

We never ignored each other, which meant she was doing it on purpose.

Because he made this seem more like an agreement than a first date. It was exactly what I wanted, but did he have to make it seem so clinical?

"Maybe we should get to that then."

His thick, dark brows tugged in, and that nose ring flashed again. "Let's order first, then we won't be disturbed. That all right?"

"Sure."

I grabbed the menu and pretended to peruse it. Not like I hadn't pulled it up online earlier to make my choices so I didn't hesitate while I was in front of this man. Darrick always laughed at me for picking out my meals before I went to restaurants, but sometimes the choices were overwhelming.

A first date with a new guy and he didn't need to see how ridiculous I could be.

"Would you like to share an appetizer?" Dawson asked, and his voice was a jolted pleasant surprise.

Damn, his voice was deep, throaty.

So much so the only appetizer I could think of was what his lips would taste like.

I hadn't thought to choose one of those....

"Calamari?" I blurted. They weren't horrible. Never my first choice. More word vomit for me. Awesome.

Dawson's lips curled at the edges. "Perfect."

His smile was perfect. Along with his teeth and his cut jawline concealed behind a shortly trimmed and sexy-as-hell beard.

Several minutes later, he leaned back and lifted two fingers. Our server must have been waiting because an older gentleman entered, dressed in all black.

"Ladies first," Dawson said, with a slight tilt of his chin down, and oh my.

I really needed to not screw this up.

I ordered the gnocchi and allowed the waiter to pour me a glass of wine when he offered because what the hell? Why not. Dawson ordered chicken parmesan with a side of asparagus and then requested salad.

"Would you like one?"

I loved salads. Hated eating them on dates. My luck, a crouton went flying across the room or a chunk of pepper from the Caesar dressing would be stuck in my teeth.

The guy would either be too much of a gentleman to point it out, or he would, and then I'd be more embarrassed.

"No thank you," I croaked out and took a healthy chug from my wine.

It was crisp. Chilled to perfection. Reminded me of apples and pears and summertime.

I was so lost in the taste of the wine, I hadn't realized our server had left and Dawson was watching me.

His face showed an emotion I'd never seen on a man's face, especially Darrick's, directed at me.

It was full of want. Confusion. Desire and need and a hint of anger.

Odd, that the hint of anger appeared, but as soon as it was there it was gone. Dawson shook it off before he grabbed his water and drained it in one large chug.

His Adam's apple worked, corded throat displayed muscles I didn't realize actually existed on people, and by the time he set it down and poured himself a new glass, I was practically squirming with desire.

"Need to stop looking at me like that," he muttered.

My eyes widened. "Like what?"

"Like if I told you I wanted you to climb across the table and sit in my lap so I could see if your lips taste as sweet as I imagine they would, you'd be over here in a second, without hesitation."

Well.

At least it was nice to know I hadn't read him all that wrong.

Too bad my emotions were equally noticeable.

"Um...do you want...?"

"Yeah," he huffed. "I'd like that, like that a lot, Hailey, actually, but that can't happen. Not here. Not ever."

Ever?

The word was a slap to my libido and my face, and I sat back in the chair, frowning.

"Then why am I here? If that isn't a possibility?"

"Because I fucked up last season and the general manager of our team told me I need to work on cleaning up my image."

Clean up his image? What the hell had he done? And how could you take someone who looked like they belonged chopping wood in the mountains and turn them into a clean-cut guy who wore polo shirts? Impossible.

"Okay..."

Dawson worked his jaw back and forth before sucking his top lip in between his teeth. Not the first time he'd done it. No less sexy seeing it the second time. A flash of white appeared before he set his mouth into a firm line.

"I need a girlfriend. A fake one. I have a season to focus on and baggage no one wants to handle and ones I'm not ever going to hand to anyone. Couldn't find what I needed on my own, so I went to Meredith. She suggested you."

"Why?"

My best friend in the whole wide world. She knew exactly what I wanted. Him. In paper form. Short-term.

A man willing to let me explore more, salacious, desires in bed than I'd ever have.

If that was off the table...

What the hell was Meredith thinking?

Dawson shrugged, the move no less fluid or graceful or sexy than any other move he'd made so far. "I figured you'd know. Considering she said she never set up relationships for short-term only goals, I was surprised when she told me she had someone who would be able to help me."

Help him.

I was supposed to be some pretty little thing on his arm for a few photo ops and then go our separate ways.

He wanted a fake girlfriend.

But if he wasn't willing to have sex with me...

"Excuse me, I need to use the restroom for a minute."

And get some space without his intense gaze pinning me to my seat and making me think of only wicked things.

I returned to the private room after rushing out of there like a terrified little kitten, but this time, I knew more.

I understood.

Time in the restroom gave me time to not only think but pull up a quick Google search on my phone.

Dawson Butler, age twenty-nine, was never seen with a woman in public. He had one sister. Parents divorced. He'd also been arrested back in January for an altercation in a bar and charges were never pressed. Dawson called it an unfortunate accident, and the other party agreed in a separate statement.

So, at least he wasn't a criminal or anything. An accident. Those happened, especially in bars. But none of it explained why he was looking for a fake girlfriend. I texted Meredith, and the witch didn't respond. An SOS text never went unanswered.

She was playing with me. It irritated me and made me think of what she said at brunch.

If you can get past the bullshit...

He needed something from me.

The least he could do was give me what I needed in return.

Dawson Butler wasn't only the perfect man to be seen with to seriously piss off Darrick, which was a lovely side benefit, he was also the man who was going to teach me how to seduce a man. How to enjoy what I wanted in bed.

He was going to be the man to take my virginity and teach me how to please men—or this was the last dinner we would share, and he'd have to find someone else, some other way.

I figured I now had the upper hand, and I was willing to play it.

Dawson stood as I reached the table, concern tightening his features. In the center of the table was our calamari.

He helped me with my chair again, and I tried not to be overwhelmed by the sexy masculine scent of sandalwood that wafted from him as he did so. "Thank you."

"I was worried you weren't coming back."

He took his own seat and lifted the bottle of wine from the ice. "More?"

"Please." I pushed my glass closer to him. "I apologize for that, but you took me by surprise in more ways than one, and I needed a minute."

His lips quirked at one corner. Sexy. There was nothing the man did that wasn't. "Now you see why I wanted to meet in private."

A loose chuckle rattled free from the tightness threatening to close my throat.

His smirk turned into a full-blown smile.

Breathtakingly wicked. I took a quick sip of my wine so the force of that smile didn't knock me off my chair.

"So, since I'm not quite sure what you're looking for. Why don't you tell me?"

He brushed his hands off on his napkin and resettled it in his lap. The man had manners, I'd give him that. "I've had some issues in the past, with a family member. Let's say she caused quite a bit of trouble for me last spring."

That must have been his sister, Crystal. She was the only person pictured online with him and she was mentioned in the article about the bar.

"Okay."

His brows tugged together. "You know."

"I did a quick search online when I was in the bathroom."

He sucked in air between his teeth and his massive shoulders rose and dropped with a heavy breath.

"Does that make you mad?"

"Only that it's out there, and it happened at all. So okay, Crystal. She won't be a problem anymore, but she's caused enough. Actually, might be more fair to say that because I kept hoping she'd get her shit together, I caused enough trouble. Enough that my coaches are still pissed at me and our team's general manager, who's best friends with the owner, wants to see some changes out of me. I even understand it. The professional sports organizations, especially football, have put in a lot of work over the years to show our humanity, to prove we're good men and not troublemakers. So when someone gets in trouble, we have to bear the brunt of it."

"How does a girlfriend help?" I popped a piece of calamari into my mouth and chewed.

"Because it shows I'm not a wildcard. Shows I've got something to work for off the field. Gives people hope I'm settling down or some shit." He sneered then, and while it wasn't directed at me, he let his anger at the whole situation slip.

"You don't want a relationship."

"I will never get married." He reached for his wine, and if I wasn't mistaken, he white-knuckled the thin glass, or probably crystal, stem a bit too hard. "Any real relationship is eventually going to want someone who begins to lean that way. I'm not going to lead them on or hurt anyone."

It was enough for me to not ask why.

He was entitled to his secrets.

I tried to quell the disappointment that rose. Meredith said he was perfect for me. Had she meant forever, or for my short-term goals? He spoke with such conviction there was no doubt he believed every word he said. I'd try to pry the truth and why Meredith was so sure of him when she finally answered my phone calls.

Probably after her vacation, knowing my luck.

"Okay. So, let's say I agree to this. How long are we talking?"

"At least through the beginning of the season."

And that would be?

He chuckled at whatever expression I gave. "Right. Pre-season starts in July. We're doing off-season workouts now, but we don't go to camp until the end of July. Pre-season games start almost right after in August."

"And it ends?"

"January if we don't make it to the Super Bowl again."

"Again?"

"Yeah, Hailey." He grinned, and it was disarmingly cute. Sweet. Like he was fully amused by me and my lack of knowledge. Made it a lot harder to not help myself to what he suggested earlier.

Couldn't be too hard—or embarrassing—to climb over a table to get to him.

"Oh. Well, congratulations on that."

He chuckled then and showed me a full smile of teeth and a gleam in his eye.

"Here's my question for you." He set down his wine and pushed away his appetizer plate. Leaning forward with his forearms on the table, he hooked his two index fingers together. "Meredith said you'd be perfect for me. That you want something short-term. So, if you help me out with this, what do you want from me?"

It was the moment of the hour. My throat was suddenly stuffed with cotton, and the preparation I went through in the restroom burned my tongue.

Tell him. All I had to do was open my mouth to tell him.

Risk it all on a stranger.

I took a sip of my water, not wine, because I couldn't lose any more sense, and licked a droplet off my lip.

He'd already admitted, basically, to being attracted to me...

"I want you to take my virginity."

CHAPTER 7
DAWSON

"WHAT?" I sputtered.

I had to have misheard her.

This woman? There was no way...and if she was, was she out of her damn mind?

She swallowed thickly. "Up until two months ago, I was engaged to a guy I started dating when we were twenty. We'd both been...inexperienced...and he wanted us to wait until we were married."

I gaped at her. Pretty sure my mouth moved and no words came out. A virgin? Her? This fucking sexy bombshell with legs for days and a seductive little smile and the perfect throaty laugh and singsong voice was a virgin?

"How old are you?" Probably not the question I should have asked based on her grimace.

Oops.

"Twenty-four."

"You dated someone for four years and never had sex with them?"

"Yeah, well." She dipped her chin, so I lost her face except for the fan of her long, thick eyelashes as they fluttered. She fidgeted with her silverware. Lined them up. Anything to not look at me, and when she finally lifted her head, there was a wet sheen in her eyes.

"I'm the only one of the two of us, considering he ran off with my bridesmaid, and since, I've found he wasn't exactly the faithful kind of type."

"Are you fucking kidding me?"

"No." She sniffed and drained her wine. It was only her second glass. Probably enough. But hell, this had to be more difficult than what I shared. If she needed to get drunk to get through it, who was I to stop her?

"Anyway, so yeah. That's why Meredith told me I'd be perfect for you. I want something short-term. Or, at least, she wants something short-term for me."

"What do you mean, she wants that for you?"

"Oh." A nervous giggle. Another fiddle with silverware. Her tells were as easy to read as any rookie opponent. "She and I are friends. I'm not, exactly, a client of hers. And she and my other two friends dared me to let her find someone for me, so we made a list..."

Well, this was getting amusing. I leaned back in my chair and crossed my arms. "A list?"

"Yeah. And funnily enough, you waltzed into her office the very next week."

A list.

"What exactly was on your list, Hailey?"

She waved her hand in a circle toward me. Cheeks turning pink, she still grinned when she said, "Well, you...all of that muscle and tattoo and piercing and...so yeah...that's why I'm here."

To fuck me.

Have a little fun with a guy who wouldn't break her heart.

There was only one problem with that, and I'd never been quite so pissed to be used for my body as I was then. "I was very clear in telling Meredith sex was off the table. I wasn't paying a woman to give me her orgasms."

Her lips parted in surprise and then pressed together. "Pay?"

"Yeah. I told Meredith I'd pay someone. Six months. Six figures. Figured that'd be worth the hassle and the time required."

"I don't need your money."

Just my body.

Should it have really pissed me off? Women I met at clubs did the same thing. Saw my muscles and height and climbed me like a tree at the first sign of interest from me.

Still...not this woman. This woman who initially assumed jocks were dumb as a box of rocks. Yeah, she apologized.

But damn.

"What else?" I asked, my irritation forcing me to grind my teeth together. "What else would you want? I imagine now you know I play pro football, that'd be a good fuck you to your ex too, yeah?"

"Well, yeah. Maybe. Darrick's into golf, but I've never really seen him watch football."

She said it so innocently like she wasn't aware at all of the shit swirling in my mind. My chest.

This should have been an easy yes. I got what I wanted and didn't have to rely on my hand.

And better...I could imagine her. Soft. Pliable. Compliant. Her hand would probably tremble the first time I showed her my cock. Her mouth would water, eyes might part in fear at my size. Her long lashes would grow wet the first time I pushed a little too deep into her throat.

I cleared my throat and vanquished those thoughts from my mind.

"In my defense," Hailey said, and she was quieter now. More timid. "When we made that list and when my friends had that idea, I truly didn't think any man would come close to meeting what I said. I only agreed as a joke, and if you're not comfortable with that, I can understand."

Uncomfortable with fucking a virgin? Teaching her how to please me?

What man wouldn't like that.

My dick already sure as hell did. I'd need a half hour in an ice bath to get rid of the erection I was currently sporting.

Thank god for tablecloths and space.

I fisted my hair at the base of my neck before letting it drop.

"Seems like we both need something from each other, then."

There was hope in her eyes as she blinked at me.

This was possibly a worse decision than not kicking Crystal out after she destroyed my house on New Year's Eve, but there I was.

Willing to bend on my boundaries for a woman who needed help only I could give.

"Fine. I'll do it. If you agree to be my girlfriend."

She grinned. That soft little nervous laugh barely reached my ears. "Fake girlfriend."

"Right. Deal?"

That time, her smile was blinding, knocking me straight on my ass. "Deal."

What did I have to lose? She knew the score. Knew this was fake with a deadline.

And for the next six months? I got to spend all my time pleasuring her, teaching her...

Before I set her off to find some guy who'd appreciate all the effort.

Fuck. Me.

Weights slammed down around me. An echoing of grunts and groans and laughter and typical bullshitting from my team. Davis was spotting Mason next to me as he worked on his bench press, and I shoved up to my ass from my finished set and grabbed my towel.

Pre-season workouts, all individually prepared and designed by our trainers and after we were done, meals were made by the team's chef specifically created for our unique macro needs. After, there'd be speed workouts. Conditioning and sprints to increase our speed off the line of the scrimmage and getting down the field.

My day was organized for me, down to the second as soon as I stepped foot into our training facility a couple miles from our game field.

Typically, I didn't mind. Helped me stay focused.

Today, I couldn't focus on shit. Four days ago, I walked Hailey to her car after dinner, waited until she pulled out of the parking lot and even though it was almost ten o'clock on a Saturday night, phoned Meredith.

"What the hell is this bullshit?"

She answered immediately, and I could practically hear the laugh in her voice when she replied, "You said you wanted short-term."

"I also said I wasn't paying for sex. And don't you think this is a conflict of interest?"

She laughed again. Actually had the gall to laugh at me. "I think I'm considering everyone's interests, and besides, you aren't paying anything. No way would Hailey take you up on that with what she wants."

That damn woman. How infuriating. How in the hell were they even friends? She also wasn't wrong. As soon as I'd brought up the money, Hailey shut me down. Refused to hear anything I said. "I can still back out of this. Ruin your winning percentage you so proudly boast about."

"You could."

But I wouldn't, was what she left unsaid.

"Anything else, Mr. Butler?"

"Yeah." Damn her and Hailey for being so utterly and completely tempting. "Call me Dawson since I'm soon going to be fake dating your best friend."

I hung up to the sound of her laughing. Infuriating woman.

That was Saturday night.

Now it was Thursday. Hailey and I hadn't spoken.

How in the hell did I set up our next date? "Hey, wanna get started on that sex stuff?"

Did we become friends? Let that happen naturally? Did we just go out in public for a few photo ops or whatever and then go back to one of our homes so I could give her a How To Give A Blow Job 101 lesson?

How in the hell was I supposed to lead all of this?

Cole stepped into my line of sight, scrubbing his hair with a towel and draping it over his shoulders. Hands on his hips, chest heaving from his own workout, he peered at me. "You okay? Haven't moved in five minutes."

I hadn't even realized I was still in the gym. "Yeah." I shoved to my feet.

Cole gives a quick glance around the room and leans in. "How's that plan of yours going?"

"Already a mess."

"You had the meeting with the matchmaker, right?"

"Yup, and I'm not saying any more."

No guy on the team was going to find out what was going on. So a few knew I had to fake date someone. Fine. But I certainly wasn't going over the terms of the agreement with them.

Cole frowned and whipped his towel off his shoulders before setting his hands on his hips. "Why not?"

"Because I don't like talking about my own shit."

"But you made me talk about mine."

True. "That's because you were acting like a fool."

He choked on a laugh. "Still helped though."

I grabbed his arm and yanked him toward the wall where we'd have more space. Not like I expected guys to sit around, waiting to gossip or anything, but surprisingly, some of the guys on my team liked to talk about their shit a lot more than any male I'd ever met.

"I met her," I said, keeping my voice low. "We had dinner last weekend. I'm calling her again soon. She knows the score, and I know what she wants from me, so it's fine. That enough for you?"

"What does she want from you? The money?" He said money like she wanted me to rip my soul straight from my body and sell it for the highest bidder.

Joke was on him.

I wasn't sure I had one anymore.

"None of your business."

"Maybe not now, but if this woman wants you to do something you're not comfortable with and that starts affecting your training, or our season once it starts..."

"It's fine."

Hell no it wasn't. I equally loved and hated the idea of taking her virginity. She'd saved it all this time for someone she thought she was going to marry, shouldn't she want to at least have it go to someone she was in a relationship with? Or hell, whatever. Her body, her choice. She wanted to give it to me, whatever. Her call. I wasn't uncomfortable with the idea. It was that I'd spent far too much time thinking about the moment I slid inside of her. The first time I went down on her and the first time I had her screaming my name. Her short, unpainted nails grabbing on to my hair while I slammed deep inside of her.

That was starting to make me uncomfortable, even in front of Cole. Not a good look in a locker room full of men.

I swiped my towel over my face and spied an open treadmill. A nice punishing run would help get my head on straight. "Talk later, Cole. If I need help, I'll ask."

"Liar."

I shrugged and slapped his shoulder, shoving him back.

So I wouldn't ask for help.

Everything would be fine once I finally called her and set something up. We'd talked at dinner about what she did, so she told me about her shop and how she rented out the apartment above it.

She worked late, usually until eight at night. The store closed at seven, but she said she usually spent at least an hour working on pieces, especially if her tenant in the apartment was traveling. I'd be out of here by four.

What better way to start seeing her than by bringing her some food or something, showing up, and getting a good look at how she lived her life.

Girls liked surprises, right?

CHAPTER 8
HAILEY

"THANK YOU, make sure you come back some time and visit again."

I smiled at the customer and handed over her purchase. She'd not only bought a set of nightstands painted in a warm, soothing green color she swore would look incredible in her guest room, but she'd then bought a silver platter I'd refinished a couple weeks ago.

Both were beautiful pieces. Both were also pieces I scored for almost pennies at an estate sale, so the sale alone was enough to pay my electricity for the week. Definitely worth the hours I'd put into them.

Not bad. Not bad at all.

As soon as the customer was gone, I turned to Misty, who'd decided to stop by after she went to the gym. She was still drenched in Lululemon gear, and her hair was plaited into two braids. She'd helped herself to my checkout counter, plopping her ass onto it and was swinging her feet back and forth like a child on a swing.

"Don't you have somewhere to be?"

"Nope." She grinned. "I want to hear more about the guy."

I rolled my eyes and grabbed a stack of tea towels I sold third-party for a local mom who entered frequent craft fairs. I took fifteen percent of her sales, and she marked them up so her percentage stayed the same. No one seemed to mind.

I needed to fold her newest delivery, and now was the perfect time.

Misty couldn't see my hands shake with nerves and fear if I kept them busy. "It's fine."

"When are you going to see him again?"

Sloane and Misty showed up Sunday afternoon when I was in my workroom, and apparently, lovely Meredith, who was now safe from me in Puerto Vallarta, had talked to them and told them Dawson and I went out. They were only slightly pissed I hadn't called them myself.

"Don't know."

He hadn't called. It wasn't a normal relationship, so I didn't expect to start checking in on each other, but the radio silence after four days was creating a cramping sensation in my chest.

Had he changed his mind? Was he ghosting me? I'd thought we had a deal, and after we'd agreed, dinner had proceeded like a more normal date. He asked about me, my family. I told him about my siblings, that my parents were born and raised and still lived in Friendswood while everyone else moved away. I told him about my business, and he'd seemed so genuinely interested, I'd gone into detail about my work, how I started it.

He hadn't seemed to be faking any of that, but maybe he went home and realized he could do better?

Maybe what I wanted from him was too much to ask?

"He hasn't called?"

"No, Mist, he hasn't."

"So call him."

I was not calling a man who agreed to help me with my sex life. And say what? "Wanna fuck me tonight?"

How absurd. And so not me.

I glared at Misty. "Don't you and Ryan have plans tonight?"

Usually bringing up her situationship or whatever was enough to get her to be quiet.

"Nooo...he's going to a brewery with friends tonight. Although I might swing by later if he's not too drunk."

She wiggled her brows. For sex. Because everyone was having it but me, and I was supposed to be a married woman by now and getting it whenever I wanted.

"Rub it in," I muttered.

Misty laughed and spun one of her braids in a circle. "Speaking of rubbing. If you called him—"

The bell above the door rang as someone came in. I shot Misty a glare to shut her up, but she'd already closed her mouth. At least, right before she breathed, "Holy shit. You have got to rub your hands all over that."

"Mist," I scowled at her and turned to see her gaping at the customer.

The customer currently headed our way—or mine—

The customer I hadn't seen since Saturday night and the man who looked entirely too brutal, too savage, to be in a tiny little shop with painted and restained antique furniture. In jeans that clung to his thighs and a long sleeve, simple gray Henley that looked fitted to every single one of his muscles. His hair was pulled back at the back of his neck, and that beard...he was the epitome of a bull in a china shop, moving with grace right for me.

"Hey," I said, and I was pretty sure it came out on a breath. My heart started racing and my fingertips turned sweaty.

"Damn," Misty whispered. "Lucky girl."

She said it quietly. No way could Dawson hear her, but still, he quirked an amused smile at my friend before his look changed to uncertainty when he finally reached us.

"How's your week going?"

Better now. So much better now.

"Um. Hi."

Misty laughed.

Dawson frowned.

"What?" I glanced at both of them.

"You already said hi, dummy."

"Thanks, Mist. This is Dawson. Dawson, my ex-friend, Misty."

He held out his hand, and I was pretty sure Misty was blushing when she reached out to shake his. "You are bigger than I pictured."

"Misty." I elbowed her, but she didn't let go of Dawson's hand.

How awkward. They were shaking hands, Misty was swinging her feet, and Dawson's fingers flexed in her grip to get her to let go, but she held on.

"Let him go, Mist. You have Ryan."

She scowled at me. "Had to ruin my fun, didn't you?"

"Pretty sure I'm taken," Dawson teased and with his free hand, he peeled Misty's hand off his before stepping back.

Good idea for him. Misty didn't always understand other people's personal space issues.

"Good." She grinned and hopped down. "I'll let you two do your thing." She kissed my cheek and waved to Dawson. "Nice to meet you. Have fun, you two!"

Dawson swiveled, watched her leave, and when the bell rang and she exited, I breathed a sigh of relief.

"Gotta say, and no offense, but so far I think you have some really interesting choices in friends."

"Are yours better?"

He scowled, and with all his brawn and muscles and beard, it was adorable. Not that I was telling him that. "Probably not, no. She taken? If she's crazy. Might know someone..."

I laughed, full-out laughed. "Misty's never taken."

"Who's Ryan?"

"The current guy she won't want to hold on to after another month or so."

"Got it. So...I meant to call or text this week but didn't know quite what to say, so I figured I'd stop by. That all right?"

Well, he was here, so it would have to be, but I appreciated the honesty.

"I didn't quite pick you as a guy who would be nervous to call a woman."

He cleared his throat, still adorable. "Relationships aren't really my thing. And this isn't exactly a normal one."

More honesty. Should have appreciated that one too, but it was only a brutal reminder. Whatever we were going to do was fake. And limited.

"Right," I said, and I couldn't hide the tremble in my voice. "So... what do we do then?"

"Figured we could talk about that in person. But show me around your store? You do all of this?" As he asked, he swept his arm in a circle, gesturing to well, my entire store.

Nerves from his arrival split. This was what I knew. What I could talk about without hesitating and worry. "Yeah."

"Show me your favorites."

"Ah. That's like asking a parent to choose a favorite child, but okay."

I led him around the store to some of my larger items. A buffet and a china cabinet. Furniture from the early nineteen-hundreds. I'd polished and kept the original hardware and found replacements from other broken antique pieces. Some of the pieces I painted, but only those were the woodwork needed too much repair to show the natural wood grain. Others, I stained. I showed him smaller silver pieces and platters, and chandelier fixtures. I pointed out the items like the kitchen tea towels and other craft and home decor items I sold for vendors. Every time I showed him something, he took time, showed interest. He ran his hand over the top of a dresser I'd painted an eggshell blue and asked about the process, how much time it took.

He was far too large, far too masculine to have his large palm on anything, and yet touched it with a gentleness I wouldn't have expected him capable of.

"What are you currently working on?"

I checked my watch and noticed it was well past closing. I'd spent almost an hour showing him my store, and he hadn't once seemed rushed or annoyed I was taking so long.

"Let me lock up and I'll show you." I grabbed the keys out of my pocket.

"You need to go?"

Isaac was out of town, so I was planning on spending a few hours in the back, but I never used my workroom when I was alone in the store with doors unlocked. I might have been independent, but I wasn't stupid.

For Dawson and whatever we needed to discuss or do, I'd put it off.

"I'm good." He waited by the counter while I locked the front door and flipped the open sign to Closed. Then I dimmed the lights, to discourage anyone else who might not see my posted hours or the Closed sign. It was amazing how often it happened.

"Come on."

I led him to the back, a narrow hallway I used for storage and a bathroom, and then unlocked the workroom door. Behind it was the door to the back parking lot, so it was always locked when I wasn't in it. I stepped in and squirmed internally.

No one had ever shown so much interest. My friends, yes, and Meredith would often sit with me while I worked especially during Tuevo's season, and he was on the road. But it hit me, I'd never had a man in this space. Certainly never Darrick. He'd never once given a shit about my passion or my business. He hadn't even shown up when I had my grand opening celebration.

Red flags. Red flags had flown in my face so often I must have been color blind to not see them.

My throat closed as Dawson stepped in behind me and sucked in all the oxygen in the large but disorganized and messy and dirty wreck of a workroom.

"It's kind of a mess," I said and spun my keys around my thumb. "And it doesn't look like much, but I guess, yeah...this is where I do most of the work."

"It ventilated?"

He had tipped his chin to meet my eyes and then scanned the room.

"Um. Yeah?"

"You work with all those chemicals. That can't be safe."

Was he...worried about me?

I showed him the masks I used, the fans. "Bigger pieces I sometimes take out back to sand, but that's just to make clean up easier, but the door opens and there's the window. I'm good, Dawson."

He shoved his hands to his hips. Frowned. "Good. That's good."

God, he was gorgeous. Aloof and growly, but so damn gorgeous. I stood by the door as he wandered around the room, not all of it, because it was half the size of my store, but I needed the space to hold everything I'd bought and was working on. He took in everything with an intensity I hadn't expected, a natural curiosity.

"I gotta say, and you don't need my approval or shit, but this is damn impressive. Really fucking cool what you do."

A knot in my chest that I hadn't realized was there loosened, making breathing easier.

I didn't need his approval, but damn...it felt good to have it.

"Thanks." I grinned then and froze as he headed my way. Our gazes met, his dark, almost black eyes and that glint of the nose ring. I licked my lips as he came closer. Couldn't be helped.

He made my mouth water and my throat dry at the same time and my fingers itched, burned and pulsed to do exactly what Misty suggested and rub my hands all over him.

"So, what should we do then?" I asked, because there were ideas flashing in my mind at a rapid pace giving me so many suggestions.

"I'm not sure what we should do," Dawson whispered, and his quiet voice was a rumble that shot a spike of arousal straight to my core. "But I know what I want to do."

"What?" He was in front of me now. So large and broad-shouldered and sexy, and damn, I really wished his hair was down.

He brought his hands to my cheeks, thumbs brushing on the soft flesh beneath my jaw, and I shivered, full-on body tremble as he swatted his thumbs against my flesh.

"This." He tilted my chin, his face moved closer.

And kissed me.

CHAPTER 9
DAWSON

I SHOULD HAVE CALLED HER. Sent a text. I should not have showed up at her store, while she looked so damn fine in torn jeans and another cropped tank top, this one a vibrant blue and shorter, showing more than a tiny sliver of skin at her stomach.

I definitely should not have followed her into the back workroom after spending an hour surrounded by her soft, floral scent and listening to her lyrical voice while she spoke with passion and such knowledge with every question I asked.

All the shit she did was impressive as hell from start to finish, and it was crazy that as she told me about some of the visions she had for the pieces, as she showed me before pictures she had set up on some of the larger dressers and such, that she'd not only seen what a piece of furniture could become, sometimes while it looked tattered and broken to hell and back, but then was talented enough to bring that vision to life.

Incredible.

So damn incredible.

So yeah, should not have followed her into a more cramped space, walked toward her.

And I definitely should not have been kissing her, with my thumbs at her jaw, her soft, parted lips opening for me in surprise.

Peppermint and sunshine and happiness. She tasted like all of it and the soft flesh of her skin was so damn beautiful. Too damn much. I barely pressed the tip of my tongue against hers before I wanted to yank her body to mine, slam her back against the wall, and speed through all the first steps she probably wanted to know about sex.

"Fuck," I groaned into her mouth, slid my hands to her shoulders, and gently peeled her away from me.

She was panting, eyes still closed. Those blonde lashes framing the top of her cheeks. I held on to her until she was steady on her feet, but she was so surprised by either the fact I kissed her or that I stopped, it took her a hot minute.

"Oh," she whispered, and her hand came up and covered her mouth. "That was...well, wow."

Wow was right.

"Sorry." I stepped back toward the doorway that would give me an exit.

"Sorry?" Her lashes fluttered in surprise. "For what?"

"I shouldn't have...I didn't know..." Fuck. I hadn't even asked if kissing was okay. If she'd be okay with it. Yeah, she wanted something from me, but this was fake.

Temporary.

"I, um, didn't mind the kiss."

Yeah, the pink staining her cheeks and the fact she kept pressing her fingers to her lips told me that.

"Should have asked."

"I'm glad you didn't." She stepped toward me. "Feel free, you know...while we're doing this fake girlfriend thing, to kiss me whenever you want, especially if it's going to be like that."

A joke. She liked it. She'd seemed nervous at dinner, at least for a bit. Was more confident now.

"I'll keep that in mind."

She laughed, that same soft laugh that shot straight to my dick. "So, while that was an enjoyable start, when I asked what we did now, I didn't mean the kissing and stuff. I meant about dates."

Right.

Of course she had, although now that kissing and stuff was on her mind, I could spend the night teaching her another thing or two.

"If you're done here, we could go to your place and talk about it?"

"We could. Or we could go grab a drink and actually be seen in public?"

Right. Because that was the whole point of this. "I think the things we need to talk about should be in private."

"Trust me. I know just the place."

I was already trusting her a hell of a lot, especially considering she was a stranger. Hell, she could still fuck me over, but she wouldn't.

Didn't know how I knew, but somehow, I figured Hailey might be the first woman I ever met who didn't fuck me over.

And that was more terrifying.

"Lead the way."

After Hailey finished locking up, she told me to leave my car parked. We walked down Main Street, full of vibrancy, families out, a huge line of them waiting out on a sidewalk for ice cream. There were breweries and food trucks parked outside, and at everyone we passed, music and laughter filtered out. The bar she took us to was only three blocks away but took a whack of time to get there considering Hailey was stopped every few yards with someone saying hello to her.

No introductions were made, although a few women eyed me curiously. She waved, said hello, and kept moving.

"You know everyone in this town?"

"Friendswood's big and getting bigger, but I grew up here, and it used to be much smaller, or feel that way. Parents still live in town. And they're friendly people. Mom teaches school at the middle school. Dad still volunteers at the fire department and works for the city. So yeah, not everyone. But enough."

"And your business."

"What?"

"You said you know everyone because you grew up here, and you might, but I'm guessing you know a lot more because of your shop?"

"Yeah." She shrugged. Almost like she didn't want to talk about it. Or maybe didn't get a lot of compliments on it? Confused the hell out of me. "Maybe."

She led me around a corner near the end of the street. I didn't notice the signage, didn't know what I was walking into, but as soon as we stepped inside, I knew exactly why she brought me here.

There were only eight tables in the darkened, small bar. An entire wall of wine bottles lined one wall and at the back was a small cashier stand. "We can go out back, there's a small patio. Or stay here?"

Inside, in the dark, where we'd have to sit so close together I'd be able to settle my hand on her thigh? Worked for me...definitely.

"Is this place even open?"

"Yeah, it's one of my favorite places."

"Hey, Hailey!" a woman called.

Hailey turned to her and smiled. "Margo. How's it going?"

"Good." The brunette wiped the back of her hand at her hairline and then grabbed a towel. "Busy out back. Can't figure out why because it is hot out there. And buggy. Cooler in here. And who's this?"

The woman glanced at me. Had to be at least ten years older than me, putting her close to forty, and the look she gave me made me think of a protective big sister—at least for Hailey.

"Dawson. Dawson Butler," I said. "Nice to meet you."

"Butler...you're..." Her brows lifted on her head. "Tight end? For Nashville?"

"That's me." I grinned, tried to fake it. I wasn't recognized a ton but the name, for any sports fan, was memorable. That and I scored a touchdown during the Super Bowl. Davis and I had both been on that stage, standing behind Cole as he took that trophy in his hands for the first time.

"Wow. Cool. So cool to meet you, great season last year. My husband's a freaking huge fan."

"Thank you."

"So, oh my god. If he wasn't stuck at home with the kids, I'd totally make him come up and meet you, but oh...you might not like that. Right?"

"Geez, Margo. I've never seen you like this?"

"Well it's not every day we get a famous athlete around here. Singers, sure, but still..."

The woman's eyes were wide with wonder. Strange, absolutely so strange to me to be looked at this way. An uncomfortable itch started at my spine. I was used to this. I could fake it, but these were also Hailey's friends. People she'd know long after I was gone.

I couldn't be my typical dick, standoff self, which left me not quite knowing how to act.

"It's fine. Cool. Actually, you want to take a pic of us?"

"Can I?"

Hailey smothered a laugh next to me, and I grinned down at her. "I didn't realize people would treat you like toddlers treated Santa Claus."

"This is minor. Trust me."

And it was. A fan excited was one thing, but the things fans tossed our way—bras, underwear, phone numbers and business cards. It got weird sometimes.

"Really?"

God, the fact she didn't know sports at all was starting to be a hell of a turn-on. "Yeah."

Margo came back over with her phone, lined us up in front of the wine case. "Want me in this?" Hailey asked me.

"Damn straight I do. This is what you're here for."

"Right." She flinched in my hold, smiled for the picture and as soon as Margo checked the screen I apologized.

"That's not what I meant."

"I know." But the light in her eyes was gone and her lips were tilted into a frown.

"So, wine? Food? What would you two like?"

Reverse time, go back thirty-five seconds where I didn't make Hailey look like I'd just sacked her to the turf.

Hailey's smile returned. Fake as hell. Still looked pretty on her though.

"You pick, Dawson."

"Sure? You've been here."

"I like it all." She waved at the wall, put her back to Margo, and scanned the wine at the far end.

I glanced at Margo over my shoulder. "She have a favorite?"

"Yep."

"Then we'll have a bottle of that. And some food? Appetizers or something?"

"There are several Hailey enjoys."

"That's not necessary."

It was. I'd cheer her up with food and drink if I had to. "Everything she likes, bring it out."

"All right." Margo was still smiling at me in that dazzled kind of way as I settled my hand to Hailey's lower back and guided her to a table. I gave her a better view of the place and sat my ass down next to her. The tables were small, four-person bar-height tables, but that would only comfortably seat two, which meant even though it was just us, we were close enough to touch.

Heaven and hell mixed in one, especially given what I'd just said.

I waited until she was settled on her seat before taking the one next to her. Given my size, even with pushing the other two stools out of the way, I could still brush my knee against hers. I refrained since she was still looking like I'd swept her feet right out from under her.

"You didn't have to do all of this."

"I also didn't have to treat you like you were some object and hurt your feelings, but I spoke without thinking, and that's exactly what I did."

"It's fine." She waved her hand in the air, flippantly trying to blow me off. Only pissing me off more.

"It's not fine. We both know what this is, but I don't have to throw it in your face, and I won't. Swear it, Hailey, you might not really be mine, but you're still mine, and while we're doing this, my job is to make sure you don't get hurt, especially by me."

"Your job is to make sure your general manager likes you again."

Yeah. That was also true.

"Doesn't mean your feelings aren't important. I'll do better. Like I said, I don't date much, and outside of hook-ups and shit, I don't have a lot of experience with women. At least not dating them. Pretty sure I'll fuck up this fake dating thing as much as I would a real relationship, but I do promise to try and be better."

"Why don't you date women?"

"Excuse me?"

"Here we are," Margo sang, and arrived at our table with a bottle of white wine in a chiller and two glasses. "Want me to pour?"

"I got it."

Another white wine. Not my choice, but this was for Hailey anyway.

"Okay, I'll leave you two alone then. Let me know if you need anything."

"Thanks, Margo." Hailey smiled at her while I poured her a glass and then one for me.

I told her why I needed her, and a bit about my sister, but maybe, if she was really going to understand, I needed a dash more honesty. She hadn't hidden shit from me the other night, not when it came to why she agreed to date me.

"There's not a woman in my life yet who hasn't fucked me over in some way. It's not that deep. And that doesn't mean I hate women, or whatever, but for me, it means my life is a hell of a lot less complicated when I'm not close to them."

She sipped her wine. Took her time. Eventually, she brought her eyes to mine and smiled. That same damn smile that made a warning shoot straight to my gut. This woman was trouble, in a vastly different kind of way than what I'd just been thinking of.

"Maybe you haven't met the right kind of woman then."

Yeah. She was right about that.

It was after an order of bruschetta came. After we finished our first glass of wine. After we talked more about her work because that's exactly where I was trying to keep the conversation headed as long as it didn't come back around to me when we finally got around to talking about Hailey's family and her three siblings.

"Your parents must have been busy. You close with them?"

"Yeah. I mean, I see them frequently. Mom occasionally pops into the store during the week when it's slower, brings me lunch or hangs out. Dad texts me random facts about his day, like how many deer he saw on their property."

"Your sister and brothers?"

When Crystal and I were younger, up until our parents' marriage imploded and took us all down with it, we'd been practically best friends. Only two years difference between us, we'd hung out all the time. Lots of weekend nights she'd come into my room, we'd turn on a movie, and she'd fall asleep. I never cared, even when we were too old probably to be sharing a bed. It was cool. She was cool.

"They were all born within four years of each other, and I came six years later. My brothers are protective, to say the least. My sister thinks she's my second mom. But they're all good. Charlie's in Portland. He's a tattoo artist and works at some like, famous tattoo shop or something. Tate's a plastic surgeon, lives out in San Diego, and Holly's a lawyer and lives in New York."

"You're the only one who stayed close to home."

"Yeah. They all craved the city life, and Portland's easier for Charlie and he loves it out there."

"Easier?"

She twirled her wineglass in her hands, and when she spoke again, her voice was softer. Almost hesitant. "Things are changing, but it's not always easy to be a gay man in the South, you know?"

Well, I didn't know. Hadn't known her brother was gay, but I guessed with how she approached it, she'd assume I'd mind. Or had people in her past who'd minded a hell of a lot. "Don't give a shit who people love, Hailey."

But maybe it had nothing to do with me at all... "Your parents okay with that?"

"I don't know if they were, originally, maybe sad for him or something, but he's Charlie. Their son. They love him, so yeah, might have taken a hot minute, but they love him just the same."

"That's good. Good you have that."

I sure as hell didn't, and it never had anything to do with my sexual orientation.

Talk about a conversation stopper. Fortunately, I was able to redirect the conversation when Margo appeared.

She set down a plate of a variety of meats and cheeses and crackers.

"Thank you, Margo," Hailey said and snagged a chunk of cheese.

She chewed on it and closed her eyes, making a humming sound that shot straight to my gut. Goddamn. The way this woman ate. She didn't hide her enjoyment and hadn't done it the other night either. She dove right in and showed her appreciation for every bite of food she enjoyed like it was the last meal she'd have for a month.

Hadn't ever realized how sexy eating could be, until I enjoyed a meal with her.

"Anything else?" Margo asked, grinning at me.

"We're good. Thanks. You send your husband that pic yet?"

"I'm surprised he isn't here yet, breaking every stoplight in town in order to get to you."

I shook my head, chuckling. Funny how grown men turned into boys when surrounded by professional athletes. At our core, we were still men.

She laughed. "Our little boys are already asleep, so he won't be here, but he's pretty damn bummed he missed you."

"Did you put it on your social media yet?" Hailey asked.

She was dropping a dollop of mustard onto a cracker and covered it with prosciutto.

Margo's brown eyes turned the color of saucers. "Is that okay with you?"

"Yeah. It's all right. Mind waiting until we leave though?"

"No. Of course. But well, thanks. I hadn't considered you'd be okay with that. Normally I don't, out of respect, you know..."

"It's cool, Margo. People will see us eventually."

"Will they?" Margo teased, glanced between us.

"Yep. I think he likes me." Hailey popped the cracker into her mouth and chewed.

She was not wrong.

"Does he?" Margo's question was asked to me.

"Yeah." I grabbed my glass of wine. "I just might."

Which wasn't a lie, and I wasn't quite so mad about it.

CHAPTER 10
HAILEY

TONIGHT HAD BEEN a whirlwind of surprise from the moment Dawson showed up at my store. It occurred to me that I should probably start looking into his career. It was impossible to miss the side-eyes we'd received on the walk to Margo's—both my friend and the name of the bar—and her reaction pretty much sealed the deal.

It wasn't like I was some moron who lived with their head buried in the sand, but when you grew up in a family where sports didn't factor into our rec time or television viewing events, I was struggling to figure out why everyone made such a big deal of seeing an athlete in person.

Was it the millions? Was it the entertainment factor?

I wasn't quite sure, but while we finished up the food Margo delivered, I tried to push past the unease of the fact it felt like everyone was watching us and vowed to learn a little bit more of his life without prying.

He didn't owe me anything other than the promises we'd made to each other the other night and as our last glasses of wine were filled from the bottle he poured and our plates were cleaned, I'd spent well over an hour with the heat of his body warming me and the scent of his masculine cologne, or maybe it was pure him, making my head spin.

He was signing the bill, and I was nervously tapping my foot in the air, one leg thrown over my knee in a way to figure out what to suggest next.

A good night? A walk me back to my store? Or maybe...

In the end, Dawson decided by lifting one hip off the chair, tucking his wallet into his back pocket and holding out his hand. "Getting late, and I've got an early morning. Let me walk you to your car?"

I stared at his hand. Then up at his face. All that hair hanging at his shoulders and all that breadth of muscle.

I wasn't the least bit tired.

Nor had I drunk too much.

"I usually walk to work."

"Then let me take you home."

Since I was now confidently knowing exactly where I wanted this night to go—with at least one of us starting to fulfill our roles, I easily agreed and slid my hand into his.

"All right."

Dawson helped me off the stool, we waved goodbye to Margo and as we were walking out, I glanced back. Her phone was in her hand, and I had no doubt by the time I got home, my face would be on her Instagram page.

I tried not to let myself think about that. Fake dating Dawson could end up with a lot more attention for me than I usually preferred.

I also tried not to think about the fact he didn't say much as we headed in the direction of my store, that he kept his hand clasped firmly with mine.

I also made no effort to pull my hand out of his hold. He was warm. Strong. And the way he held my hand so tightly I figured if I tugged on mine, I wasn't going anywhere anyway.

He held the door open to a tricked-out, matte black Tahoe, shut it after I was in and buckled, and followed my simple, two-turn directions to get me to my home. An old bungalow with a shaded front yard from the magnolia tree out front, a wooden swinging bench at the edge of the front porch I'd had my dad come over and help me hang early this spring. I'd had visions of sitting on it with Darrick, leaning against his chest while we had a drink after a long day at work and catching up, reading outside on Saturday mornings before he went golfing.

It swayed gently with the breeze, reminding me of all of it. That sting I always felt when I saw it didn't hurt quite so bad in the passenger seat of Dawson's SUV.

"Cool place," he murmured and cut the engine, and he barely spared me a glance before he went back to taking in the front porch. It wasn't done, but I'd added a line of railing planters and had more on the steps leading up to it. In front of the window, I had a small bistro set, originally a rusted-out white metal I'd painted a bright yellow that now matched a yellow door. The front landscaping held bushes, but they were minimal. I'd cut most of them down and taken out a handful when I first moved in to keep the walkway clear to the door.

"Would you like to come in?"

Dawson pulled his eyes off my yellow, probably way too girly for him front door, and stole my breath with a look. "Yeah."

It came out as a rumble, and I felt that rumble all the way to the tops of my thighs.

I waited until he opened his door, and then I hopped out and met him at the front.

"You always walk to and from work?" He scanned the street. Lots of streetlights, lots of front porch lights on. There'd never been a time I felt unsafe walking home, but that rumble in my thighs only grew deeper, warmer, while he checked everything out.

"Unless it's raining or too cold, usually." I headed up the steps and Dawson followed, still scanning the street as he did, head turned over his shoulder. "It's a safe area."

"Looks like it, doesn't mean things can't happen. And there's always a chance, we go public, you could get some attention you aren't prepared for."

I'd already considered, but I hadn't thought of bad attention.

I opened the door and pushed it open.

"Should at least get a storm door, so you can see who's here before you answer."

"Thanks, Dad," I teased.

His lips quirked. "Smartass."

I walked in and flipped on the light switches even though my kitchen light was already on. I might have been joking, but I wasn't naive. Bad shit happened anywhere, to anyone, so I always left lights on when I left my house. The door closed behind Dawson as he followed me in, and I dropped my purse on the side table as soon as I entered. "I was teasing, but my dad says it to me all the time. I'm having a hard time finding the right one."

"There's a right kind of storm door?"

"Of course." I kicked off my white Converse platform shoes. "Do I want one full sheet of glass? Do I want one that's half and half with a screen? The screen would be lovely in the spring, on nights like tonight, but then just a screen sort of defeats the purpose of security. Someone could slash right through it and get to my handle anyway. With all glass, I might hear it shatter. But the screen would come in handy on Halloween, make it easy to hand it out without giving people access to my house. But then, if it's a screen, and I look outside, that blurs the view across the street and of my magnolia tree."

When I started talking, I'd headed toward the back of the house, straight through the open living room you walked right into to the kitchen and grabbed two bottles of water from the fridge. By the time I turned back, Dawson was standing in the middle of the living room, jaw slack, and he bounced his dark gaze from the door to me.

"Um."

"Don't get me started on the frames. Or the kick plates. Those could hide the view of my yellow door and I love that yellow door."

I handed him a bottled water.

"Yeah, Hailey. Can see now how that'd be a difficult choice." His lips twitched like he was fighting a laugh. Not meanly, and okay. I'd definitely gotten carried away a bit.

"Occupational hazard in my own home," I admitted. "I put a lot of thought into wanting things to be perfect."

"Yeah. I can see that. You do all this to your house, or did you and your ex work on it together?"

"Darrick was supposed to move in after we were married." Darrick also hadn't touched a tool in his life. "The flooring and kitchen were all updated when I moved in."

Thank goodness, because the previous owners had taken a small kitchen in the back right corner with a closed-off dining area and put the kitchen at the far back of the house, fridge and pantry close at the ends, and then placed a giant island.

Dawson took a drink of his water and walked straight to my bookshelves.

My pulse kicked up a notch. Not from him, but the fact he was as interested in my home as he was my shop, and my home bookshelves did not hold knick-knacks I'd refinished or refurbished.

They held books. Romance books. A boatload of them and they were not at all my mother's kind of old-school romance.

"I like to read," I sort of mumbled, sort of whispered.

"You like to read a lot." His finger brushed along the spines of not one, not two, but three shelves before he pulled out a book.

"Um." I stepped toward him, the book in his hand. Probably figured I could grab if I moved quick, but Dawson spun and held it against his chest. Title out.

"Dominate Me" clear in red, bold font against the black cover and the almost entirely naked man.

"You can try to take this from me but should probably know I'm one of the fastest tight ends in football, and I've got no problems tackling two-hundred-pound men if I need to."

The threat probably shouldn't have sent a spike of arousal down my spine. I stayed glued to my spot.

"This is embarrassing."

"What? That you might not have had sex, but you liked reading about it? Nothing embarrassing about it." He flipped through the book and my cheeks turned the color of a fire engine.

"They're tabbed." His thumb brushed along the pages, and the tiny pink and blue stickers I'd put on some of the spicier parts flickered along with him. "Wanna explain why?"

"Not particularly."

He chuckled.

I shuffled back and forth on my feet. I could not believe this was happening. Hadn't expected him to look at all or notice.

Darrick never had, and I'd read the books in front of him. He definitely never asked why I highlighted and marked some of the sex scenes.

Research. It was all research. Once we broke the seal on our celibacy, I figured we could do all the fun things together. And what better way to start than to show him some of the things I was most excited about trying?

Except he'd been doing fun things the whole time.

My throat grew tight, and like every time I thought of Darrick's betrayal, my nose stung along with my heart.

"Will you drop dead of embarrassment if I see what they are myself?"

"Probably?" The heat searing my cheeks was spreading to my neck and my chest.

He watched me for a minute, two, while I fought against squirming beneath the weight of his gaze before he turned and set the book on the shelf.

"Pick one you want me to read."

"Excuse me?"

"You want to learn shit, you honestly have ideas of what you like. Pick one, something simple and small to start. Show me what turns you on, Hailey."

He stepped back, putting space between him and the shelf that would now, forever be renamed in my head as The Shelf of Doom.

Then I took one trembling step forward.

CHAPTER 11
DAWSON

IF YOU'D TOLD me the sweet but sexy woman who wanted to learn about sex had a naughty side buried deep, I wouldn't have believed you. But in that moment, while I focused on Hailey stepping toward me like she was walking to her execution but gathering her courage every small step of the way, my dick was hard, and I was fighting against grabbing her and slamming my mouth to hers.

Sex books. Romance. Whatever. From the titles and the quick description on the backs of the books, this girl read shit about bondage, BDSM, being kidnapped and forced into marriages.

Not sure how any of that had to do with actual romance, but it was fucking hot as hell. I wasn't into BDSM, not as a formality anyway, but did I like the thought of her tied up, unable to escape while I tortured her with my tongue, my hands, and my dick, drove her to the edge and back again before throwing her into a blissed-out orgasm where she went limp afterward and thought of me for days?

Certainly was now.

"This is embarrassing," she whispered, but she was still doing it, now at the bookshelf. "I thought maybe we'd start with a kiss or something, you know...get used to each other before diving right in."

I wanted to dive my hand into her thick blonde hair and slam her mouth to mine. There was no warming up when it came to my thoughts of what I wanted to do to her. Knowing there was a freaky little minx beneath her wholesome exterior only made her sexier.

She'd banked all that for one man who didn't deserve it. I might not have deserved it, either, but I would enjoy the hell out of it.

"We'll kiss first," I assured her.

Hailey whipped her head toward me, cheeks still flushed, no longer trembling as she pulled a book off her shelf and handed it to me. I took it and she stepped back, like the book had burned her.

"What's it about?"

I glanced down at the title, but like all the other books I could see, it was a title and a mostly naked man. Not the kind of thing I could read on a plane, nor anything I ever thought I'd have in my hands.

"Um. Football, actually."

My brows rose in surprise. "This doesn't look like football."

"He's a football player. She's a sports reporter. They meet, um, at a sex club. And she's blindfolded."

I added "blindfold Hailey" to the list of things to try.

"You like this stuff? Sex clubs and stuff?"

"In theory? Maybe?" A nervous little giggle escaped her. "Obviously, I don't really have a frame of reference or anything."

My guess, she liked having the guy take charge. That was what did it for her. If she was worried she didn't know what she was doing, she'd want someone to guide it.

"You and your ex. How far did you two go?"

Didn't want to bring him up, but in order to know how fast I could go with her, I had to know.

"How far?"

"Yeah. Oral? He go down on you?"

She shook her head, sucked her bottom teeth between her lips. Jesus.

"Use his fingers on you? Fuck you with them?"

"I'm not sure..."

"No joke, Hailey. You gotta know this, we'll be talking a lot about this shit, things will need to be said. I'm not trying to embarrass you. I'll never be embarrassed by anything you have to say, or judge you for it, but in order for me to give you what you want, what you need, I need to know where I'm starting from."

"It's embarrassing, and it's not because it's sex, but because it makes me feel stupid for thinking he was trying to make everything special for me when he was lying and betraying me the entire time."

Shit. "Fuck, I'm sorry. I hadn't thought of that."

I gave her space, tossed the book on the couch and opened my water. Gave her a minute. "We can slow this down, give it time."

Hailey shook her head again, not liking that idea. "Outside. Sometimes. He used his fingers outside. But I have a toy..."

That would definitely help. For when we get to the really fun stuff and to make the fun stuff even better. For now, I tried not to picture her long legs spread, feet braced on the bed with her knees bent high and wide while she used it on herself. Bet that fucker never watched her get herself off, but I sure as hell would be.

"Okay. Now, I've got an early morning tomorrow, so I need to get going, and apparently I have some of my own homework to do with that book of yours, but before I leave, how about you come here and let me give you a good night kiss."

She didn't want to be in charge, but if she really wanted this, me, and was ready for it, I needed her to take that first step.

Although, it would be the last first step she took, all night, or for the rest of this arrangement.

"Dawson..."

"Scared?"

She shook her head. "Terrified, and more excited than I probably should be."

She took that step, though, and that one small move toward me was all I needed. I reached out and took her fingers in my hand and gently pulled her to me.

I brushed my other hand up her arm. She shivered beneath my touch and her lips parted with my hand resting at the side of her throat, my thumb sweeping along her jaw.

"Dawson—"

"Sh...I'll make this good for you."

I let go of her hand, placed my other hand on the other side of her throat, and tilted her chin up. Only a little, because she was already tall enough, I barely had to move her. She inhaled a quick gasp, tongue darting out, and I took the invite.

Teasing her, I brushed my lips over hers and pulled back. Kissed her again. I kissed her softly, and was invaded by her soft, sweet scent and the softness of her lips, the skin beneath her jaw.

God, she was incredible, tense in my hold, so I kept the kisses soft and light, didn't push for more until she succumbed. The tenseness slid out of her body, and her hand settled at my hip right before she leaned in, pressed her body to mine and slipped her other hand around to my back, and pressed me against her.

"Thatta girl," I murmured and sealed my lips to hers, tongue slipping inside.

"Oh." She gasped and kissed me back, and my blood turned to fire, racing through my veins, as the kiss quickly grew in speed, in ferocity, and in passion.

I twisted, pressing her back to the bookshelf, and grabbed one of her thighs, draping it over my hips.

Fuck slow. This was going to become a problem if I got my hands on her and lost control.

"Oh, Dawson."

I pressed my hard dick, pulsing and angry it was confined inside my jeans right against her sex, and another beautiful and fucking electric moan slipped from her lips.

"Ride it," I grunted, and a shiver raced through her.

She rolled her hips, hesitant at first, but then she moved, went wild.

"That's it, Hailey." I kept kissing her, pressed my hands into her hair, and groaned at the softness of it. Smooth, soft, smelled like flowers, and as I held her head still and devoured her mouth, I dropped my other hand to her ass.

"Fuck," she gasped against me, pulled off, and shoved her face into the side of my neck.

"Dawson."

"Get there, Hailey. Use me."

I rocked back into her, grabbed her ass, and helped her along.

The tip of her tongue came out, swiping along my neck, and my gut clenched with my own demanding need.

Need to have her. Need to see her face as she unraveled. Need to figure out how to continue going through with this without fucking it all up.

"Shit."

Her teeth came out next, scraping along my neck, and then the most beautiful, needy little sound escaped her throat as her entire body trembled with the force of her orgasm. Her hand clung to my back, fingers curled into my shirt. She came fast. She came hard.

She came and responded to me like an absolutely beautiful goddess I couldn't wait to be inside.

Her lips pressed to my throat, and I turned my head to kiss her temple while the aftershocks subsided, and a husky laugh vibrated against my skin.

"Sorry. I tried not to bite you."

"We'll work up to the freedom to bite me whenever and wherever you want," I murmured against her temple.

She froze, then relaxed, and she pulled back. She flashed me a dick-hardening grin. At least, would have been, if I wasn't still a cement brick in my jeans.

I loosened my grip on her, gently guided her leg off my hip and back to the floor and smoothed down her shirt. "You okay?"

"I think that today I learned Darrick really sucked at kissing."

I chuckled along with her. She was okay.

"How about you?" Her gaze flicked down back to me.

"I'm good."

"Are you sure? Because—"

She reached for me, and I grabbed her hand. "Not trying to be a gentleman right now, but if you touch me, I'll blow in my pants or all over your floor, and I'm definitely sure we're not ready for that. I'll be fine, and you can make it up to me another day."

And I had actually come to her tonight instead of texting because we needed to talk. We'd done a lot of that, but none of it is what we needed to talk about.

"I have an event to go to next Friday. Can you be free to come with me?"

"What?" She blinked, still coming down either from her orgasm or my denial to get her hand on me, so it took a second before her gaze cleared. "Friday?"

"Yeah. Cole, the quarterback on our team, hosts a summer camp for kids every year. It ends on Thursday and then there's a dinner and dance after the last day to raise money for next year's camp."

"Is it...like fancy? Black tie?"

"Don't worry about that. I'll take care of it."

It occurred to me I still had her back pressed to the bookshelves and stepped away.

"I can buy my own dress, that's not why I asked."

She probably could.

"Yeah, but this is last minute, and you'll be busy, but you can come with me? Media will be there, and my coach."

"And the team's manager?"

"And owner," I confirmed.

It'd be my first night out doing what he expected of me. Figured by now, we at least knew each other well enough we wouldn't look fake.

"I'll make it work. So yeah, I can be there."

"Good." And because we were still close, and I couldn't help myself, I leaned down and kissed her forehead. "I really do need to get going. Thanks for a good night, Hailey."

"Thanks, for, um, you know..." She waved her hand in a circle in front of her, that blush returning.

"You haven't seen anything yet. Trust me."

I grabbed the book I'd tossed to the couch, and she walked me to the door.

"Make sure you lock up behind me. I'll text you the details about Friday once I confirm them."

"Okay." She licked her lips, looked too damn sweet for me and oh so perfect. "Night, Dawson."

I turned and left before I did what I really wanted to do, which was take her back to her bed and spend the rest of her night teaching her everything she wanted to know about pleasure and everything she hadn't considered yet.

The sun beat down on me, even standing in the shade. It was hot as hell outside, and I still couldn't figure out why I agreed to head up to Marysville to play cornhole with Cole and Davis and one of Cole's friend's, Scott, but there I was, sipping a beer, tossing around a bean bag and removing my ball cap every few minutes to wipe away the sweat.

Good news, which was the only kind of news I was focusing on, was the general manager's text I got this morning. It included a screen-shot of a photo with Hailey curled up to my side at Margo's. All Rick said was **Nice to see. Will I meet her next weekend?**

I responded with a simple yes and promptly turned my phone to silent, only looking at it again when I got the thank you text from Hailey about the details for Friday's event.

I didn't particularly enjoy cornhole.

But I liked the fact that since we were in the small town where Cole and Eden grew up, people mostly left us alone. There was always the occasional camera out and pointed our way, but if one of the workers saw it, they stopped it.

Since it wasn't my turn, I was hiding in the shade along with Maggie, who was not only visibly pregnant but planning her wedding to Davis, sitting with Eden and Scott's wife, Cassy.

"You in need of a plus one to the fundraiser next week that Eden's been stressed to the max about?" Cassy laid her hand on my arm playfully. "I'll go with you. Always wanted to hobnob with the who's who of Nashville."

I peeled her hand off mine and gave it a friendly squeeze. Cassy was laid-back, living her dream with her husband and in their first year of starting their own small farm. I knew this because she was constantly talking about the treehouse Scott built for her and the goats she wanted for her homemade goat's milk and cheese.

"I'm good. Got a woman. Hailey."

I'd told Davis and Cole to keep their mouths shut about what Rick was forcing me to do, but assumed they told their women.

"But any suggestions on where to get her a dress for it would be appreciated."

I knew where Crystal would have gone, but Hailey didn't strike me as the same kind of girl as my sister. So far, I'd seen Hailey dressed nice. But casual. She had a comfortable feel to her. Didn't mean she didn't like to get dressed up, but I saw her in something sleek and classy more than shiny and showing all the skin, trying to do anything to get the attention on her in any way she could.

"I've got someone you can call," Maggie said. "Belle has a personal shopper she adores."

Annabelle Connolly wasn't only Maggie's best friend, but she was heir to a massive recording studio and music agency. Belle's father was the guy who insisted Maggie take the stage last winter. She was loaded and classy. And I had no doubt Maggie wouldn't steer me in the wrong direction.

"I'd like that."

As she spoke, she pulled out her phone. "Gimme your number and I'll text it as soon as I get it from Belle. She uses a woman named Josephine to dress her every time she has some fancy shindig she has to go to."

"Thanks, Maggie."

She grinned at me. "No problem. You bringing her to the wedding?"

They were getting married next month. Definitely something I'd need a date for. "Probably, if that's all right. I know you're keeping it small."

"Of course it's okay with me." She grinned. "You guys are okay, though, I mean, with everything? Davis told me..."

"Told you what?" Cassy asked.

"Nothing. It's new is all."

Next to Cassy, Maggie flinched and mouthed *sorry*. So she knew.

Which was fine.

Didn't stop the uncomfortable itch beneath my skin when I thought about what I was doing with Hailey, what she wanted from me, and how fucking good she'd tasted and felt the other night.

Hadn't stopped thinking about it. Thought about her that night when I got home, when I woke up. Thought about her in the shower after I worked out and again, later, when I was trying to do some cooling laps in my backyard pool.

She was everywhere, jumping into my thoughts at every inconvenient moment, and I was pretty damn certain it was only going to get worse the more I was around her.

This is what we signed up for, but now I had to focus on us both getting what we wanted, without getting tangled up and complicating things further.

CHAPTER 12
HAILEY

"I NEVER KNEW you could get more beautiful than you already are."

I blushed at Meredith's compliment from the reflection in my full-length mirror. She was tanned and happy and had come over to help me get ready.

"Don't be nice. It'll make me cry."

"Fine, then bitch, you look a lot less skinny than you normally do."

I grabbed my eyeliner pencil off the table next to me and flung it at her. "Thank you."

She laughed, and I joined her before brushing my hands down the most gorgeous dress I'd ever worn, outside my wedding dress, but that wasn't going to be thought about tonight.

Not when I was preparing to head to Dawson's house.

Two days ago, in a complete surprise to me, a woman showed up at my door at eight o'clock in the morning. I'd just gotten out of the shower, wore nothing but a robe and a towel wrapped around my hair when I saw her through the glass, holding on to a small garment rack full of dresses.

The only reason I hadn't been at work already was because Dawson told me he had a delivery scheduled for me and asked if I could be home to receive it.

I'd expected to have to sign for a box, not open the door to a woman who called herself Josephine and pushed that garment rack straight into my living room. She had no hesitation before she scanned me up and down, inspecting me, and spent the next hour having me try on a dozen dresses, even more shoes, and then after we declared the beach-blue dress I was currently wearing "the one," spent more time sticking pins in it. She ran out to her car, hauled in a small sewing machine, and by the time I had to leave to open my store, Josephine had not only secured me such a gorgeous dress, she'd altered it and steamed it to perfection.

Thin, silky straps with a draped low-cut front. The tops of my rounded breasts showed, along with more than a mere hint of cleavage before it tucked in at my waist, made me look two sizes smaller which I appreciated on my size eight frame due to boning I could feel but was invisible through the thin, satiny fabric. It clung to my hips and then fell to the floor, leaving a whisper of a small train at the back even while I was in the three-inch open-toed gold shoes.

The back? Completely bare. It scooped down to just above my backside leaving me unable to wear a bra or underwear under normal circumstances but even with that, Josephine proved she was a miracle worker.

She'd provided me an open back corset type top that was one-piece, a thong at my butt, thin enough that somehow, even with the fabric of the dress, not a single line of it was visible when I swished and swayed in front of the mirror.

"I'm surprised he's not coming to get you," Meredith said.

"It's not really a *date* date." I was convincing her as much as me. After the other night, a night I couldn't stop thinking of, not to mention the fact he'd taken one of my books to see what kind of sex scenes I liked, I needed to continually remind myself that Dawson was only helping me out for his own reasons.

It was obvious we had chemistry, but that was as far as I would let my mind go.

"Besides, we have to drive downtown and he's on the way. I don't mind."

"Hmmm." She tapped her lips with her neon pink painted fingernails. "And do you have a bag packed?"

I held up my gold clutch. "Yes."

She rolled her eyes and shoved off the bed. "Such a novice. Man like that is gonna spend the night seeing you in what you're wearing, there's no way you're coming home tonight, Hails."

As she spoke, Meredith helped herself into my closet. From inside, she continued, "If things are going the way I expect they are and with the little you've already told me, you're going to at least need comfortable clothes and shoes to wear home in the morning."

To prove her point, she walked out of my closet with a pair of slip-on sandals, a lightweight sweatshirt and cutoff sweat shorts. The sweatshirt was so old, the screen print on it was faded, but the fact she'd grabbed me a top that said, "I'll ride that cowboy," above Ripp's face—a character from the show *Yellowstone*—made me roll my eyes.

"Can you find me anything cuter?" Those shorts were what I wore to clean my house in.

Meredith smirked at me. "So picky."

"Well, if I am spending the night with a guy, I don't want to leave his house looking like some kind of scrub, do I?"

"You have a point. Grab your face wash and bathroom things. I'll find something cute, but it won't matter. After he catches sight of you in that dress and those shoes, he's never gonna think of you in anything else, unless it's thinking of you in nothing at all."

She disappeared back into my closet.

I vanished into the bathroom and tried not to have a panic attack.

If she was right...could I finally be counting down the hours until I was no longer a virgin?

The twenty-minute drive from my house to Dawson's should have given me all the time I needed to prepare to see him. I was doing pretty good until I reached his gated entrance neighborhood and was allowed entrance by the security guard manning the gate. The last half mile, I fell apart. By the time I pulled up his driveway, my hands were sweating, my heart was racing so fast there was no amount of deep breaths that could calm me down, and I was pretty certain that as soon as I stepped out of my car, I'd face-plant onto the cement from my trembling, quaking knees.

Nerves were a bitch, and I was experiencing the worst of them.

Worse, I hadn't taken the time, not even a second, to consider that if Dawson went to all that effort to deck me out in a designer dress, he would take the same amount of time for himself.

I shoved my car into park facing his four-car garage, his large, double door and curved wooden front doors were to my left. It was still light enough out, but the sun was setting behind Dawson's house, giving the white-painted brick and black-lined windows and shutters an ethereal glow from the shadows and fading light of the sun behind the house.

The front door opened.

My heart jumped straight into my throat. I tried swallowing, but I couldn't over the growing ball of nerves and instead of smiling at Dawson as he appeared, I choked.

I bent over in my car and hacked up a lung.

Damn it. Damn it damn it. That was how I was going to die. Choking on my own spit in the front seat of my car. EMTs would have to pry me out.

Dawson's plan would go up in flames, and there I'd be, pronounced dead in a blue silk dress.

"Hailey."

Oh god, he was close. Close enough to hear me practically gagging with nerves.

"Yeah?" I cleared my throat and covered my mouth as another round of the coughing fit from hell hit me.

A very large, warm hand settled on my back with only a small amount of pressure. And dear god, I prayed for the coughing fit to take me right then. Right there.

No way could I face Dawson after this.

"Sorry," I croaked, coughing again.

His hand ran lightly up and down my back. "It's okay. You all right?"

I nodded, carefully wiped my eyes as the fit subsided. I was still alive, which was both fortunate and unfortunate.

Now I had to sit up.

Moving was difficult seeing as how his hand was still at my back, covering almost the entire exposed area. He had a strange reaction on my nerves. With every sweep of his hand against my spine, the trembling in my legs subsided. My heart rate began returning to normal, and the sweaty palm situation resolved itself as I placed my index fingers beneath my bottom eyelashes to hopefully swipe away any unfortunate mascara mishaps.

"I'm good," I managed to say.

Dawson's hand drifted from my back to my left arm. He curled it around my bicep and gave me a gentle tug.

I resisted, only minimally because his hand was still creating those miraculous calming effects, and when I was finally sitting in my driver's seat, I rested my head against my headrest and rolled my head in his direction.

"Hey," I said stupidly, and with that hand on my arm, I was pretty sure I looked drugged. Felt like it.

Dawson was bent over the opening in my door, his other hand braced on the top of my Camry. He was imposing. His dark hair was loose and created a shadow of his hard edges and deep set dark eyes. He'd shaven and cleaned up his beard. The darkness made him appear dangerous.

My mouth watered to run my lips along his jaw and risk the danger.

His tie swung loose, and I blinked. Double-blinked.

"Your tie matches my dress."

His lips, full and lush, curled up at the corners. "Had Josephine kit me out after she got you sorted. She thought you'd like it."

I did. Very much so. His suit was dark. Either a midnight blue or ebony black, hard to tell with the lighting and the stark white of his dress shirt made the blue tie pop.

Could have been the light from my car.

"Gotta question for you."

"Anything." I'd tell him anything he wanted to know. Probably do anything he asked. No limits. No questions.

"You going to get out of that car so we can get going, or are we hanging out in here all night?"

"Right." I chuckled and pressed the button to turn my car off.

The country music I'd had playing went silent and all that was left was the sound of our breathing and cicadas in the background. The quiet rumble of a distant engine that could only be the typical kind of Tennessee tricked-out massive truck.

I was no longer certain I'd survive the night if I left my car.

"I vote for staying in my car all night."

He let loose a soft chuckle and gave my arm a gentle tug. "How about you undo the seatbelt, grab that purse in your passenger seat, and I'll grab the small bag in your backseat. We'll go in, have a drink or some water so you relax, and then we'll get going."

That sounded very much like the original plan I wasn't sure I wanted to continue with.

"Okay."

Before I could undo my own belt, Dawson let go of my arm, bent down, released it for me. As he moved back, he opened the back door behind me, reached in, grabbed the small tote bag and was back in front of me as I turned and settled my heels to the cement.

The wobble came back in my knees, until Dawson closed the back door, held out his hand.

As soon as my small, cold hand was in his large, warm and firm grip, that wobble went away.

Crazy.

He guided me out of the car, waited until I closed my door and brushed my hand over the handle to lock it. Once it beeped, he held on tight to my hand and walked me toward his house.

"Your home is gorgeous."

"Just a house," he replied, but there was an angle of his jaw that wasn't quite right.

Didn't seem all that happy with it which was odd. What was there to be unhappy about when you could afford a home like this while living alone.

"You like all this space for you?"

"I like being alone and I like to have room, so yeah. It works for me."

"I can only imagine the parties you could have here."

"Last one didn't work out so well for me," he muttered, and dropped my hand only to grasp elbow as we reached the brick stairs leading up to his front door.

"Why not?"

"Crystal."

It was all he said, but with the trouble he said she tended to cause, it said more than enough.

And then my jaw fell to the floor as we crossed the threshold. "I'm really going to need more than a glass of water."

CHAPTER 13
DAWSON

I WAS TRYING to keep myself in check. Trying to be a gentleman. Trying was the operative word. The strain it was taking to not toss Hailey up against a wall, slam my mouth to hers and dive my hands beneath her silk dress I was going to murder Josephine for putting her in was more than the amount of work I put into the entirety of our summer training camp. And the energy required for that full week was deadly.

So was Hailey's dress.

It was either murder Josephine for having her wear it, or risk murdering every single one of my teammates I'd see tonight that let his eyes drop below hers.

I was going to end up in jail. Again. No doubt about it. She wasn't going to be the woman who saved my image and cemented my next contract with the team.

She was going to be my ruin.

She also went from nervous to normal to shock so damn quickly it was a wonder my head didn't spin in a full circle from the constant changing of her emotions.

"Wine?"

I'd stocked up on more white for her. Considering it was all Crystal drank, she'd emptied my fridge of it before I kicked her out, or she hid the remainder with her in her suitcases when I did. Every time I saw it, it was a reminder of the hell that swirled around my sister and the destruction she left in her wake.

Done. I was done with her.

"Please. Thank you."

I gestured with my arm for her to head to the kitchen, although it was unnecessary. My home opened to a living room on the left, a wide-open dining room on the right, separated by two pillars for support. Beyond that was the butler pantry that took us straight back into the kitchen where it was all white and light gray and a double island, one for food prep, one for seating to the windows that went floor to ceiling beyond.

The windows sold me on the place. The entire back of the house, including a study tucked back past the main family room area was all floor to ceiling, tinted glass mirrors so I could see out to my acres of land while no one could see in.

"Your house is beautiful." Hailey's hand trailed along the marble counter while I went to the end of the food prep island, crouched down and grabbed a bottle of wine for her.

"Thanks. I like being able to have the land."

I turned and reached for the wine opener and when I turned back, there was a soft smile on Hailey's lips and a pink color to her cheeks.

She grinned up at me. "That's the wine I had at Margo's."

"It is," I told her and poured her a glass.

Instead of wine, I grabbed a Stella Artois beer.

"You remembered."

It wasn't rocket science to remember the label and order a few bottles online for her. The way she said it, though, made me think of that dickhead she'd been with.

What kind of guy would not only throw away a woman like this but treat her like such shit.

My guess, he didn't even know how she took her coffee. Or knew what made her smile light up a room, probably because he'd spent so much time thinking of himself and juggling all the women he was cheating on her with, he didn't give too much time to thinking about anything Haley might find important.

I took my first drink and set it down on the counter. "I feel like you should tell me exactly how big of a dick your ex is if this impresses you."

She smirked. "I'd rather have toothpicks shoved beneath my fingernails than talk about him, if it's all the same to you."

Fair enough. At least for tonight. No sense in ruining the night before it began. I walked around the corner of the island until I was facing her. The memory of what we'd done in her living room hit me hard and fast, and I forced it down before I ruined her dress and we skipped the dinner.

"Wasteful," I muttered, and her eyes narrowed. "Whoever the man was who had you, he was wasteful to not take care of the beauty he had in his hands. Bet he didn't even realize what he had, did he?"

"Dawson," she breathed my name.

I reached out and trailed a finger from her shoulder to her arm. Bumps rose in the wake of my touch, all the way down her arms and across her exposed chest, the rounded covers of the tops of her breasts.

"I hope you know that. I figure you're probably still hurt, and you have every right to feel what you need to feel to move on from him, but under all that pain, I hope you know you're worth more than a man like that."

She was sipping her wine, and the glass froze at her bottom lip. Blue eyes, brighter than her dress because as beautiful as the fabric was, nothing could beat her blue eyes. "I do, thank you."

"Good." I stepped back, put space between us, more for me than her. "I finished the book you gave me."

A book that gave me more erections than I could ever remember getting in a few hour time period. That shit was hot, and if we stayed progressing, someday, I was going to have her reading out a scene she wanted to reenact while we were reenacting it. My dick pressed against my suit pants.

We needed to finish these drinks and take off before I blew my shot at impressing Marchand.

"You did?" Her eyebrows arched into points as she sputtered out the words.

"Yeah. And I'll let you wonder what scenes I liked the best so you have something else to think of tonight."

"Charming. Because I hadn't made it clear I was nervous enough?"

She had, what with the coughing fit and the flushed cheeks. I was trying to pretend it didn't happen for her sake.

"Trust me. There's no reason to be nervous about what we'll be doing later...or rather, what I'll be doing to you."

Her tongue darted out and licked her glossy, bright pink lips. "Can you give me a hint, at least?"

I leaned in, close enough to whisper in her ear and inhale the floral scent mixed with vanilla that made my brain foggy. "Let's just say it involves some rope."

"Oh."

Not exactly. I was leaning toward using my tie, but by the end of the night, sexy and sweet virgin Hailey Monaco would be writhing beneath me, unable to do anything but take all the pleasure I would be solely focused on giving to her.

We pulled up to the event center fashionably late after I'd given Hailey a warning, and then given her a reason to need to redo her lip gloss. My own still tasted like her cherry-flavored lip gloss, and I was not complaining.

Every time I caught a taste of it, I thought of how sexy she was. How undeniably ravishing she looked in the dress sitting next to me, and the threat of what I was going to do to her later along with the kiss seemed to evaporate her earlier nerves.

Was she spending her time thinking of what particular scene I'd referenced? Had she read the book often enough that she knew there were only three scenes where the heroine had been tied up in some way. One of them, on her knees and blindfolded...

I shoved my Tahoe into park as we reached the valet parking area and hopped out before the workers, all young, male, probably college-aged reacted to our arrival. "Keys are in the ignition." I rushed to the other side and opened Hailey's door.

I barely managed to shove the other worker out of the way before he could help her slide out of the car and slipped my hand into hers.

Once I got her on her feet, I helped her up the curb. In her heels, I barely had to dip my chin to meet her gaze and when her crystal blue eyes blinked up at me, I tugged her closer. "By the way, since I'm pretty sure I forgot to tell you earlier, you are absolutely stunning in that dress. Although, I still can't wait to take it off you later and see how it looks on my bedroom floor."

To my surprise, she didn't flush. She didn't even blink. Instead, she flashed me a blinding smile. "That's funny, considering Meredith said the only other thing you'd want to see me in besides this dress was nothing at all."

"I think I might be beginning to like your friend."

She laughed, which meant as we walked into the lobby of the event center that was decked out in our team's black and red and silver and white colors, we were greeted by no one other than Rick Marchand himself. Hailey's smile was beaming, her gaze fixed on me.

Out of the corner of my eye, Marchand flashed a look of surprise, and then grinned.

"Cole. Nice to meet you."

"Hi, Cole." Hailey shook his hand and smiled at Eden, standing proudly next to her husband. "Nice to meet you, too."

"Eden. Cole's wife."

"They just got married this spring," I told Hailey.

She was tucked into my side, and my hand had settled on the curve of her hip like it was the most natural thing.

She'd settled there as soon as Marchand walked our way into the entry area and introduced himself to us. If she was an actress, she deserved an Emmy, but part of me was hoping this wasn't all pretend.

While she sipped on champagne I'd snagged off a tray of a passing waiter, she'd barely had half the glass while I introduced her to some guys on the team, and their girlfriends or wives if they had them. Cole's fundraising event was one of the few events I actually enjoyed. And that was because Cole didn't act like he had a stick up his ass because he was rich, but like the small-town Southern guy he was raised to be and still was. Which meant there was not one, but two popular country singers taking the stage, the dinner was going to be real food, filet mignon and scallops and shrimp and food that actually had taste. The bar was open, stocked with everything from Coors to Dom Pérignon, and the appetizers were more normal mozzarella sticks and stuffed mushrooms. There wasn't a hint of étouffée or ceviche in sight anywhere like the stuffier events we had to attend, including one over Labor Day weekend, where our owners, along with the Avengers owners, held a joint gala promoting breast cancer research ahead of October so they could spend all October talking about how cool and pro-women they were.

Outside the cause the money was raised for, the entire night was an event of trying not to gag as I sucked down slimy, cold fancy food that had no taste whatsoever.

"Congratulations." Hailey smiled, but her eyes weren't shining like they'd been all night and shit...I hadn't considered bringing it up would make her think of her own wedding she was supposed to have. "That must be really exciting."

Damn it. I couldn't pull her away or excuse us without looking rude, and that wasn't any impression I wanted someone from my team to have with Hailey. I squeezed her hip and pressed her against me.

She tilted her head and flashed me a quick wink. It happened so quick, I figured Cole and Eden missed the silent exchange, but when I caught Cole's look, I was dead wrong.

His lips were curled into a smirk and Eden was hiding a smile behind her wineglass.

"Long time coming," Cole murmured, grinning down at his wife. "You see him yet?"

"Marchand or the new coach?" Our last coach, Bowles, drop-kicked our asses to the floor during last season's playoff game when we were getting our asses handed to us and told us he was finally retiring. He told us whatever last game we played that season would be his last game and there was no way he was going out with a game like that. I figured we gave him the best send-off with a Super Bowl ring, his first and only in his thirty years of coaching. Man was a beast, had come close more than a handful of times before he was brought in to coach the Steel. He turned our team and entire program and fan base around in less than five years.

An incredible man who'd leave large shoes to fill.

Management and ownership decided Logan Caldwell was the guy to do just that. I'd met him once. Decent guy. Positive. Young, though, and untested, and while we had a fucking kick ass team, that could all fall apart if Caldwell wasn't able to step up and lead us. Keep us at the level we were capable of.

I was still uncertain, as were many veterans on the team.

Cole, however, had met him already several times and felt better about him than I did.

"Marchand. Caldwell bowed out. Didn't want to show up and take any attention off the purpose for tonight since he hasn't met everyone yet."

"He seems really nice," Eden said.

"Nice doesn't mean shit if it isn't coupled with wins," I returned with a shrug, my gaze still on Cole.

"He'll be fine. Just wants to wait until it gets closer to OTAs."

"What are OTAs?" Hailey asked.

"Organized team activities. The start at the end of the month. We have weeks of meetings and organized strength and conditioning programs to follow to get ready for the season and training camp. And yeah, we saw Marchand, but he hasn't approached. My guess is right now he's keeping watch, and I feel like I'm being fucking babysat."

All this over one single bar fight. Big fucking deal. It happened and so what if it looked bad. It happened to other players, too. If Bowles hadn't been leaving and I hadn't had to be worried about some new coach swooping in, I probably would have told Marchand to shove his "settling down" plan up his ass.

Not that it wasn't working out well for me...

"He's at the bar right now, talking to someone."

"You know where he went?" I asked Hailey.

"Been keeping an eye on him, just in case."

Nice. I hadn't even tagged where he'd gone, hadn't wanted to know, but it was nice to know Hailey had my back. It was so simple, so damn small, but my chest swelled with pride, and it wasn't the only thing that was swelling.

When was the last time anyone, outside my teammates on the field, had taken my back, looked out for me?

Not since I was twenty and my relationship with my dad frayed.

"We should go get seated for dinner," I told Cole and Eden.

"Our table's up front with my parents, but yours is next to it on the right."

"Thanks, man." I fist pumped Cole. Eden and Hailey said they'd see each other later. Thankfully, no one was at our table yet, so we found our name tags and slipped into the chairs.

Good thing, since it gave me the chance to lean over and settle my hand at Hailey's thigh and lean in close to her. "Thanks for that, keeping an eye on Rick."

"You'd do it for me," she whispered back.

Yeah. Yeah, I would. And if I was willing to admit it, I'd probably do just about anything for her, too.

I was so freaking fucked.

CHAPTER 14
HAILEY

DINNER WAS A GORGEOUS AFFAIR. The food, the music, the company. I was absolutely blown away when Bethany Carlson, a country singer who hadn't toured in four years stepped out on the stage and played during our dinner, slow songs and some covers. I was so enamored with the fact I was sitting twenty feet from a country singer icon I would have forgotten to eat altogether if Maggie, Davis's fiancée and very clearly pregnant, hadn't leaned close to me at one point and teased me about my food going cold.

"I have a friend who knows a lot of people in the industry," she said to me, "and I still get tongue-tied every single time I'm at one of her parties."

"It's crazy. I mean I've lived near this city my whole entire life and I never stop getting awestruck when I see someone famous."

"And yet you didn't seem impressed at all when you met me," Dawson teased.

How wrong he was. I was impressed all right. With his body and his hair and his smile. There'd been a lot to be impressed about when it came to him, but considering we were in public, I couldn't exactly tell him that.

Instead, I teased him right back. "Yeah, but you play football. That's not nearly the same thing."

"Ohhhh," Davis groaned. "Please, please Dawson, tell me you didn't find a woman like I did who doesn't know a thing about our favorite little hobby."

"Hobby, my ass," Dawson snorted. "And I did. You also don't hear me complaining."

As he said it, he pressed a gentle kiss to my shoulder and slid his arm over the back of my chair.

I forgot words. The company. I stared up at him, probably gawking.

It was an affectionate gesture. Something he was probably only doing to play his role.

But damn, I wished some of that was real.

I turned back to my food, and tried to ignore the talk about Maggie's wedding they were apparently having in Cole's parents' backyard.

Dawson's finger brushed along my exposed shoulder. Probably meant to comfort me. Maybe he just wanted to touch me.

But every swipe of his thumb over my flesh sent shivers down my spine.

I was supposed to be married. Supposed to be back from my honeymoon. Darrick was supposed to have moved in and we were supposed to be enjoying the first few months of our life together.

Instead, I was there. Surrounded by strangers and fake dating some apparent god in the football world and there were so many weddings going on.

So much talk about happy marriages.

Babies.

All the things I'd been expecting to have at my fingertips and...

I needed air.

Space.

"I've told Dawson you have to come with him to the wedding," Maggie said.

She turned to me so abruptly, or maybe I'd been so spaced out her words sounded like they were coming through a tunnel.

I flinched. "Pardon?"

Her hand settled on her large, rounded belly. "I told Dawson you should come with him to the wedding."

"Oh."

"Maggie..." Dawson's voice was a thick rumble, cascading over me, and no...

There was no way I could...

I shoved my chair back so quickly, Dawson's arm went flying off my chair. Conversation stopped on a dime.

Maggie gaped at me.

Space.

Air.

Escape.

"Sorry. Excuse me, please. I need a minute."

I rushed out of the elegant conference center, barely recognizing a handful of heads swiveling in my wake as strangers watched me high-tail it out of there like my ass was on fire, straight toward the long hallway and into the women's restroom. It wasn't until I was inside, my back against the wall, cooling from the cold wood behind me I finally breathed again.

"Damn it," I muttered and shook out my hands and arms to relieve the tension building faster than a forest fire.

I'd run out of there, didn't even look at Dawson. Probably looked like I was rushing to escape him in the middle of a freaking dinner with all of his teammates. His coach and owner. All the people he'd needed to impress and now I'd completely, one hundred percent not only screwed up, but tears were gathering in my eyes faster than I could stop them from falling.

Shit shit shit.

This was bad. Really, really bad.

No wonder Darrick left me. Cheated on me.

I couldn't even make it through a dinner without losing my mind.

"Oh god," I groaned and went straight to the paper towels sitting in a basket next to the sinks. I flipped on the faucet taps and soaked it in cold water, squeezed out all the excess and pressed it to my forehead.

My makeup would probably be ruined.

My mascara destroyed. Dropping the paper towel to the counter I shoved my hands under the ice-cold water to help calm the hell down.

I was drying my hands, staring at my pale face, mesmerized by my pulse racing at the base of my throat when the door opened.

Great. A witness to my complete and utterly humiliating breakdown.

Instead of one of the hundreds of strangers, it was Maggie.

"I'm really sorry."

"You have nothing to apologize for." I flipped off the water and grabbed a fresh paper towel to dry my hands.

She stepped forward. "Dawson told us how you met, you know, or well Davis told me. So I know this thing between you isn't exactly organic."

"Okay." I was focused on drying my hands but glanced up at her through the mirror's reflection.

"He also just told me that you were supposed to be married a couple of months ago."

"Right." Of course he did. "Like I said, it's not your fault, and just because my life imploded doesn't mean I don't want other people to find their happiness."

"Yeah, but if I'd known before I wouldn't have kept talking about it. So I'm really sorry I hurt you, even if it was unintentional."

"Thank you. That's very sweet."

"He's really worried about you."

"Dawson?"

"Yeah. And I'm pretty sure if I can't get you out the door so he can see you're okay in the next minute or so he's going to bust it down."

She glanced at the door as if to prove her point, but it was unnecessary. "If you know how we met, then you should know this isn't really real. We have an understanding."

"Yeah, so did Davis and I, at least at first." She chuckled and rubbed her hands over the top of her protruding belly in her skintight, black dress. She was so tiny her belly stuck right out in front of her I had no idea where she'd fit anymore with all the growing she still had left to do.

"What does that mean?"

"It means, I got pregnant on a one-night stand and when I went to tell Davis about the baby, he insisted I move in to help me. And then about two weeks later we couldn't keep our hands off each other. Understandings and arrangements only last for so long when you start to really like the person or fall in love."

Oh, that was where she was wrong.

"Dawson won't fall in love with me."

He'd all but guaranteed it.

She tilted her head to the side, another soft smile. "I wasn't talking about him, but I've also never seen him like this. He keeps to himself. Is quiet. Hangs with the guys occasionally but usually it's under duress. And I know he only contacted that service to keep management happy, but that doesn't mean things won't change."

I'd balled up the paper towel in my hands when I dried them and tossed it into the garbage.

I didn't need any more hope for a happy future. I'd already lost it once.

"That's very sweet, Maggie. Really, but Dawson and I know exactly where each other are at."

After all, I'd been trying to remind myself of our agreement for the last week.

Maggie wasn't wrong.

Once I used the restroom, rewashed my hands, and Maggie and I stepped outside the bathroom, Dawson was still there, pacing back and forth.

He rushed to me, curled his hands around my shoulders and his gaze scanned my face for any sign of duress. "You're okay?"

Maggie chuckled. "She's fine, big guy. Calm down."

He scowled at her, a look that would have had my ankles wobbling in my heels if it was directed at me and Maggie laughed again. "You two take all the time you need. I'm going to go find Davis and make sure all the kids are okay."

She skirted off and I frowned at Dawson. "Kids?"

"Yeah. She has like four of her siblings or something living with them. Don't know, but it's a boatload of them. Crazy shit we can talk about later. Be honest, you really all right? We can leave. I don't give two shits if sitting there is going to make you uncomfortable."

For the briefest moment, Maggie's warning whispered through my mind. Arrangements only last for so long...

I kicked it straight to the curb. Dawson had been very clear with me.

"I'm all right. All that wedding talk just got to me."

"Figured. It won't happen again." He leaned down closer, and I inhaled the quick scent of his spicy, woodsy cologne before he brushed his lips over my cheek. "If I'd been thinking, I would have warned them to keep all that shit to a minimum, but I wasn't. Sorry."

"It's fine, Dawson. Really. It's not like I begrudge other women getting married, it was just a little soon to hear it all."

"We can leave."

He'd been waxing poetic about the food Cole always ensured he had at these dinners. Dawson had said on the way here it was one of the few events he didn't mind attending because of it. I wasn't going to take that from him, or the time with his team because I got stupid for a hot minute.

"And miss the best steak on the planet you promised me?"

I went for a smile but probably failed because Dawson's thumb brushed along my bottom lip. "You don't have to fake shit with me, you know."

This whole thing was fake. I didn't tell him that.

I reached up and grabbed his hand still at my shoulder and laced our fingers together. "I'm hungry."

He fell into step beside me and thankfully, salads were still being served. Good sign. At least I hadn't ruined the entire meal for him.

No one glanced our way, at least not in a way it was obvious, and by the time we returned to the table and Dawson pulled out of my chair, Davis and a guy next to him, Mason, were giving each other crap about which one was a better golfer.

"Don't listen to either of them," Dawson muttered next to me. He slid his hand to my thigh and sparks burst beneath the burning touch of his palm. "I can kick both of those kids' asses in any sport they choose."

"Not all of us has a putting green in our backyards." Davis scowled at him.

Dawson rolled his eyes and pointed his salad fork at him. "So build one."

Dawson slipped my clutch from my hand, tossed it to the counter, and then curled his hand around my bicep, steadying me while I flicked off the ankle strap of my heels and slid out of them.

"Oh my god," I groaned. "A man will never know how good it feels to take off high-heeled shoes."

Dawson chuckled in my ear and made sure I was steady on my feet before he let go. "Are you worn out or would you like a drink?"

My limbs were tired from all the dancing. My throat sore from all the talking. Once we got past the snafu at dinner, the rest of the night had flown by. And Dawson was right. Not that I had a whole lot of experience with galas and fundraisers for the richest of the rich, but Cole Buchanan put on an incredibly entertaining event. Not only did Bethany Carlson sing during dinner, she came back out during the dancing portion and played a few of her most popular favorites. I laughed more with Eden and Maggie. I met more wives. I even met Cole's parents, whose mom was named Kate but she quickly insisted I called her Mama B like everyone else and his dad who introduced himself as "Dave. Just Dave, darlin'."

Dawson danced with me, his hand searing into my lower back when he pressed me tight to him, and more than once I'd felt a thickness behind the zipper we both tried to ignore. On the way home, he'd settled his hand on my thigh like it was the most natural place for his hand to belong, and I'd broken out in full-body shivers every time his thumb did a gentle brush along my inner thigh.

If he was trying to relax me, his touch spurred the opposite effect, and right then, with all the touching and laughing and talking and thumb sweeps, I absolutely did not want a glass of wine.

Except, as he walked away from me, my nerves settled in.

This was it. Or hopefully was it.

The night I'd finally see him naked. Have my hands all over those muscles...

"Hailey?"

"Yeah?"

Dawson was removing his jacket, standing at the end of the island in front of the wine fridge. "You all right?"

No. No I am absolutely not okay. My head started shaking back and forth before I commanded it to, and Dawson's brows furrowed as he folded and set his coat onto the counter. "No? You upset about the dinner?"

"No." I swallowed over the quickly growing lump of nerves in my throat.

"Then what's wrong?"

"I'm not thirsty and I don't want wine."

His eyes widened and then his tongue appeared, sliding along his full bottom lip. God, they were good lips. And when he'd kissed me before they'd been warm. Soft.

"Something else you're in the mood for then?" He slunk toward me with panther-like grace, his large fingers going straight to his tie. He grabbed the knot and tugged.

I felt that tug at the joining of my thighs and swallowed. "Um."

He ate up the remaining steps while I forced myself to remember to breathe and as he reached me, he was already flicking open the buttons of his dress shirt. "You need something from me?"

And oh god. Skin was revealed. A light smattering of hair as he tugged his shirt out of his waistband and the shirt dropped open.

"Oh god," I whispered and reached out, slipped my hand beneath his shirt and for the first time felt him. His stomach tightened and he blew out a breath.

Muscles hidden beneath a thickness. His abs were defined, but there was weight over them too. Which told me he was large and strong and so damn sexy, but he didn't look like he spent all his time counting protein and macros and lifting. He used his body as a machine, and it showed.

I swallowed, licked my parched lips and jumped when his thumb brushed along my chin and tipped my face so I was forced to look him in the eye.

And they were molten. Already dark eyes with large pupils. "I've had a lot of time to think about what I could finally do with you here."

"You have?"

"More ideas than probably all of the books you have tabbed and highlighted."

My cheeks flamed at the words. The teasing. "That's a lot of ideas."

"Ready to get started?"

CHAPTER 15
DAWSON

I COULDN'T KEEP my hands off her. It wasn't the dress. It wasn't her body. Every time Hailey was near me, my body craved some kind of contact with her. If I'd driven her crazy with all the ways I'd already touched her, it was nothing compared to my need to have her. Every time my hand or thumb or body brushed against hers it screamed at me to take. Demand she give me every inch of her body for my pleasure—which would only ensure hers in the end.

She was a temptress. Seducing me every minute I was in her presence, and the only thing that made me feel marginally better about my newest obsession was that she was a shit liar, had the crappiest poker face of any woman I'd ever met, and she didn't hide a damn thing about her attraction to me.

Even now, cheeks flushed, that crystalline blue in her eyes three shades darker, and those damn plump lips glistening from her tongue, all I could think of was destroying her in a way that'd leave no man after me capable of comparing.

It was that thought that had me yanking my thumb from her and stepping back.

Fucking hell. What was happening to me? An itch beneath my skin burned to ravish her and make her scream so loud with pleasure that my neighbors two acres away heard her scream. Never before had my attraction to a woman been so visceral. They were disposable to me, not disrespectfully, but I'd never allowed a woman to come close to touching anything besides my cock and my flesh and that was where it ended.

Somehow, Hailey was burrowing herself beneath the flesh to my veins and my marrow and I hadn't even fucked her yet.

"Dawson?" She peered up at me with confusion, rightfully so.

If I was throwing her for a loop, she had no idea what rollercoaster I was experiencing.

This shit had to stop. My need to see her. My desperation. The ache clawed at me to tear down my pants, bend her over the counter and flip up her dress.

I didn't want to teach her. I wanted to train her.

And fuck...what a glorious student she'd make, even to my own detriment.

"Give me a second. Sorry. It's not you." I stepped back, scrubbed my hands over my face and shoved my hair back off my shoulders.

"What's wrong?"

I barked out a harsh laugh. Wrong?

She was upending my entire worldview standing there in a silky blue dress I wanted nothing more than to tear off with my teeth and she didn't have the faintest clue.

"Nothing's wrong, Hailey." I yanked my hands down my face and pressed them to the counter. The cool marble did nothing to cool the inferno raging inside of me. "I want you so much I'm terrified I'll hurt you. Show you a side of me I'm not sure I recognize right now."

How was that for honesty? Jesus. I needed my head examined.

Her lips parted in a perfect circle and an ohhhh sound escaped. "Is that bad?"

I laughed. It was cold, brutal, and did not help wipe away the confusion knotting her brows together. "I have no fucking idea."

She swallowed sharply and chewed the inside of her cheek. A more patient man would teach her all the things she wanted in slow, patient steps.

Patience flew out the door as soon as she stepped out of her car tonight in that godforsaken dress.

After I tore it off her with my teeth, I was burning that fucker to ash.

She stepped toward me and settled her hand on my arm. Her touch was soft, hesitant, and somehow, even through the dress shirt's crisp cotton fabric, it cooled my flesh in a way the counter hadn't. I inhaled a deep breath and was arrested with the floral scent of her perfume and her gentle presence.

"You won't hurt me, Dawson."

I dropped my head and stared at the marble. Not purposefully. Not permanently. But did I want to see my handprint on her ass? Hell yeah, I did.

"Want to know how I know?"

I twisted my neck so I could see her. My hair fell, blocking my view, so I shoved it back.

"You're too good."

I scoffed. Like she knew anything. "Hailey."

"You've already protected me. You kept our first meeting private so we could talk without eyes on us, knowing it might be a hard conversation. You've warned me about being spotted with you, and tonight, you were upset when I got upset. That's how I know. You won't do anything to me I don't want."

She was killing me. Daggers straight to the chest couldn't have hurt more or woken me up. So I wasn't an asshole. I knew that. Didn't mean I was nice, either. At least before her, no one would describe me that way.

"What do you want then?"

"I want you, and whatever you want to do to me because I know you'll think of me first."

Odd how my freakout seemed to settle her nerves. Gone was the trembling woman from earlier. She was replaced with a confident vixen in ocean blue who settled her hand at her hip.

"If I hurt you—"

"You won't."

"Tell me to stop."

"You won't."

"Hailey." Her name was a growl, part animalistic as it left my throat.

"Fine." She rolled her eyes, sass I hadn't yet seen vibrant in her eyes and her tone. "I promise to stop you if you hurt me, but only..." She held up an index finger to make her point. "If it's a hurt that doesn't also feel good."

Damn her. Damn her to hell and back. She was young, but not stupid. She was also inexperienced, but my guess from the books she read, at least the one I read, she wasn't naive. My control broke, unleashed, and I closed the space I'd put between us, flung my arm behind her lower back, and yanked her to me.

"Just remember you asked for this," I warned her, and right before I kissed her, she broke out into a huge smile.

"I have, multiple times, I believe."

I slammed my mouth to hers, taking her by surprise, and she gasped into my mouth. I took advantage of the opening and didn't kiss her slowly but speared my tongue into her mouth. Our lips pressed together, teeth clinked, and I shoved my other hand to the back of her head, beneath all that thick, silky platinum hair, and adjusted her so I could take the kiss deeper.

She was on me, instantly, responding exactly how I craved, how I needed her to, and she rolled her hips against me. My dick was stone behind my zipper, begging for release, and as her hands went to my shoulder to shove off my dress shirt, I grunted my satisfaction. I pulled back only far enough to shake it off me and then returned to her.

She tasted like sunshine and fresh air and summertime and everything bright and cheery and good in the world.

It was no place for a man like me to be, but hell if I didn't want to revel in the gift she was giving me. And the kitchen was no place for a woman like her to be, the first time we experienced that gift together.

"Upstairs," I grunted and pressed kisses along her jaw, down the column of her throat where her pulse was a horse stampede.

"Yes, oh god, that feels good."

I bent, slipped my hand beneath her knees and back, and carried her to my room, kissing her throat the entire way, the sounds she made while I was doing it only made me harder. Needier. Hungrier for her.

My lights in my room were off, so still holding on to her, I carried Hailey to the nightstand closest to the bathroom and flipped one on.

Once there was a light glow, I set her on her feet, and like I'd wanted to do, used my teeth to tug down the thinnest strap of her dress.

Her hands clung to my sides, shoved up my rib cage, and whispered little pleasured sounds that had my cock aching.

"Dawson." My name was a muted rasp, filled with pleasure, and even better, only certainty.

"I've waited all night to do this." To prove it, I trailed my lips across her collarbone, to the other side and used my teeth, gazing along her skin, relishing in every shiver she made from my touch.

"There's a zipper," she whispered. "On the back."

"On it." As I bit into the second strap, I reached out, found the zipper at the top center of her ass, and slid it down while I tugged down her strap. "Step out of this for me."

I waited until she'd stepped away from the pool of blue that looked perfect against the cream rug and dark wood floor.

"What the hell," I rasped as soon as I caught what was beneath her dress. It was strapless, cups barely covering her nipples but doing their job of lifting her breasts. Hailey's hands went to her stomach, and I stopped her. "Don't, don't cover up for me, let me see the back."

"There isn't really a back."

Couldn't have been, considering her dress, but she still turned. I kept my hands on her hips to steady her, brushed them up and down the outside of her thighs as she spun. There was nothing to the back.

Absolutely nothing except for two thin, nude straps that moved along the top curves of her ass and then between.

"At least that answers my earlier question if you were wearing underwear," I muttered.

Hailey looked at me over her shoulder, and her smile lit up the room. "You wondered that?"

"Baby, with what you had on, and how little was there, yeah, I was wondering all night what you were hiding beneath."

"Oh."

Yeah. Oh.

I took her hand in mine and settled both of ours at my chest. My heartbeat was a steady thump against her palm and her fingertips curled in. "Nothing happens here tonight without your okay. Got it?"

She nodded, licking her lips. I'd skip this, but it was important. Now that we were in my room, and her nerves had stayed downstairs, I was less afraid of hurting her, more worried about ensuring everything we did was good for her. Wasn't sure I'd ever been with anyone who'd been so untouched, but my mouth watered to taste her everywhere. Have her crying out my name with her legs spread on my bed.

I skimmed my hands along her sides. Found the tape sticking to her ribs that held up the bra. My brows furrowed, and I tried my finger along the curve of her breasts. "Will this hurt?"

"Only one way to find out."

"Come here." I turned her so her side was facing me, pulled the skin taut and like a Band-Aid, tore it off fast. She hissed in a breath, and I quickly followed the pain with my kisses, licking away the sting until she'd softened against me. I did the same toward the other one and inhaled a quick, calming breath before I shifted her so she was facing me, her back to the bed, I moved her back, kept my eyes on her until the backs of her knees hit the bed and I guided her down.

Her breasts were incredible. Tan, pebbled nipples and more than a handful, I brushed my hand over one, and she gasped as I moved her back to the bed. The garment had folded in half, and I left the bottom part on while I bent over her on the bed. My hair shaded her face from my view so I tore off the band I always kept at my wrist and tied it back.

"You all right?" I asked while my tongue circled one of her nipples. My hand cupped the other, and she nodded, licking her lips. Her back bowed off the bed, and I continued working them both. Taking turns, keeping my movements soft. I kissed every inch of her body and with my free hand, I tore off my belt, shoved my pants down and kicked them to the floor before dropping to my knees, and slowly peeling off the contraption covering her sex.

And oh dear god. Thank God I was already on my knees. Had I been standing, I would have fallen to the floor right then. She was perfect. Beautiful. She was soaked. So damn wet her inner thighs glistened with desire. Only a small patch of neatly trimmed hair.

"Dawson." Her hand still at my head, pressed against my hand that was helping hold her thighs open.

I met her gaze, knitted brow, lips parted.

"I've never—"

"I know. Trust me when I tell you this will be the best part."

She laughed softly, half a laugh, half choking sound. I ran my hands up and down her thighs.

How did I get here? On my knees, worshipping this woman. I couldn't remember the last time—if ever—I'd been on my knees for any woman. I kissed her thighs, trailing my lips down her soft, silky legs. Both sides, until her nervous sounds changed to whispered rasps and puffs of air and slowly, her legs fell open as she relaxed. I propped her heels on the edge of the bed, leaned forward, and almost died from the pleasure of that first whiff of her scent.

As sweet as the rest of her, I pressed a finger to her clit, swollen, drenched with her own arousal and relished the way her hands clung to my mattress.

I didn't ask if she was ready. But I waited until our eyes met, hers already half-blown with pleasure and she nodded. The tip of her tongue peeked out from her lips.

God, that look.

So damn innocent. So damn ready.

I ran my finger over her clit, kissed the juncture at the tops of her thighs and then I did what I'd been craving to do.

Flattened my tongue against her opening and ran it all the way to her clit.

CHAPTER 16
HAILEY

I WAS GOING TO DIE. Right there, right then. Dawson Butler was going to have to call the cops for a woman who died of extreme pleasure asphyxiation on his bed. The story would hit the news. He'd become known as the man with the most talented tongue in the world.

No toy, no matter how good it was could have prepared me for the moment where Dawson swirled his around my bundle of nerves while sliding a finger inside of me.

Sounds tore from my throat as he continued driving me absolutely mindless, and I peeled one of my hands off his sheet and settled it in his hair.

He grunted his approval, and my fingers dug in. It only made him go harder, eating me like he was trying to win an award for the orgasm he could give me. My thighs were shaking, my hips rolled and searching until he braced an arm over my lower stomach, speared me with a glare, and with my wetness shining from his cropped beard, growled. "Take what I'm giving you, Hailey."

"Oh fuck." My head fell back to the bed, and my mind spun.

I would do anything to hear him boss me around in that growly, rough voice of his.

A second finger entered me, and there was a slight burn at the stretch while he moved his fingers out of me and sucked gently on my clit.

Thank God, I'd stocked up on toys. His fingers were large, but as my body grew comfortable, he added a third, and "Oh god, Dawson."

"Do not come yet."

How could I stop it? I clamped on his fingers and tried to stave it off, but he was too good.

Too perfect. He shoved his fingers in roughly and slid them out slowly. He curled them inside, and I knew exactly what spot he'd found —thank you, erotic romance books—when a cry escaped my throat before I could stop it.

His tongue was gone, replaced with his thumb, and he was standing over me, mouth slamming to mine right as he commanded, "There you go. Let loose, I got you."

Oh shit. There was. No stopping it. An inferno raced down my spine, spread out to my limbs, and my entire body convulsed with the intensity, the white-hot blinding pleasure, as my first not provided by me orgasm raced through me.

"Shit." I clung to him as my hips rolled while his fingers kept moving. Wave after wave rolled through me, bringing me down, and I laughed stupidly against his mouth before tearing my mouth from his and shoving my face into the crook of his neck and shoulder.

"There you go," he crooned in my ear, bringing me down. His fingers slowed, gently slid out of me. "You okay?"

I wasn't sure I was okay.

I was positive I would never be the same again.

It took a moment to catch my breath, and when I managed to peel open my eyes, Dawson was hovering above me, one arm braced to the mattress next to my head, the other resting gently at the curve of my waist.

"Did I hurt you?"

"No." I ran my hands down his sides, felt the heat of his body and the cotton of his boxer briefs. My hands stilled there. I hadn't realized he still had his boxers on. And...now what?

I slipped my fingertips beneath the waistband, and he bent down, brushed his lips over mine. Hair that had come loose tickled my cheeks. "Tonight was for you, Hailey. I wanted to give that to you. Show you how good it could be."

That was more than good. It was phenomenal. Life-altering.

I didn't say anything to that but brushed my hand down the front of his boxers and felt the hardness pushing against the thin cotton.

"But you..."

"I'm a grown man. I can take care of that."

"But what if I want to?"

I'd never even jerked Darrick off before, just rubbed him through his pants, because he'd always stopped me when I went for more, but he was nothing close to being comparable to the weight I was currently feeling. The thickness.

No wonder why Dawson didn't go straight to sex. Probably terrified he'd tear me in two.

"You done that before?" Dawson asked.

I pushed through the embarrassment of the question. Twenty-four and never held a man's dick in my hand. "No."

"All right then. Up you go." He shoved off me and held out his hand. As soon as my palm was in his, he tugged me to my feet, and for the first time, I truly got to take in all those muscles he'd always managed to poorly hide beneath his clothing. In fact, Dawson should never wear clothes again. Not in my presence. I'd failed anatomy and biology in high school, but I was pretty certain if a model like Dawson had come in to give us a visual of where every muscle was located, I would have been the star pupil.

"Go where?"

"Shower. I don't want to leave a mess I'll have to clean up. You watch. You can help. Do whatever you feel like doing to me while we get cleaned up."

A shower? Naked? Where'd he soap himself up, and I'd get to see my first ever real-life dick while he was soaked beneath soap suds and water and bright lights?

Where he could stare at my body? Maybe touch me again?

It was that thought that had me hurrying after him and when we reached the shower, my mouth opened. "You throw parties in there?"

His shower had not one, not two, but five showerheads. Two waterfall showers. Two at each end hooked to a hose, and one on the wall between them.

All glass was on one end, opposite a soaking tub that could have been custom-built for his large frame. The long side where we entered was totally open. On the inside's longest wall was a bench I was pretty sure six could sit on and watch a shower show.

"Never been anyone in this shower with me before."

"What?" I spun in a slow circle.

He shrugged, reached inside around the corner, and flipped on both of the shower heads at each end. "Never bring women to my house." He smirked. "Crystal might have used it, but definitely not when I was in it with her."

"That would be weird," I admitted, and his smirk grew.

"You're nervous again." He came to me, curled his hands over my shoulders and slowly brushed them down my arms. "You sure you're okay?"

"Well, I'm standing naked in front of a man for the very first time after having possibly the best orgasm in history known to womankind, and you're still clothed, so...yeah. I'm a bit nervous."

He dropped his hands from my shoulders straight to his waistband and shoved down his boxers. "That help?"

Oh dear god, no that did not help. His dick was huge. Larger than any toy. Larger than some of the toys I'd viewed online that made me wince. Thick. Veiny. There was also a drop of shimmering liquid at the tip and... oh my god...another piercing.

Two tiny silver balls were at the ends of a metal rod that went straight through.

"That'll hurt," I whispered, definitely not nervous but scared out of my hand.

"First time, probably. That's why tonight was for you. I'll need to take time getting you ready. As far as the piercing goes, that'll only feel good."

Goddamn, his confidence and his complete lack of embarrassment about any of this was a turn-on. "You going to come in the shower with me?"

Watch him wrap his hand around that?

Like he read my mind, he wrapped one of his hands around himself, and my mouth watered. Two slow, firm strokes and that fluid at the top grew.

Before I could stop myself, I reached out and swiped my fingertip over it.

"Fuck," Dawson grunted, and my gaze jumped up to meet his. "What?"

"Taste me," he grunted again, and his hand was still moving, but I couldn't resist.

I wanted to know what he tasted like.

As soon as I sucked on my fingertip, he had his free hand around my bicep. "New plan, you're gonna help me take care of me, I'm gonna take care of you again, and this time, with only my mouth, and then we're going to find that tie I threw off earlier because I have a lot more planned for you if you're down for that."

Down for that?

Had he hit his head somewhere?

Nerves and fears aside, I was down for anything.

"Yeah," I said instead, and dutifully followed him straight into the shower that would forever be remembered in my dreams.

A tickle on my arm made me squirm. Another tickle at my side. I opened my eyes and jumped.

"What are you doing?" I tried to move my arm, but it wouldn't.

"Dawson?"

I glanced up at him and realized the tickle felt was either the soft brush of his hair or his lips along my skin. And my arm? Well, something light blue and silky dangled in my vision as I twisted my neck.

He'd tied me to the headboard.

Holy freaking crap. Sleep vanished, and I shifted as Dawson bent down again. This time to my breast, and a delightful warmth spread to the juncture of my thigh.

"Oh..."

"You need to use the bathroom? I'll untie you quick, but we didn't get to this last night, and I couldn't wait any longer."

Oh. My. God. Talk about something right out of my romance books. I did need to use the restroom. But I also wanted to see where this was going.

We had a glorious shower. My best shower ever. A shower where last night, I got to touch him all I wanted, rub my hands over all that was him, including his thick, rigid cock that was now currently brushing against my inner hip. The piercing was cold, a direct contrast. I'd liked everything he'd done to me, but that piercing freaked me out.

"Dawson," I whispered. At least he'd left one hand free because I was able to shove hair off his face. "What are you doing?"

"Woke up needing to taste you again," he mumbled as he slid down my body, taking sheets with him. I'd fallen asleep in one of his T-shirts after the shower and it was now shoved above my breasts, exposing the rest of me to him.

I spread my legs.

He'd turned me into a fiend in less than twelve hours.

He wanted to go down on me? I wanted him to live there. We hadn't even had actual sex yet, and I wasn't sure how it could possibly be better than his mouth on me.

"Please." I arched my hips toward him and slid my hand from his hair.

"Good. Then hold on to your other hand, and don't let go until I'm done."

A full-body shiver rolled through me, and I whimpered. Then hot, warm breath was at my core, and his tongue appeared, gently lapping at my clit. "Already so wet for me, Hailey. Gotta say I love this pussy of yours." He inhaled. Deeply.

I couldn't even think straight as he pressed his hands to my inner thighs, spread my legs until they burned from the stretch and then he dove right on in.

Sparks of pleasure ignited down my spine and behind my closed eyelids. I forced them open, not wanting to miss a single millisecond of everything he was doing to me, and when he added his fingers, crooked them to my G-spot, I was an absolute goner.

I clamped my hand around my tied wrist so hard it was probably going to have bruises, but I didn't care. I braced my feet into the bed and lost myself to the intensity of everything he was doing to me and when my orgasm hit me this time, it spread as a fire to my core, shooting to the tips of my fingers and my smallest toes. I cried out his name, words with no meaning, and my entire body trembled as he tossed me over the cliff and brought me gently back to a safe landing.

When I could think straight again, Dawson was straddling me. All those muscles above me, his hair, the dark expression in his eyes as he unwrapped the tie from his headboard and then massaged my wrists.

"You all right?"

It was sweet, he asked all the time. Unnecessary. I was way more than all right. One night with Dawson and I wasn't sure how any man, ever, could match these skills of his.

"Wonderful." I sighed as he brushed my cheek with his fingertips and bent down, pressing his lips to mine. The kiss was soft. Tender.

As if he actually cared, and that was a dangerous thought that had no place in my mind. I reached between us, felt his hard, thick and so long dick in my hand I wasn't sure it could all fit inside of me. "Can I help with this?"

"Babe, you can practice this on me all you want."

My mouth watered to taste him again, but before I could ask, Dawson slipped a hand beneath my back. He rolled us, reversing our position, and I squealed in surprise as I ended up straddling his thighs. My hand was still wrapped around him, and he kept a hand at my lower back while he lay in the bed, the other hand brushing up and down my thigh.

"Whatever feels good, Hailey. Whatever you think you might like. Do that."

"Are you sure?"

He huffed a laugh and squeezed my thigh with his hand. "Definitely."

Hmm. He'd shown me how he liked it last night in the shower. Firm long pulls that grew faster and harder the closer he got. I started that way, keeping my eyes on him, the flexing of his stomach muscles, and reveling in the sounds I drew from him. He encouraged me with yeses and right there and just like that, honey, and I was pretty certain he hadn't meant the endearment, but as precum appeared at the tip of his reddening head and the vein in his shaft pulsed beneath my touch, I definitely needed more than my hand on him. I scooted down, and Dawson's gaze jumped wide.

"Hailey, you don't—"

"Teach me," I murmured right before I slid out my tongue and took that first, quick taste of his cum and him. And oh dear sweet heaven he was beautiful. All of him, large balls I cupped on instinct with my hand while I swirled my tongue around the head. And thank you erotic romance genre for teaching women with detailed, visual words, of how to do all the things when it comes to pleasing men.

I played with his piercing, lapped at it with my tongue, both the one on top and the bottom.

"Oh shit. Yes. That's it. Take me in your mouth. Just the tip. Suck, apply pressure. Fucking, hell, your mouth feels good."

I listened to every compliment, every command, and soon I had my hand wrapped around the base of Dawson's thick, silky cock and my other covering the rest. I bobbed up and down on it, tried to match the rhythm with my mouth that he'd taught me with my hand, and he reached down, cupped my cheek, pushing hair off my face.

"Gonna come, Hailey. Be ready...you can..."

I sucked harder. I was in this. No stopping now. That first hardening and pulse of his cock almost had me gag as he hit the back of my throat, but then he groaned, a rumble of pleasure that vibrated straight through my body and the first taste of him hit. Salty and warm, but not bad, I swallowed it down and slowed my movements when it seemed like he was done, until his hands grabbed my hips, and he yanked me up his body.

When my gaze hit his, he was smiling. Pleased. Relaxed.

And that was the moment all hell broke loose.

Next to him, his phone started ringing. At the same time, mine started vibrating on the nightstand next to where I'd slept. He'd gone and gotten my purse and phone after the shower, and we both stared at each other as our phones interrupted us.

"Fuck," Dawson grunted.

He grabbed his phone, and I climbed off him to grab mine. "It's my dad." And that wasn't all. A quick flip through my screen showed I'd missed several texts. "My brothers have all texted. And my sister."

Dawson flashed me his phone. "My dad, too. Damn it."

CHAPTER 17
DAWSON

I HADN'T TALKED to my dad since I was arrested earlier this year. I hung up on him after he continued to remind me that Crystal was Crystal, and she was never going to change because she was too damn intent on being just like his ex-wife. I hung up on him once he started the mom bashing. Not that I liked the woman or had anything to do with her, but I didn't need to hear it.

The last person I wanted to hear from at that moment, my dick still wet with the taste of Hailey all over me, before I could tell her how incredible she sucked my dick, was that man.

But there he was. Showing up at the least convenient time.

Not much different than the last ten years, really.

"I'm guessing your family saw some pictures of us." I quirked a brow, tried to keep my tone light.

Hailey's cheeks were still flushed from the orgasm I couldn't not give her when I woke up with her sleeping next to me, but her pleased expression after swallowing my cum like it wasn't her first blow job was long gone.

"They don't watch sports," she muttered, and I fought an eye roll. Sure, men didn't follow sports. I could totally buy that. But her dad was a firefighter. I didn't know what he did for the city, but in my experience, he had to have at least caught a few games at the fire station. "Doubt they know who you are."

God her naivety killed me. "I'm on billboards all over the Nashville area, Hailey, and Cole's more of an icon than a quarterback. You might want to realize that people do know me."

I pushed up to sitting, trying not to laugh at her. She was too damn cute, and I wasn't even insulted she kept acting like my job was no big deal.

"Really?" She had awe in her voice, and I chuckled, unable to hold back the laughter.

"Yeah, honey." I kissed her forehead. "Remember how your friend Margo reacted? That happens."

"A lot?"

"Sometimes. You need to call them back?"

She worried her lip in between her teeth and then a pretty pink blush rose on her cheeks. "You're right. My dad knows who you are and he's not really happy."

"What do you mean?"

She curled up next to me and held her phone out. On her screen was a text message, and I quickly scanned it.

At your house and you're not here which only tells me you're one place. We need to talk about this association you have with Dawson Butler. ASAP.

Damn. Her dad probably didn't like me all that much to begin with, but until this year, I'd never made the news for anything bad. I'd never made the news at all except for being called rude to reporters. Excuse me for not wanting to sit behind a table and answer idiotic questions after we lost a game. We played bad. The other team played better. I should have been able to say that, but instead, social media critics started claiming I wasn't a team player and didn't support my QB or coach. Total and utter bullshit.

"Don't think your dad likes me very much."

"Doesn't matter." Her thumbs started wildly flying across her screen, and she hit send before I could catch more words than dare, not your house, and call you when I feel like.

"Hailey. What was that for?"

She flung sheets off her waist and practically jumped out of the bed. If I thought she was cute not giving me credit for who I was, or not knowing, she was glorious as she started pacing next to my bed.

"Twenty-four years old, Dawson. I am twenty-four freaking years old, was supposed to be married this year, and my dad thinks it's okay to show up at my house? The house I worked for? The house I paid for to lecture me about a man I spend time with? It's absurd."

Well, yeah. She had a point. "Is it bad he's worried?"

"No." She spun, faced me and slammed her hands to her thighs. The loud slap of her palm against skin echoed in the room. "No, it is not bad he's worried, but they treat me like a baby. Still, all of them. Hell, my brothers freaking texted and it's what? Five in the morning there? It's freaking ridiculous. I'm allowed to live my life the way they've always had the freedom to. Ugh!"

She spun on her heels and rushed to the bathroom. She slammed the door so hard it rattled the hinges.

I didn't quite care about her parents being concerned about me. I didn't quite care what many people thought of me, period. With how hot she burned, how quickly, I took it this wasn't the first time her parents crossed a boundary she didn't appreciate.

At least she had a family who cared.

Unfortunately, in a few months when we ended this, her parents would probably give her the *I told you so* speech, and that sucked.

Although the knot in my chest tightening at the thought made me uncertain. Was I actually concerned about them liking me? Or was it the thought of us ending things?

"Damn," I groaned and climbed out of bed. After pulling on a fresh pair of shorts from my closet shelves, Hailey exited the bathroom. She'd washed her face, probably brushed her teeth.

After our last round last night, I'd gone downstairs and brought up the overnight bag she'd brought with her and she went straight to that on my dresser, grabbed her clothes, and marched right back to my bathroom before slamming the door again.

A clear stay out message to me. Awesome.

I gave her the time she needed and hurried downstairs instead. After I used the bathroom there, I was in the kitchen, making coffee when she entered. The plunk of her bag on my floor alerted me to her presence first and when I faced her, she was gently laying her dress over the back of my couch.

"You all right?"

"No," she sighed. "And I'm sorry for that, you didn't need to hear all of that, but my family...they're a lot. Great people, but boundaries and remembering I'm no longer thirteen come harder for some than others. But now my dad is still at my house, claiming he's not leaving until I get there and I'm debating whether to stay away for the entire day, and go to Meredith's just to let him stew in his own anger that's ridiculous and completely unhinged, or if I should head home and deal with him so it's over."

I was not a fan of her father putting his adult daughter in either position.

"Want me to come with you?"

Her eyes turned huge. "Why?"

"It's my shit that's got you in this mess."

"No it's not," she scoffed. "Again, it was my own decision. To agree to this with you and to stay here. You didn't twist my arm or manipulate me or force me to stay here."

Outside me tying her up, I hadn't, but my point remained. "What would be easier for you?"

"I don't know." She huffed and plopped her ass onto one of my barstools.

We had an excellent night. A damn good morning. If she didn't get this taken care of, she'd be the one stewing on it all day and I was not letting her handle this on her own, not when her dad was pissed because of me.

"You drink coffee?"

"What?"

"Coffee. You drink it? Need some before you meet with your dad?"

"I'm not sure I want to see him."

I waited, and she must have seen my impatience growing because she finally shook her head. "I don't really drink coffee before I eat."

"All right then. Let's go."

"Go?"

"Yeah. I'm going to throw on a shirt. We're going to your house, and then we'll deal with your dad. Then I'm taking you for breakfast before you need to get to your store. Whatever your dad wants to say, he can say it to my face, but he's not ruining what we had last night or this morning."

Fake or not, it'd been important to her. It meant something to me she gave me all she did. Especially this morning when she took control.

"Dawson..."

"You're still not moving."

She slid off the stool, lips twitching before lifting into a smile. She came straight to me and set her hand on my bare chest, right at my heart. "Thank you. You're the best fake boyfriend a girl could ask for."

My chest squeezed and not from her touch. Fake. I was anything but fake.

She rolled to her toes, I met her halfway seeing as how I didn't have to dip very far and brushed my lips over hers. "Tell him you'll be there in twenty, but you don't appreciate the game he's playing with his adult daughter. It'll take me a second to grab a shirt."

"All right."

I ran up the stairs, skipping two of them in my rush and when I reached my room, took the time to brush my teeth and grabbed a hair tie for my hair. I changed my athletic shorts into pale-blue chinos and threw on a gray T-shirt.

I didn't like what her dad was doing, but I wasn't going to meet him looking like I just rolled out of bed with his little girl.

It took thirty minutes, not twenty, and based on the way Hailey's dad popped off her swinging bench on her front porch, he didn't like to be kept waiting.

His scowl was furious, aimed immediately in my direction even though Hailey was pulling in the driveway in front of me. Since she had to open her store after breakfast, I'd followed her in my Tahoe and with the F-150 at the curb, I pulled into the driveway behind her. I ignored him, like Hailey seemed to be doing, while she opened her garage door and pulled her car in.

I hopped out of the truck, waited for Hailey to climb out of her car and as soon as she reached me, took her hand in mine. She was trembling like a leaf, and based on the press of her lips and the fire in her eyes, it had nothing to do with nerves.

We headed up her front walk and her dad dropped his scowl as he caught Hailey's gaze. Her hand in mine flinched. He spied our clasped hands and that scowl returned to me, softer this time, but noticeable.

"I'd like to speak with my daughter alone."

"That's funny because out of the two of us, I was the one invited."

His eyes turned round, a complete mirror image of Hailey's look earlier and she squeezed my hand again. "Good morning, Dad. How are you? Maybe before talking to Dawson like I'm not here, even though you are, as Dawson pointed out, on my front porch uninvited, you can at least tell your daughter hello."

His nose twitched, and he licked his lips. The fact he cared was obvious. Dressed in an outfit similar to mine, he wasn't a bad looking guy. Graying at his temples. Jet-black hair that had somehow skipped over Hailey entirely, but the rest of their features made it clear he was her father.

Just not one I liked all that much.

"Good morning, baby girl," he finally said. "Came over so we could talk today."

"It'll have to be later," Hailey said, and she pulled me up the stairs. Her dad was forced to step back. "But if you'd like, you can come in while I get ready so Dawson and I can go eat breakfast before I need to open my shop." She stopped at her front door, key out, and then faced her father. "Oh, Dad. This is Dawson Butler, my boyfriend. Dawson, this is my dad, Ken."

I had to pry my fingers out of Hailey's grip to hold out my hand. Not that I wanted to.

"Boyfriend?" Ken's blue eyes bounced between the two of us. "Hailey..."

"Nice to meet you, sir." I held out my hand and waited a beat. Then two and right when I thought he wasn't going to shake my hand and be that big of a dick in front of his daughter, he clasped on to mine. Firmly. A man who was about my size, at least my height, thinner, and shook it firmly.

"Nice to meet you, Dawson. Been a fan of yours on the field for years."

Could have fooled me.

"Thank you."

"You don't watch football," Hailey stated, her key in the lock forgotten.

Her dad smiled, and it was again so similar to hers it made my head spin. "Of course I watch football. Every Sunday. You and your mom were always working in the garden or out shopping, or you probably had your nose buried in one of your millions of books."

He was teasing her, gently, lovingly. Helped me forgive the game he was currently playing but it was clear to see when he looked at his daughter, talked to her, he had nothing but love for her.

Maybe a bit too much overprotectiveness in him, too, but I wasn't sure I could fault him for that much after seeing the way he looked at her.

"Huh," was all Hailey said, and opened her door. "I never knew that."

I rolled my lips together to keep from laughing. I *knew* her dad watched football. She glanced back at me, scowled playfully. "Don't start."

"I didn't say anything," I told her and lifted my hands, and then held out my arm for Ken to follow her inside.

He shook his head, watching our interaction. "You first, son. She's right. You're the invited one here."

Technically I'd said it, but whatever. That son hit hard and fast. I wasn't his son. But he seemed like the kind of man who said it to every male his children's age, so I tried to let it go.

Once we were inside, Hailey went straight to her kitchen where she pulled out a container of orange juice. "So, what's Mom doing?"

She poured herself a glass and held up the bottle to me, but I shook my head. I wouldn't let him be a jerk to her, but I wasn't going to interfere as long this visit stayed cordial.

"Pissed I'm here to be honest. Said it's none of my business who you're...dating...these days."

"At least one of you has some sense."

This time, it was my chest that swelled. Damn, she didn't hold back much, and in a heartbeat, it told me the kind of relationship they had because her dad chuckled, shaking his head and was now smiling.

"We've been worried about you, Hailey. Ever since Darrick, and there was no mention of this until your mom saw some pictures on her Instagram or whatever it's called."

Least that explained the phone calls.

"So did you call my brothers and get them all riled up or did they find out on their own?"

Ken had the decency to flinch. "Like I said, we were worried."

"It was probably four in the morning out there! Aren't you worried about their sleep? Their health? Hell, Tate was probably up all night long..."

"He was still finishing up a twelve-hour shift."

Hailey's eyes grew so round and large I worried they would leap right out of her sockets, or she'd get so angry she would throw herself over the counter to strangle her own family.

I stepped in, maybe not my place, but she wasn't going to blow her top. Not if I could help it. "We're new," I said. "Only had a few dates. I'm sure she was going to get around to telling you."

"And yet she stayed at your house last night, obviously."

"Oh my god, Dad!" It wasn't even an embarrassed groan. Furious. She proved it when she shoved a finger in his direction from halfway across her house. "You have never called any of my brothers or sister out on their behavior like this. This isn't just humiliating, this is horrific. You being here doesn't say anything about Dawson or me. It says everything about you, and I will not stand here, in my kitchen, listening to you question me or discuss my sex life or the choices I make with who I spend time with. I am twenty-four years old, and I have every right to fuck the entire Nashville Steel team if I so damn choose."

"The hell you do," I growled. Growled. An actual growl escaped my throat like I was some kind of wild animal. It rolled up deep inside my gut, let loose before I could stop it.

But there was no way in hell, even once this was all said and done, any of my teammates would go anywhere near her.

Fuck no.

Hailey rolled her eyes. "You know what I meant, Dawson."

I knew the gifts she'd given me and the gifts she was going to give me and hell if I would stomach even the thought of her giving that to another man, much less a teammate. Ever.

Ken, possibly seeing the fight brewing between me and his daughter, wisely, or unwisely, changed the subject. "You've been arrested. Spent a night in jail."

An accusation that had his lip curling.

And just...the hell with this. I hadn't fully told Hailey all the shit about why I didn't want a relationship. Why I didn't trust women but if it got this man out of her home so I could take her upstairs and do things to her she'd never allow another man—especially a teammate—to do to her, then he could have it. They both could.

CHAPTER 18
HAILEY

"GOT A MOM, OR HAD ONE," Dawson started and as he did, my dad's gaze flicked to me.

I only had eyes for Dawson, even if he wasn't looking at me. Even if his gaze was glued to my dad's and his entire body was locked, ready for fight mode. He said Mom like a cuss word, the worst kind of cuss words.

"Also have a dad, and a sister, Crystal. She's two years younger than me. Dad's a pilot. Flies all over the world for his airline and so when we were kids, he wasn't home all that much, but when he was home, he was a good dad. A great one. Totally into both of us and every time he left town, he settled his hands on my shoulders, chuffed my chin with his knuckles and said, 'need you to be the man of the house, Daws. Got it? Need you to take care of your mom and sister. Precious jewels we have in them that need to be taken care of. Make sure they stay out of trouble and stay safe, okay, son?' So I did. I was eight the first time my dad gave me that speech and every week, he did it."

Dawson inhaled a breath, and he might have still been staring at my dad, but he wasn't there. Not in my living room in my house or hell, I bet he wasn't even in the town or the state of Tennessee.

He was somewhere else. Probably back to being that eight-year-old boy with a cute little statement from his dad that had become way too serious to him.

I hated Dawson's dad.

"Every week, until I was fourteen, anyway, when he got back from a flight early, Crystal and I were at school, and he caught my mom in their bed cheating on him with the neighbor. His best friend since we'd moved in."

Shit. "Dawson..." That was none of my dad's business.

"Son," my dad said, because he knew it too.

"Not your son," Dawson clipped. Still as a statue, he continued, "Dad yelled at me that day when I got home, yelled at me for not letting him know it was happening. My mom was fucking some other man for who knows how long, and my dad blamed his teenage son for not doing his job. Did he get pissed at Crystal? Fuck no. Did he get mad at my mom? Kicked her ass out that very day, said he hadn't married a whore and wouldn't stay married to one. She moved out. That guy and his wife also got divorced and Mom moved Crystal and me right on in."

I couldn't take it. Dad's jaw was tight. Eyes laced with pain, but it was the coldness coming from Dawson making me shiver.

"Hey." I ran to him, set my hands on his arms but I might as well have been in Egypt for all he cared. "Crystal took after our mom. Apparently Mom liked Dad because he was a pilot, but this other guy was some COO. She stayed with him until she found the CEO of an even larger company. By the time I graduated, Mom had moved Crystal and me into five different homes, each one larger and richer than the previous and we went from seeing our dad every weekend to once a month until we barely saw him at all. Who knows who's she fucking now, fleecing them for money and jewels. Crystal decided she wanted to be like our mom, so that's what Crystal does. Causes drama, causes problems, fucks married men and gets them to be her sugar daddies until their wives found out. Three times I've paid off seriously pissed off, rich women, on her behalf."

"This isn't any of my business, son," my dad said, and he flinched as soon as he said it. Given Dawson looked ready to tear someone's head—anyone's—straight from their body I didn't blame him. It was his habit.

Dawson let that one go if he even heard my dad talk. I brushed my hands up and down his arms and still got no response from him.

"You wanted to know why I was arrested," he snapped back. "You wanted to know so you could tell your daughter here, who already knows some of it, why I'm no good for her. Maybe I'm not. I won't even argue it, considering it's clear you love her more than your own life even if that love comes with crossing boundaries I don't quite respect."

At that, Dad's jaw sharpened, and I rubbed my lips together. I didn't know many men who told off my dad like that. Or who my dad would take it from, but before he could snap back, Dawson kept going.

"Crystal shows up, every couple of years, destroys my home, ruins my life, and I pick up all the goddamn pieces because Dad hasn't spoken to her since she was eighteen and pulled enough shit on him he got sick of it, but me? I'm still that damn kid, looking at her like she's my responsibility. So yeah, I went to jail. More bullshit of Crystal's got out of control when she blamed that guy at the bar for doing shit he didn't do but it was my sister, and I'd been conditioned to protect her since I reached my dad's hip, but I didn't mean to hurt that dude. Not lying there, either. The dude, slipped, both of us did, and it was bad fucking timing, bad damn luck, so yeah. That's what you wanted to know."

My phone rang on the counter, and I ignored it. At least, until my dad's phone rang immediately after. He didn't ignore his but pulled it out of his pocket.

Dawson's flesh was burning beneath my touch.

"Yeah, should have listened. I'm headed back soon..."

"Dawson," I whispered, and his chest shuddered with the weight of his breath. "Calm, honey. It's okay, breathe."

I inhaled a deep breath, and waited for him to follow, but he did, so I did it again, and by the time Dad ended the phone call with my mom, Dawson's hands were loosely resting on my hips, and the cloud coloring his past was fading from his steely gaze.

He settled me at his side, and my hand went to his lower back, my other to his stomach.

He was still breathing like a bull in a china shop, but it was better. Not as scary.

Dad slipped his phone back into his pocket, barely glanced at me, before he said, "That wasn't on you. Your dad never should have put you in that position."

"Didn't realize he had until I just said it out loud."

Oh. My heart. It squeezed so tight I feared it would shatter.

"Right," my dad muttered. "First, I want you to know what you said here today won't be repeated. And you're right, I crossed some boundaries today, which I'll try not to do in the future." He glanced down and winked. "Your mom and I have had a time since everything with Darrick, wondering if you were okay, and how you've really been. But it wasn't my place to handle it this way today, but well, with everything Charlie went through, and we couldn't help him, we just...we worry."

Charlie fought depression for a long while after he came out as gay. Or maybe he became depressed and anxious because he was gay and then was able to seek help once he came out. I wasn't really sure considering I was ten when it happened, but it'd been hard on them for a long time.

"You don't have to worry about me, not like that," I told him. "And I don't even think of Darrick anymore. What happened happened and it's done. I'm moving on."

"Yeah." A soft, warm smile stretched his lips. The kind my dad was famous for. "I can see that."

"My apologies again, Dawson," he said to him. My dad stepped closer, and I went to step back, but Dawson squeezed me tight to his side. "This won't happen again, and my wife Sue said she'd love to have you for dinner sometime."

"Dad—"

"When you're ready. Whenever that may be."

"Thank you, sir."

"Ken, Dawson. That'll be good for now."

Dawson dipped his chin. My dad leaned in and kissed my cheek. "Sorry, baby girl. Won't happen again."

"Love you, Dad."

"All my heart, precious. You know you have it."

Dawson didn't let me go until the front door closed and even then he only did it to bury his face in my hair.

"What do you need?"

"This."

I gave it to him. Stood there and let him squeeze me tight and breathe in my hair and I let him do it for as long as he needed, rubbing my hand up his back every time he shuddered.

"So what happened after?"

Sloane was helping me in my shop, and by helping me, it meant she was picking up every tool and brush I owned, fiddling with them, and setting them back down in spots I'd never find them again. We'd only been able to connect via texts for the last couple of weeks, so she declared she was helping me today since she didn't have a shift at the hospital and then we were going out tonight for a couple of drinks.

We had the doors opened because I was painting a dresser. A dusty, smoky blue color I adored. Eventually I'd add gold handles. It was a small, six-drawer side-by-side dresser that could also be used in a large entryway or as a buffet side table in a dining room.

People didn't come to my store for typical furniture they could find in any bookstore or online shop so I always took the time to ensure my pieces could be used in multiple places if possible.

"I'm not telling you what happened after my dad left."

"Is he good? You know? At the whole cherry popping thing?"

She popped her p's much more dramatically than necessary.

I wouldn't know, not yet. A week had gone by since that Saturday morning. We'd checked in with each other almost daily, and he'd come to my house for dinner once. I'd gone to his once. Both of those included more sleepovers and hands-on tutorials, but I was still, technically a virgin.

It was driving me mad, which was why I called Sloane and told her she had to come to my store and hang with me to get my mind off things. Except she was doing the opposite and kept needling.

"You were supposed to be helping me," I told her. "And talking about cherries isn't helping."

"So you're still a card-carrying member of the V-Club?"

I rolled my eyes and dipped my brush in more paint. "Sure, Sloane. You could say that. We've done other things, but he keeps stopping before that."

And all the other things he did, he excelled at. Wednesday, we'd been watching a movie on his couch. There'd been touching. Flirting. Teasing kisses. I'd then found myself thrown onto the couch, hands on the cushions at the back of the couch. Dawson had thrown up the skirt of my dress, yanked down my underwear to my knees.

He'd then dropped to his knees on the floor and ate me from behind.

Incredible. Absolutely incredible. It was like he'd taken his homework seriously. Hell, maybe he hadn't needed the help of ideas of what I'd like in the first place because every time he touched me, he worked miracles.

The problem was that it was all starting to feel a little too date-like. Good morning texts. Good night phone calls. Earlier this week, he had me FaceTime him and then walked me through stripping for him, masturbating while I saw him make himself come. And it was Dawson making the effort, all the way.

He was either taking his job of teaching me about sex incredibly seriously, liked the idea of having a willing sex partner at his beck-and-call, or the final possibility I was trying very hard not to think about...

I wasn't the only one catching feelings.

Wishful thinking, so I chalked it up to him enjoying spending time with me.

"Have you asked him?"

"What?" I stood. Paint dripped off my brush, and I set it in the paint tray before I made a mess.

Sloane grinned. "Have you asked him to actually finish, you know... pop your..."

"Please don't say cherry again. And no, should I?"

"Maybe." She shrugged. "Maybe he's holding back because he's worried you're not ready or something."

That was a theory. My own fears and doubts were rising. Two weeks of all the making out and touching and it was spectacular, but I'd wonder why he held back. Why he always finished with his hand, or mine, or my mouth. Doubts had crept in. Was I not good enough...again?

I certainly hadn't been for Darrick.

"Just a thought." She jumped off the table. "I'm going to grab us dinner. Need anything?"

"Sure." I placed my order for The Tavern on Main, their gyro meal was to die for, and while Sloane was gone, I finished up the last coat of paint on the dresser before stripping out of my painting overalls. After a quick clean-up, I was back out in the front of the store.

Grace was working that night, and since it was getting late, the shop was winding down. The weather had also been threatening storms all day which kept foot traffic away, but so far, the streets had stayed clean and dry.

"Busy today?" I asked her. She'd shown up as soon as her last high school class ended and allowed me to spend time in the back.

"I think it was a good day. A few bigger purchases—that headboard and then the side table by the front—" She pointed to them. "Sold. I have them on hold until tomorrow at five."

"Awesome."

The headboard was all wood. I'd stripped off the old seventies walnut stain, restained it to a lighter wood and then white-washed it. Sized for a king bed, it took up a ton of space which made decorating around it difficult. It'd be perfect for a lake home, or a beach theme bedroom. I was glad to have it gone. The dresser I was currently working on would fit great in the space it'd leave behind. It'd also been in the store since winter, and I'd been starting to worry it'd never sell.

Our bell rang, and Grace scooted off to chat with what looked like a mom and daughter pair and Isaac strolled in. "Hey, neighbor," I sang to him.

He gave me his standard cocky grin and held Peanut Butter closer to his chest. "Where's Jelly the Cat?"

"She didn't feel like a walk today."

"Ah." That made sense. "Cats and their temperaments, right?"

He made some sound of acknowledgment. Isaac didn't like to be teased about his cats, much. Odd little duck was he. "You're dating Dawson Butler?"

"What?"

"Sorry, didn't mean it to sound bad or anything, just heard from some guys on my team you were dating him."

I was thrown. A team? What in the hell did Isaac do?

"Um. Yeah, I mean, we're dating. What team are you talking about?"

Because oh my god...did he play on the Steel too? If so, what were the odds...and how had I not known?

"No, Hailey." He was chuckling, a soft quiet laugh. "I play for the Avengers. Tuevo's team? I thought you knew."

"Why would I know that?"

"Because Meredith was the one who told you I needed a place to live?"

Oh...well, sure. Damn. I might really need to start paying attention to sports and things going on in my life. He'd been living here for well over a year. "I must have forgotten," I mumbled, cheeks burning.

"He's a good guy from what I hear. But after Darrick, you know... are you sure he's good for you?"

I'd now gotten that from my brothers and my sister. After the day my dad showed up, I'd had to call back my sister and my brothers. I should have scheduled a family Zoom call for as much as I'd had to repeat myself that day.

Hearing it from Isaac, who was more tenant than friend, didn't really want me to repeat myself again.

"It's fine. We're having some fun, is all." Maybe the more I repeated it the more I'd believe it.

"All right. Just make sure you take care of you first, right?"

I hadn't had to take care of myself since Dawson showed up in my life. I figured Isaac and I were thinking different things.

"Will do, Isaac. And thanks, I guess, for your concern."

"Wouldn't be a good neighbor if I didn't let you know."

He turned to leave, and Jelly let out a little meow so I scratched the top of his head before Isaac left.

"Take care, Isaac."

"Have a good night, landlord!"

He stopped the door from closing, and Sloane swooped in under his arm. "Thanks, Isaac! Sorry about you guys missing the playoffs."

He mumbled something and Sloane lifted two white bags of food.

Good grief. Did everyone know more about my tenant, and sports, than I did?

I really needed to start learning.

CHAPTER 19
DAWSON

"I'M BEGINNING to think you're the only person alive who would not know Isaac Svechnikal was living above them."

This girl. I was almost laughing too hard to speak, and that had never happened.

But Svech? What the hell was he doing renting a second-floor apartment? He had the money to be living in a neighborhood like mine. It was all strange, but it killed me how Hailey could remain so clueless about professional sports when her best friend was married to one of the best defenders in the NHL. And Svech? He was breaking records left and right in his second year since being called up from the AHL league in Wisconsin.

"Well, no one told me!" she shouted into the phone and then humphed, threw herself back onto her couch. "I'm going to need lessons, Dawson. All the lessons. And maybe quizzes on faces or something. I mean, I didn't even know my own dad watched football. It's like my brain has some kind of blockage whenever a sport is mentioned. Just goes in one ear and out the other."

One of the many reasons I was really beginning to like this girl. Outside her willingness to not only try everything I mentioned when it came to sex, she loved every damn thing. Might have had more excitement than I did.

"Do you not even watch the local news?"

"Ugh. No...it's depressing. Or lame. Or hell, maybe I do, and I just don't remember."

At least she could laugh at herself. Another thing I liked about Hailey.

Truth be told, when it came to her, there wasn't anything I didn't like yet.

"Next time we're together, I'll start going over the basics of hockey and football. Okay?"

"I think that'd be either great, or a complete waste of time for both of us."

Spending time with Hailey was never a waste of my time. She was consuming all of it. I'd found myself thinking about her all week. When I was eating. When I was working out. When I was placing my weekly grocery order. Wondering what she was doing. How her shop was going. If she was remembering to eat lunch, something she confessed she often forgot before she lost time. Yesterday, I'd been so damn consumed with it, I'd called Margo's, asked what Hailey's favorite lunch was and had it delivered to her.

Later, I received the cutest selfie with a thumbs up while she held her caprese flatbread as a thank you.

I'd been so focused on the picture, Cortland had shoved me in the shoulder as he passed by me, and I almost slammed my face against my locker. Considering Cortland had one hundred pounds on me and was almost butt-ass naked by the time I collected myself, I couldn't retaliate.

This fixation on Hailey wasn't supposed to happen, but I couldn't quite bring myself to stop it. I was going to take all the time she was willing to give me and when it ended, I'd figure out how to deal later.

"You ready for Sunday, then?"

A pool party at Cole's to officially welcome our new coach Logan Caldwell. Now that our conditioning was in full swing, he wanted a day to get to know us better on a personal level.

For the first time, I was bringing a date, and more shocking, I wasn't hating the fact I had to go. After all, it gave me an excuse to see Hailey in a swimsuit.

"I think so..."

"You'll be good. Eden and Maggie will make sure you have a good time."

"Will your manager be there?"

"Probably not, but he'll hear what goes on."

"Right. So I better be on my best behavior then, make sure everyone knows we like each other."

My heart thumped a strange beat in my chest. Was she planning on faking liking me? Yeah, that was the deal, but I was starting to think she actually did. Outside the bedroom, was all of it an act?

It hadn't been. No way. Not with the way she'd let me hold her after I threw all that bullshit about my dad to hers. Unless that was her general reaction.

Fuck. I shoved my hair back and fisted it at the nape of my neck. This fake shit was turning into a nightmare. And uncertainty wasn't something I usually dealt with.

My phone buzzed, and my dad's name blared on the screen. Shitty timing, like always.

"Hey, I gotta go. My dad's calling."

"You still haven't talked to him?" Her blue eyes widened with surprise.

After the baggage I threw at Ken's feet a couple weeks back, I couldn't bring myself to return my dad's call. Then I needed time, but for once in the last twenty years, it seemed my dad wasn't willing to give me the space anymore. He'd been calling every day.

Since I didn't need him showing up announced, like other family members tended to do, I needed to deal with it.

"Yeah. See you Sunday?"

She grinned, and for the first time, I was wondering if it was a fake smile. She hadn't sounded like she wanted to go, but I'd assumed it was nerves. Maybe I'd been wrong. "I'll be ready by one."

"Good. See you then, Hailey. Have a good night."

"You too." I ended our FaceTime call and brought the phone to my ear. "Hey, Dad."

"Are you planning on avoiding me forever?"

Awesome start to a conversation I didn't want to have. I didn't apologize. Probably another first, but since I realized my dad was the asshole to blame me for his wife's affair and I'd let him, for all these years, apologies no longer felt so necessary. "Figured I'd take a play out of your own playbook for once."

"What does that mean?"

There was no point in explaining. The day he kicked my mom out, Dad vanished in his own way. Worked longer hours when he should have been flying less. Suddenly taking international flights when he'd always promised he never would. They were longer, meant more time away. He lost his wife and quit giving a shit about his kids, making me not only believe he blamed me for the explosion of our happy family unit, but that he'd never really liked us all that much, either.

Odd that I was now having the same doubts about Hailey.

Perhaps I should see a shrink.

"Nothing, Dad. What can I do for you?"

"I was calling to discuss this new woman in your life."

He went silent. I wasn't telling him anything without him actually asking a question.

"And?"

"I'm not sure this is the right time for you to get involved with someone. Your season is starting soon."

It was never the right time for me to get involved with anyone. First it was high school, and I couldn't let a girl distract me from a scholarship. Then it was college, and I needed to focus on the pros. Then it was my rookie year, and I needed to earn my spot.

Now, I was almost thirty, staring down the end of my career, something that hardly ever lasted after a tight end was thirty-five. I had max five years left. Realistically, more like two. I made a shit ton of money which affected our team's salary and trading cap and while I was good for this season, I wouldn't be surprised if they started to ask me to reduce my salary next year to bring in new talent. I'd do it, to finish my career in Nashville, but that didn't mean the end wasn't in sight.

It was almost like my father enjoyed the thought of me alone and miserable my entire life—like I'd made him be.

"Not quite sure I need your opinion on women, Dad." My mother had destroyed him. He'd never dated as far as I knew. His opinion of women sullied for eternity.

He sighed like I was the one exhausting him instead of the other way around. "I'm worried."

"Don't be. Anything else you need?"

"You talk to her lately?"

"What do you care? I mean, honestly, Dad. You bitch at me if I talk to her and then you always want to know if I've heard from her. You haven't seen me in well over two years and Crystal in ten. How about we just stop acting like you give a shit about either of us, and you keep doing what you've done best since Mom fucked a neighbor and leave, yeah? It's not like we've had you in our life since that day anyway."

I hung up. Pissed. My hand burned, and I threw the phone into the couch and shoved to my feet.

I needed a drink. Just one. Two would make me slow tomorrow and hell if I wasn't well aware that the younger guys kept getting faster and stronger—or I kept getting slower.

Whichever.

Conversations with my dad never went well, and I'd practically dared him to show up. He'd do it, too. Just so he could see Hailey in person and find a way to criticize everything about her.

"Fuck that. He's not going to say a damn thing about it if he doesn't want my fist in his face."

Which would exactly ruin everything Marchand wanted from me but fuck him too.

Hailey would be worth protecting from my family, consequences be damned.

I grabbed a glass from the cupboard and pulled out my Effen Vodka from the freezer.

Just one drink.

My phone rang from my living room. I should have known he wouldn't let that go.

Fine.

Maybe two.

In addition to the two calls I didn't answer Saturday night, Dad called four more times over the next three days. Two in the middle of the night which told me he was probably in Japan or some shit and not paying attention to what I had going on in my life. I didn't return his calls, but I only had one glass of vodka that night, so I was counting that shitty end to a night a win.

I was outside, dressed in swim trunks and a pale-blue shirt, leaning against the frame to my front door when Hailey pulled up into the curved drive. Security phoned to let me know she was close, and for a moment, I'd considered that she really needed a pass to get in whenever she wanted, and then promptly changed my mind.

One more thing to get back from her when this blew up.

Which was not what I wanted to be thinking about as she parked her few-year-old Camry in my driveway. Like the first time she came over, I hurried to help her out of the car. This time, there wasn't hesitation like the night before Cole's fundraising gala, and I barely met her at her door before she swung it open.

"Hey." She smiled up at me, eyes hidden behind a large pair of tortoise-shell sunglass frames and a smile so blinding I should have worn my sunglasses before seeing her.

"You're early."

"Mad?"

"Not a chance in hell." I bent down, unclicked her belt and waited for her to turn off her car before grabbing her hand and getting her out of the car. "Means we have some time for fun before we have to get to Cole's. Better yet, let's have a whole day of fun and forget about Cole."

God, she made me stupid.

She was laughing as I yanked her to me, and her hand slapped to my chest right before my mouth closed on hers.

Jesus. The taste of her. Sweet and sexy and her lips were so damn soft. Her skin was silk, and whatever kind of summer dress she had on was way too much.

Hailey was still laughing as she pulled away from me, breathless, lip gloss smeared.

I wiped my thumb over my own lips to clear away the grease from it and then fixed hers. "Sorry."

"And that's exactly why we're not going to have any fun before Cole's. No way am I showing up to his place with messed up hair and ruined makeup."

"He won't notice."

"No." She shoved me playfully, and I stepped back. The space gave me time to breathe. To think straight. To check out her long, trim legs that I loved wrapped around my waist when I—

"Dawson." Her tone was scolding. Somehow it only made my blood burn hotter.

I couldn't tear my eyes off her legs. "What?"

"Stop staring at my ass and help me with my bag?"

She had a point. "It was your legs, not your ass, I was staring at."

As I reached around her to open her back door, she kissed my cheek. "Later."

Fine.

Later.

Cole's thing was supposed to last four hours.

We'd stay for one, be back here in two. Naked in two hours and five minutes.

I could wait.

"She fits right in."

"Looks like she belongs."

"This is temporary, remember?" I swallowed the nasty taste of my own words with a bottled water and tried to find a way out of this conversation with Davis and Mason.

"Doesn't need to be," Mason replied. "You can't take your eyes off her."

I couldn't take my eyes off her because her dress was shorter than I'd first thought. Tight at her chest, slim little straps I could tear with one quick tug, and every time the breeze blew, the skirt lifted to give me a peek at her creamy thighs.

Also because Hailey kept laughing. With Maggie Eden so massively pregnant, Hailey was trying to help her out with her little kids, which currently meant she held one of the youngest ones by the hand and was helping her grab a plate of snacks from the long buffet table on Cole's back patio.

"I will discuss my situation with Hailey when you find a woman who can stand you for more than one night, Yeets."

"Aw. That's not fair. I don't want any woman for more than a night." He scratched the scruff on his chin. "Maybe two if they're really bendy."

I rolled my eyes. Kids these days. So he wasn't a kid, he was actually Hailey's age, but when I was with her I didn't feel that small gap like I did with Mason. Maybe that was because he was still thinking with his smaller brain. Hailey had her head on right.

Today hadn't been horrible, even if we'd now been here for much longer than the hour I'd wanted. As soon as we were welcomed into Cole's house by Eden, she swept Hailey out to the back patio where the rest of the women had congregated. Kids chased each other, husbands brought their wives fresh drinks or snacks, maybe an errant child who'd escaped the backyard.

Jasper, Cole's son, was currently jumping his life away in one of the three inflatable bounce houses and the smaller ones were alternating between a small bounce house and a splash pad that included a sprinkler that somehow, forced them to squeal at the tops of their lungs like the water was acid every single time they darted through it.

Kids were madness.

I glanced back at Hailey who was crouched down in front of one, smiling as she wiped their cherry juice-stained cheeks off.

Kids were madness, but were they as horrible as I always thought they were?

Fuck. I took another swallow of water. What was going on with me?

"You talk to Caldwell yet?" Davis asked.

"Trying to avoid him." I shouldn't have. He was my coach. OTAs were coming soon, and it'd be best to be in a good position with him when they started. From what I'd heard, he seemed to understand our team was tight and didn't need any major overhauls. Perhaps I should have given him more credit for not changing up the assistant coach or coordinators. Bowles retired, but he retired on top.

We could stay there without a massive change in coaching staff. Either Caldwell saw that, which would earn my respect, or he was giving them a chance to screw up before canning them.

Either way, it still felt strange to take coaching direction from a man who would have been eight when our old coach started coaching thirty years ago.

"I like him," Mason chimed in. "Talked with him yesterday after practice, seems like a cool guy. Wants what's best for us, which is winning, and I don't fault him for that."

"We already win almost every single game."

"Yeah, he said that too. Said he wanted to fine-tune the lines to get better blocks for offense to keep us on top. But likes our plays. Knows the way we run them."

Which was exactly what I would have done. We'd lost a starting cornerback and the right tackle. One was traded, one retired. Their drafts and trades had so far filled in those gaps and the new guys to the team slid right in.

"I'll go find him."

Had to sooner or later.

Play the role. And maybe see exactly what Marchand had said to me, how much he was buying this shit with Hailey or how necessary he thought it really was.

CHAPTER 20
HAILEY

I WASN'T sure I'd ever spent this much time surrounded by so many children since I stopped volunteering in my church's preschool when I was in high school. Dawson wasn't joking when he said that Maggie's story was a doozy. She filled me in as soon as her oldest sister Ruth walked up, two younger kids with her and then I'd heard another was running around somewhere.

As soon as she told me a brief story, it'd all clicked. Her family had been related to a different one that was on a reality television show. I'd seen it before, but it started giving me the creepy-crawlies after a few episodes. But I did vaguely remember reading one day, probably on a magazine cover at the grocery store checkout, that a bunch of them had been arrested. It hadn't occurred to me her parents and older brothers were included in that until she got further into the story.

Martha, her youngest, had practically claimed me as soon as she met me. Everywhere I went, she was there, asking me for juice or a snack, and the little girl was so adorable with curls in her waist-length dark-brown hair I couldn't resist. She skipped when she walked, and those curls happily bounced right along with her.

Maggie had grown more than when I saw her two weeks ago. If she made it to her wedding in two weeks without bursting open at the seams, it'd be a miracle in itself.

"It's like the world's largest pumpkin in there." Eden rubbed her hands all over Maggie's belly, while the rest of us laughed with Maggie.

"Shut up. Short people problems for sure." She groaned and when her sister, Joy, spilled carrots all over the ground from holding her plate sideways, made an entirely different kind of groan. "I can't see my toes, or my ankles, much less pick this off the ground."

Eden crouched down and gathered them up. "It's fine. That's why we're outside anyway." She tossed the carrots into the trees. "Squirrels and deer will take care of them, see?"

"Thank you, Eden." Maggie glanced behind my shoulder. "And I think you're being summoned by a big grumpy looking guy."

"What?" There was only big grumpy guy here who knew me, except for me, he wasn't all that grumpy.

I'd seen it though. In the harsh stance of his shoulders and spine, the furl of his lips downward. As soon as we stepped outside and teammates started talking to Dawson, he'd closed himself off.

Stupid, considering others seemed to like him despite his reserved personality.

As our gazes met, he gestured with a dip of his head to the side for me to come to him. "I'm being beckoned."

"Might as well crook his finger and growl 'woman' like some caveman," Eden said.

I bumped my hip into hers. "I like those kinds of growls."

I stepped away from both of them with their laughter following me and a get it, girl, from one of them. My guess, it was Eden. She didn't seem to have much of a filter. Sort of reminded me of Sloane.

"You rang?" I drawled to Dawson when I reached his side.

"How's it going?"

"You pulled me away from your friends' wives to ask how I was doing?"

He scanned the backyard, filled with forty men, half as many wives or girlfriends and dates, and said nothing, but there was a look in his eye. A twitch in his cheek.

I splayed my hand on my chest and gave him a dramatic sigh. "Dawson Butler. Did you miss me?"

He rolled his eyes and took my hand in his. "I have to talk to our new coach. Wanted you with me. Need a fresh drink or anything?"

Ah. So there was a reason he needed me next to him.

He also didn't deny the missing me part. If I wasn't mistaken, Dawson was actually starting to like me.

Problem was, I didn't think he liked it all that much.

Logan Caldwell was a stud. Dawson had told me he wasn't sure of him, but I was starting to believe Dawson simply didn't trust many people. And he didn't like change. Considering I didn't know anything about football, I had no idea if Logan would be a good coach or not, but it didn't take me long at all to believe he was a sincere guy.

It was obvious as soon as he shook my hand, told me it was great to meet me, in a way that made me truly believe.

Maybe I was too naive.

Maybe Dawson was too cynical.

Regardless, Dawson kept me tucked to his side while phrases flew over my head.

"You're vital," Caldwell said. "Absolutely vital to the success of the team. And I plan on keeping you that way for many more years to come."

"Thanks," Dawson said, and maybe he was finally beginning to trust this guy. Although, I figured Dawson didn't trust anyone easily. Given what I now knew of his family, I couldn't blame him.

Logan glanced at me, then to Dawson and leaned in. "I'm also well aware of what happened this past winter. I've talked to Rick. Frankly, I agree with him on some things—"

Dawson's fingers dug into my lower back. "Like what, exactly?"

"Like the media. I'd like for you to give more interviews, spend more time with the press. First time or two they'll probably ask about last year, but I'll end that shit immediately. Guys look to you as a leader on the team. Everyone I talk to. You and Cole are the two they take their direction, drive, and motivation from. I'm standing here, well aware you don't really like me all that much yet, but I'm not saying all this to you just to blow smoke up your ass. I'm not that kind of guy. I'm saying every time I ask the men who's a leader, it's you and Cole. Especially on offense. I'd like my leaders to be talking 'bout the game and team. As far as the other shit Rick told you to do, that's whatever. You keep being the player you are, you help me out with the media, and everything else is whatever you want to do with it. I'll have your back come contract renegotiation time."

Those fingers at my back loosened, and wow. That sounded great. Except, if Logan was telling Dawson this could end, that having a girlfriend wasn't necessary, where did that leave me?

"I'll think about it," Dawson said.

That was it.

"Good. Now, talking to me wasn't so painful, was it?"

I rolled my lips together to hold in a laugh. I had a feeling Logan was a good coach, a good man, because he could read people like an open book, even one as closed up and locked down as Dawson.

Dawson's lips kicked up at one corner. "Not the most painful thing I've ever experienced, no."

"Good. That's good." Logan smiled and wiped his hand over his mouth like he was trying to hide the grin, but instead, I caught sight of a tan line. A tan line on his fourth ring finger.

"Are you married?" I asked, more like blurted. Both men looked at me. "Sorry, that was rude, but I didn't see a wife around, and your finger..."

Might have been a red flag warning for me, all things considered.

"Ah." He glanced at his left hand and frowned at the tan line. That frown didn't change when he met my eyes again. "Jackie. My ex, or soon-to-be, wife. She liked our life in San Diego, liked the family we had out there. Chose to stay there and not make the move with me."

"Oh, I'm so sorry."

"Yeah, well, I can't say she liked me all that much, at least not the last couple of years. So it wasn't a shock."

Didn't make it less painful, especially based on the look in his eyes.

"I shouldn't have been so rude in asking."

"You're not the first, won't be the last, especially until this line fades a bit more but that'll probably have to wait until winter, so...I'll get used to it."

Right. Shoot.

Dawson ran his hand up and down my back but stayed focused on Logan. "We good?"

"You tell me."

It took a beat. Maybe two. "I think we'll be all right." He held out a fist, Logan bumped it, and then slapped his shoulder. "Enjoy the party, Dawson. Great to meet you both."

"Darn," I whispered once he walked away. "I feel like I just shoved my foot straight into my mouth."

"Don't worry about it. I've heard he and Jackie didn't have a real close marriage, at least from the outside looking in, so you're all good."

"Not sure a marriage ending is ever a good thing. At least, not for most." There were always exceptions.

And considering I was supposed to be married...well, I guess I was the exception. If a man was cheating on me for years, that wasn't any kind of guy I wanted to marry anyway.

"Can we get the hell out of here yet?"

We were going on two hours, longer than Dawson had teased me about staying on the way up here.

"I suppose you've paid your dues." I wasn't really in the mood to party anymore. "What else do you have in mind?"

"Tossing you in my pool right after I rip that dress off so I can see what surprise you have on for me under it."

Oh. Well then.

"Dawson!" I shrieked as I flew through the air and then gasped as I swallowed a mouthful of water. I jumped out of the pool with a splash and thrust my hair back.

Dawson was nowhere to be seen, and I spun in a circle to find nothing. No hint of him.

Until something warm grasped my ankle and I was tugged beneath the water again.

I kicked out, and those hands came to my waist. The dress he hadn't bothered stripping me out of before he tossed me into the water wrapped around my legs.

This was madness! I went to shove him, but his grip grew tighter. He pushed off the pool floor, and I was thrust out of the water. My legs wrapped around his waist and the hard length of him pressed right to where I'd been wanting him since that first time I kissed him.

He leaned back, shook his wet hair out of his face.

I shoved mine out of my eyes.

"You're insane," I breathed out.

"Not the first time I've been told that." He pressed his cool, wet lips to mine, and my body instantly boiled in his arms. He used his legs to keep us afloat, moving us through the water. My eyes closed, and a hum escaped my throat as he slid his tongue into my mouth. Wet, cool hands pressed between my shoulder blades and then the cool cement of the pool was at my back. His hand moved from my back down, cupping my ass before he shoved the dress clinging to my thighs out of the way and slipped his fingers beneath the thin string of my thong.

"Fuck, Hailey. I can't keep my hands off you."

"No one's asking you to."

I barely managed to rasp out the words before he stole my breath with a kiss and his fingers slipped inside. I'd always thought water was supposed to dry a girl out, but I'd been primed for Dawson since I first saw him.

And I intended to enjoy every moment I spent with Dawson because if what Logan said earlier was true, this fake thing between us wasn't necessary anymore.

Which meant my time with Dawson was, most likely, quickly coming to an end.

And I wasn't walking away until he gave me my marching orders, I just hoped I wasn't still a virgin when that time came.

CHAPTER 21
DAWSON

IT WAS after I made her scream in the pool then brought her to my shower. After she dropped to her knees and sucked me off like she couldn't *not* do it. And it was after we'd dried off and I threw her back on my bed and teased her with my fingers. My mouth. She came that time while I slid my dick over her soaking wet slit, her ankles hooked at my lower back, begging for more.

I couldn't do it.

Despite how much I wanted her, I still couldn't bring myself to give her what she'd originally asked of me, knowing I'd have to say goodbye to her eventually.

She deserved more, and I wasn't that guy.

But that didn't mean I was ready to let her go.

"Do you want to stay? I can order some dinner?"

Damn. What was going on with me? I hadn't been inside her yet, but she had me more worked up than any woman I'd ever been with. Maybe it was because the woman I was with didn't spend so much time talking, trying to understand me.

No, that wasn't giving Hailey nearly enough credit. She was extraordinary, in all the ways.

She was as shaken as I was, and her hands trembled as she ran them through her still wet hair. "I should go home, actually. I have some work to get caught up on."

I could go with her. Sit in her office. Probably wouldn't be bored at all while she worked and ordered us some dinner. Go back to her place...

"Right."

We didn't have to do this anymore. Caldwell all but said it, in front of her. And maybe she was relieved, but I'd wanted to punch him. Then thank him. We could end this today, essentially, according to him. Before it went further.

I wasn't ready.

A couple more weeks.

It wouldn't kill me to have a date to Maggie and Davis's wedding.

She was dressed, her damp hair thrown and twisted up into some kind of clip.

There was no reason to keep her there anymore. Not if she wanted to go.

"I'll call you later?" It shouldn't have been a question. I'd called her almost every night.

I'd called her. Not Hailey. I was the one reaching out.

Damn it. Was I the one getting caught up in this?

"Okay," she mumbled and dug through her purse until she found her phone. It hit me that it was ringing, and she stared at the phone. "It's my mom."

"Answer it."

"I can wait."

The phone rang again. I was torturing myself, but I wanted to know why her mom was calling. Her dad had said something about dinner with the family. A week had come and gone without an invitation, but this might get me more time.

No, I couldn't do that to her. Not to her family.

"Hey, Mom," Hailey all but whispered, like she was trying to hide from me when I'd just had my hands and mouth all over her slick, sexy curves, and she wasn't standing in my bedroom feet from me. "Oh. Yeah, I'd forgotten about that."

She bit her lip, turned to me, and her face paled. That beautiful blush I put there seeped away as she continued staring at me.

"Maybe I can skip this one. Meredith or Sloane, or heck, even you can do it."

She sighed. Unhappy.

"Yeah. I'm sure he'd be happy to."

She glanced at me as she said it, before looking down to her toes on my carpet.

"Sure, bye, Mom. Love you too."

Love. It rolled off her tongue so easily. So sweetly and purely. No one had ever said those words to me like that and an ache pinched the left side of my chest.

Hailey dropped her phone to her side. It was several beats of that ache in my chest before she lifted her chin. "I forgot, but there's something...city recognition night for small businesses, mostly women-owned small businesses."

"Okay..."

"It's a big deal. They have it every year in May, around Mother's Day weekend. I totally forgot about it, but Darrick and I obviously RSVP'd months ago."

Hearing that dumb fuck's name made my blood boil. "You're not going with him."

She scoffed, but a flash of pain flared across her face. "Of course not. But he'll be there."

"When are we going?"

"What?"

"When is it? And what's the dress?"

"I told my mom I can skip it. It's just...he'll probably be there with Bianca, and I don't know if I'm ready..."

Fuck that. I said those exact words, and she gaped at me. "You're not skipping out on something like this because of that shithead. If it's to celebrate women-owned businesses and you own one, then you're going, Hailey. We're going."

So much for slowing this down. Not hurting her. Hell if I was going to let her go to this alone, and she definitely wasn't skipping out on something for her because of some guy.

"You don't have to do this, Dawson."

"I know." I crossed my arms over my chest, dared her with a look to argue with me. "When is it?"

"Friday." She mumbled the words, defeat stamped all over her.

"All right. Friday night. I'll be at your house at..."

"Seven?"

"Six thirty. I'll be there." Get a drink in her. Get her to relax.

Then I'll happily shove her in Darrick and Bianca's fucking faces all night. Show him how much happier she is away from him.

"You don't have to do this," she said again, but her spine was straightening. Her color returning.

"I know."

A hint of a smile appeared. "All right then. Friday."

I was in front of her before she could blink. Bending down as she gaped at me with surprise.

"Dawson..."

I stole the rest of her words with a kiss, keeping it slow and light. I didn't slam my mouth to hers like I wanted, and I kept my tongue firmly inside my mouth. If I unleashed it, I'd take her again.

Not sure that was safe for either of us anymore. But I could give her Friday.

"See you soon, Hails," I murmured against her lips. "Drive safe."

She left shortly after, giving me a small wave and smile as she pulled her Camry out of my driveway.

I stood in my doorframe long after her car was gone.

We could take a step back, but I could support her on Friday. Be there for her in a way that wasn't what we agreed, but she needed. And then we could end things.

Screw the wedding.

Management wouldn't know if I brought a date or not, and Caldwell wouldn't care.

Yeah. That's what we'd do. We could walk away Friday, even if I hadn't done the one thing she truly wanted.

I wouldn't be that guy that fucked her and dumped her.

She was too good to do that to her.

She was too good for me.

CHAPTER 22
HAILEY

I SHOULD HAVE BACKED OUT. I should have called my mom and told her there was no way I was going to this event. She could accept the award for me. She could say a speech, thank everyone who nominated me as one of the best women-owned businesses on Main Street and she could sip my champagne. Hell, I could have sent Misty or Sloane or Meredith.

I definitely should have called Dawson and told him he didn't need to do this with me. That I didn't want him to go through this with me. He was going to meet my mom. See my dad again. Hell, Dawson didn't even know I was getting an award tonight, but I already knew as soon as he heard, he'd be on his feet, clapping louder than everyone else.

Selling this charade. Making my parents fall in love with him.

Making me fall harder for him.

It was an undeniable fact even if I'd been kicking my own butt for the past week. I was doing the one thing I couldn't do. And the irony of it all hurt more than the reality.

I was falling for another man who wouldn't have sex with me. Wouldn't sleep with me. Wouldn't stay with me.

I really needed better taste in men.

"You look mad on a night when you should have your revenge face

It wasn't his Tahoe. Not any car I'd seen before.

"This is your night. Figured we should arrive in style."

He beeped the locks on his gleaming, shining black two-door coupe with a black racing stripe down the front. It was so low to the ground I worried once I fell into it, I'd never get back out.

"You didn't need to do this."

"I know. Damn glad I did though seeing as how it matches your dress and those fucking shoes."

It almost sounded like a complaint.

"What's wrong with my shoes?"

I twisted one of my feet and glanced down. They were black. Glossy. A mid three-inch heel. It was the straps I loved most about them. They crisscrossed over the top of my feet, wrapped around the ankle, and at the back, they had a red butterfly outlined in black. The butterfly was a surprise when I saw them at Nordstrom's, and I'd had to have them. I bought the shoes before I bought the dress but as soon as I saw that butterfly they had to be mine.

"Nothing's wrong with 'em," Dawson muttered. "Just every man who sees you tonight is gonna be thinking about fucking you wearing only those damn things, having those long legs wrapped around their backs and your heels digging into their ass is all."

I almost fell right off the soles of my feet.

Dawson walked to my door, opened it, and gave me a look that said he was two point three seconds from doing the same thing. A flutter rose in my chest.

Maybe I'd been wrong about tonight.

Problem was, he still wore that same conflicted face which told me he might want to do all those things, but he sure as hell wasn't going to.

"Right. Thanks for that," I muttered and collapsed into my seat. The door slammed shut, rocking the small car, and I closed my eyes as my head rested against the back of the chair.

This was going to be one long, exhausting night.

The Longview Country Club, where the event was held, was the oldest and most elite country club in the area. The only one with thirty-six holes, it cost a fortune only Dawson and those who made millions like him could afford. The only time I came to this country club was on nights like this, mostly because most citywide galas and fundraisers were held here. A gorgeous turn-of-nineteenth-century mansion held the dining room and events center, and the streets were lined with fairways and greens on both sides, along with a smattering of trees.

After Dawson talked about the effect my shoes would have on men and then slumped into the car like it'd personally offended him, he went silent. Twenty minutes of driving with only Siri giving sporadic directions and the muted rock station radio and I wasn't only a bundle of nerves for the night to come, I was seriously regretting my date choice, along with Meredith's ridiculous bet and plan.

Not only was I going to end up a virgin again, but another man was also going to break my heart.

I couldn't even bring myself to protect it. It'd already happened. Dawson had stolen pieces of me before I knew he owned them and there was no way I was asking for them back.

That'd give too much away. The best I could hope for was making it out of this night with my dignity intact.

Stupid. I was a stupid, stupid little girl.

"Anything special going on at this thing other than celebrating women's businesses?"

To me, it was enough since women only owned thirty percent of the businesses in town. That was a higher number compared to other cities and towns of the same size.

"There'll be a reception hour, a speaker promoting the importance of economic diversity and ways to help a town thrive amid change in both economy and culture. Then there'll be some awards. Celebrations. Dancing."

"Awards?" He turned to me, just a flash of his head turning in my direction before he glanced back at the clubhouse we were growing closer to. "You getting any?"

on," Meredith told me from my iPad screen. She called to make sure I was getting dressed and wasn't halfway to Destin or something.

Her hair was done. Makeup beautiful as she stood in her and Tuevo's kitchen sipping a glass of red wine.

A drink. That was what I needed. I grabbed my iPad and headed to my kitchen.

"I don't need revenge." Until my mom called on Sunday, I hadn't thought of Darrick much at all. Certainly hadn't cried over him. Definitely hadn't gone to his or Bianca's Instagram pages. It'd been weeks since I caught myself stalking them on social media.

At least Dawson had healed that for me.

"You don't think so now, but it'll feel good when it happens, I can guarantee that."

I rolled my eyes and grabbed a bottle of wine from the fridge. Pulled out the cork and filled my glass. One large one. That'd settle my racing nerves and the hornets swarming in my gut.

"This is stupid. I'm getting an award from an event his company hosts. It's almost nepotism or something."

Darrick owned, or well, was inheriting but currently worked at a commercial real estate firm in Friendswood.

"His parents will be there. He'll be there. And you look hot enough to remind him of everything he's lost."

"Thanks." It wasn't exactly a compliment. He'd moved on to Bianca. Thinner, shorter, bustier. She looked like every Victoria's Secret catalog cover model.

"And he's totally going to shit himself when you walk in with Dawson."

"Nice visual."

She laughed, and Tuevo came up behind her on the screen, kissed the side of her neck and rested his chin on the top of her head, smiling at me.

"Hey, Tuevo."

"Hey, Hailey. She is right, you know. Remember how that dipshit acted around me?"

"Yeah." I sipped my wine and flinched, not from the crisp, fruity taste of it, but the reminder. When Meredith and Tuevo started dating, a random run-in at a bar in Nashville, Darrick all of a sudden decided he was the largest Avengers fan ever even though I knew he'd never watched a game. But suddenly, he and Tuevo were besties. Darrick was always hounding him, asking him for tickets.

That was probably a large enough red flag I'd missed.

"You are gorgeous. Dawson is a bigger star than even me. Darrick will not like it, and I cannot wait to see how he reacts."

Sometimes, Tuevo was a bigger gossip and girl than Meredith. He lived for our stories.

"You'll be there before us, right? Promise?"

I didn't want to show up without friends already there for support. Misty and Sloane promised they'd be there. My parents. We all had a table at the front of the room, right off the stairs to make the trip up to the stage quick and easy for me.

"We're leaving as soon as I finish this." She lifted her glass.

My doorbell rang, and I jumped. It was early. Not quite six thirty. "That's Dawson. We'll see you soon."

"Head high, Hailey. Even if this does not work out with Dawson, you deserve much better than any man who treats you like Darrick."

"Thanks, Tuevo." I blew Meredith a kiss, ended the call, and hurried to the door.

Dawson's jaw dropped, and those dark eyes of his widened to large saucers. "You look...holy shit...Hailey. I wasn't sure a dress could ever look better on you than the one you wore for my thing, but hot damn. That dress looks killer on you."

My dress wasn't nearly as fancy or rich or luxurious as last week's, but I'd bought it for tonight. Two thick black shoulder straps crossed over my chest, making my breasts look plump and full and exposed some cleavage. The bodice was tight, ruched in a way that made me look ten pounds slimmer. The skirt part flared out at my hips with an A-shape, tulle beneath to keep it the black taffeta material fluffy and flowy. I'd spun in it at the store when I bought it months ago, thinking

I'd be wearing it as a married woman, and had danced a little jig in the dressing room.

Putting it on tonight had brought those memories back to the forefront of my mind, part of why I wasn't in the best mood.

Dawson's compliment wiped all of that away.

I made the dress look good. It was such a subtle compliment, but I felt my shoulders roll back at the praise, standing tall. He didn't just say I looked good, like I'd put enough covering on to be pretty, but that I made the dress stand out.

He made his tuxedo look like it was sewn directly on his body for as tight as it was.

His nose ring glistened in the light. And all of his tattoos were hidden.

His lips were full. Bottom lip wet like he'd been running his tongue over it, and I still hadn't invited him inside.

"Come in, come in. Sorry. And you look...well, you always look good."

An admission. One that made his lips press together before lifting at a corner. "You ready for tonight?"

"Just had a pep talk from Tuevo and Meredith. It's all good."

We walked through my living room and I beelined it straight toward my wine. "Do you need or want anything to drink?"

"I'm good." He rocked back on his heels, hands in the pockets of his tuxedo pants. "What'd Tuevo say?"

"Um. Called Darrick a dipshit and said I deserve better than that."

"He's right."

It shouldn't have felt so good. Still, the warmth of his tone made my toes curl into my heel. "Thanks. He'll be there tonight. They both will."

"Good. Don't know him well, but it'll be good to see him again."

It was strange. Too strange how closely we were connected.

A silence fell, heavy. Stretched and thickened the space between us and Dawson's chest with heavy, slow breaths that made my own pulse kick up.

I hid behind my kitchen island, sipped my wine, and Dawson

seemed at a loss for words as I was. Last Sunday had been weird. A great day and then...I still wasn't sure what happened, but it happened in the shower, when he'd cupped my cheek, two of his fingers still inside me. I was pulsing around him, and his eyes hadn't just gone soft, they'd melted when he met my gaze. He'd brushed his nose along the edge of mine, and then he'd held me to him. Slipped his fingers out of me and pressed my chest to his and sighed so deeply in my ear, I was still hearing that contented sound a week later.

He'd shut it off so quick I wasn't sure I'd imagined it, wasn't sure he'd done it at all until that contented look was replaced with a coldness.

He'd started to feel something and shut down before the water in the shower was turned off and by the time we were both dried off and dressed, he was just a man. Staring at me. Conflicted.

It was the conflicted look that had hurt the most.

And it wasn't altogether that different from the look he had on his face now.

He was going to end this soon, right after I'd realized I was falling for him, and he was going to walk away, leaving me a virgin.

Tonight was going to suck.

I dumped my wine in the sink and grabbed my clutch, double-checking to make sure my lip gloss and phone were inside. "We should go."

Might as well get it over with.

Receive an award.

Be celebrated.

See my ex.

Get dumped.

What a fun night this was going to be.

"What is this?"

It wasn't his Tahoe. Not any car I'd seen before.

"This is your night. Figured we should arrive in style."

He beeped the locks on his gleaming, shining black two-door coupe with a black racing stripe down the front. It was so low to the ground I worried once I fell into it, I'd never get back out.

"You didn't need to do this."

"I know. Damn glad I did though seeing as how it matches your dress and those fucking shoes."

It almost sounded like a complaint.

"What's wrong with my shoes?"

I twisted one of my feet and glanced down. They were black. Glossy. A mid three-inch heel. It was the straps I loved most about them. They crisscrossed over the top of my feet, wrapped around the ankle, and at the back, they had a red butterfly outlined in black. The butterfly was a surprise when I saw them at Nordstrom's, and I'd had to have them. I bought the shoes before I bought the dress but as soon as I saw that butterfly they had to be mine.

"Nothing's wrong with 'em," Dawson muttered. "Just every man who sees you tonight is gonna be thinking about fucking you wearing only those damn things, having those long legs wrapped around their backs and your heels digging into their ass is all."

I almost fell right off the soles of my feet.

Dawson walked to my door, opened it, and gave me a look that said he was two point three seconds from doing the same thing. A flutter rose in my chest.

Maybe I'd been wrong about tonight.

Problem was, he still wore that same conflicted face which told me he might want to do all those things, but he sure as hell wasn't going to.

"Right. Thanks for that," I muttered and collapsed into my seat. The door slammed shut, rocking the small car, and I closed my eyes as my head rested against the back of the chair.

This was going to be one long, exhausting night.

The Longview Country Club, where the event was held, was the oldest and most elite country club in the area. The only one with thirty-six holes, it cost a fortune only Dawson and those who made millions like him could afford. The only time I came to this country club was on nights like this, mostly because most citywide galas and fundraisers were held here. A gorgeous turn-of-nineteenth-century mansion held the dining room and events center, and the streets were lined with fairways and greens on both sides, along with a smattering of trees.

After Dawson talked about the effect my shoes would have on men and then slumped into the car like it'd personally offended him, he went silent. Twenty minutes of driving with only Siri giving sporadic directions and the muted rock station radio and I wasn't only a bundle of nerves for the night to come, I was seriously regretting my date choice, along with Meredith's ridiculous bet and plan.

Not only was I going to end up a virgin again, but another man was also going to break my heart.

I couldn't even bring myself to protect it. It'd already happened. Dawson had stolen pieces of me before I knew he owned them and there was no way I was asking for them back.

That'd give too much away. The best I could hope for was making it out of this night with my dignity intact.

Stupid. I was a stupid, stupid little girl.

"Anything special going on at this thing other than celebrating women's businesses?"

To me, it was enough since women only owned thirty percent of the businesses in town. That was a higher number compared to other cities and towns of the same size.

"There'll be a reception hour, a speaker promoting the importance of economic diversity and ways to help a town thrive amid change in both economy and culture. Then there'll be some awards. Celebrations. Dancing."

"Awards?" He turned to me, just a flash of his head turning in my direction before he glanced back at the clubhouse we were growing closer to. "You getting any?"

I nodded, paying more attention to the valet parking signs than the man next to me. Any other day, his presence would consume the small space of this vehicle. His scent would overwhelm me.

I was blocking it all out.

"Best retailer on Main."

"No shit? That's awesome, Hailey."

I tried to mumble a thanks, but it wouldn't come out. All too soon his car was stopped beneath the covered drive, two men dressed in all black were headed in our direction to get the keys, and my escape was near.

"What are you worried about?" Dawson asked.

Now? Now he wanted to talk? "Nothing, Dawson."

He hit the lock button on the doors and reached out, grabbed my forearm. His touch was firm, but not harsh. Commanding but not overly domineering. I melted beneath it, wanted to lean into it and let him erase every worry racing through me.

"You been acting weird since I showed up. Wanna tell me why?"

He could tell me why he cared so much, but I doubted I'd get that out of him.

"I'm not. I just want to get through this night, all right?"

He sighed.

I held my breath.

The doors unlocked.

"You're lying, and we both know you are, but I'll let you only because I know it's not mine to have, but that doesn't mean I like it."

He hoisted himself out of the car, all bulk and muscle and long limbs and it wasn't until he practically shoved the valet worker out of the way he opened my door.

His touch this time was gentle, dark eyes soft warm pools as he gazed down at me and held out his hand. Lips kicked at the corner, and I would have thought this look was for show, except there was no one around to see who'd matter to him.

"Let's go get you that award, Hails."

Hails. My brothers called me that. Sometimes my friends when I was having a really bad day and needed a hug and a few glasses of wine.

Hails was the last thing I needed now.

CHAPTER 23
DAWSON

HAILEY DIDN'T PULL BACK from me. She read my mood from the moment I stepped into her house, hell, she read my mood before she left my house the last time and responded accordingly.

It fucking killed. I was already hurting her, and it was the last thing I wanted to do.

I was pretty damn sure if I called up anyone who knew me longer than six months, they'd be surprised as hell that somehow, I'd gone and stepped in some feelings that were now stuck to the bottom of my soles. No matter how much time I spent over the last week trying to shake them off, scrub them, hell, bleach them, they weren't going away.

If anything, they grew worse as soon as I saw her. Her dress was more modest than the event for Cole's fundraiser. It was classier. More professional. It made me want to skip her around the dance floor to watch her skirt fly up. It made me want to cover her with my suit coat so no one could get a glimpse of her...least of all, Darrick.

Her hand was still in mine, but it was tense. Warmer than usual, and while she held me back, curling fingers toward the back of my hand, as soon as we stepped into the country club's event space, that grip turned to a vise grip.

"I cannot believe them," she hissed.

"What?" Her eyes had narrowed into slits, and she was sucking in a breath that seemed to go on forever.

"My family," she growled.

The room was packed. Hundreds of people were already there, and more were coming based on the line of cars that had been behind us. How in the hell could she spot her family in this crowd was anyone's guess.

"Ah. My little sister!"

Oh. That was how. The guy who called for her rushed to us, wearing a dark, eggplant-colored suit with a gray shirt. His hair was blond and thick like Hailey's and his eyes were the exact same.

"Charlie." She grinned. "What in the hell are you doing here?"

His arms curled around her bare shoulders, and he yanked her into a hug. Her hand was still in mine, and I tried to let go, but she gripped me tighter.

Fine. She wanted to hold on to me, I'd hold her right back.

"Couldn't miss out on this. It's not every day you win an award, proving once again how awesome you are, baby sis."

"Please stop calling me a baby," she mumbled, but her cheek was pressed to his shoulder and a soft smile had taken over her face. "Miss you, Charlie."

"Miss you, favorite sibling of mine."

He let her go, and his smile flatlined when he took me in. Charlie was probably equal to Hailey's height without her heels, slimmer than her, too. Average size for a man, but next to me, I not only towered over him, I out-bulked him by far.

He took in my nose ring. Stalled on my hair I had styled at my shoulders and the fresh shave on my beard and sideburns.

"You must be Butler."

There was no hug for me. No grand smile. Hell, he held out his hand like it was against his better judgment.

"Dawson." I shook his hand firmly, kindly, and released. "Nice to meet you, Charlie."

"Is it?" His eyes narrowed.

Hailey's hand came up, smacked him in the chest with the back of her hand. "Be nice."

"Hmmm," was all he said. "Tate and Holly are here."

"Great." She did not sound at all like it was great. "What did I just say?"

"I'm nice to everyone if they deserve it." Which meant I didn't. Or hadn't earned it, yet.

If this was my welcome from the nice one, I was pretty certain I didn't want to meet the others.

"Come on," Hailey grunted and tugged my hand that she still had a firm grip on. "Might as well get this over with."

"Need a drink?" Charlie asked her.

"Probably six of them," she replied.

He threw his head back and laughed. She tugged me toward the front of the room where I could now see her father watching us from the far end. There were groups of people we had to greet on the way to get to him, many Hailey stopped and did a quick cheek kiss and hello and a "we'll catch up soon, let me go say hi to Mom" before moving on without missing a step.

Everyone watched her. Everyone smiled at her. Men and women both grinned when she came near them and frowned when she walked away quickly.

Hailey had been downplaying herself. Her store. The fact she knew everyone.

These people might know her because of her parents and their long-standing life in Friendswood, but she'd enamored them all.

A witch. She had to be. She had a town in love with her and a man who had no heart finally feeling his beating while being dragged behind her.

We finally made it through the melee, and she stopped in front of her dad. A woman, much shorter than Hailey, with her darkt-brown hair twisted into curls and pulled back from her face, stood next to Ken.

"Mom, this is Dawson."

"Dawson." She flashed me a warm smile and gave me a quick hug. I froze beneath it while she continued, "It's nice to finally meet you."

"Mrs. Parillo."

"Oh please, call me Sue. Mrs. Parillo sounds so stuffy."

"All right. Nice to meet you, Sue. You must be proud of Hailey tonight."

That warm smile grew. "Well, a mother is always proud of all her children, but yes, tonight is definitely Hailey's night. And you look absolutely lovely, dear."

"Thanks, Mom." With her hand still in mine, she gave her mom a one-armed hug and stepped back. "Any reason why the whole family is here?"

"Why wouldn't we show up to see our sister win something?" The man who spoke stepped out from behind Sue. His hair gelled back and to the side, he had his mother's coloring and a California tan. "Tate Parillo. Nice to meet you."

He shoved his hand out before I could say my name, a smile that was anything but similar to his mother's warm one plastered on his face. I shook his hand and when he squeezed tighter, matched his strength before letting go. Why men tried to out-muscle each other with handshakes, I'd never figure out. Did the man want to take me outside and throw a punch?

I'd let him. I'd deserve it soon enough.

"Tate," Hailey growled low in her throat.

"It's all right, Hailey." I was speaking to her, but I didn't take my eyes off her brother and his fake smile and extra-whitened teeth.

"If my family is going to be here for my night, then they should at least be kind to my date." She spoke it to me, but like me, she was glaring at her brother.

Making her point clear, she slipped her hand out of mine and slid it to my lower back. I did the same with my arm and tugged her tight to my side.

"We were worried," Tate said. "You can't blame us."

She scoffed. Behind Tate, her dad Ken wore the same chagrined expression he'd worn the day I put him in place and spewed my baggage all over his tennis shoes in Hailey's living room.

"I think I've already had this conversation with you on the phone and you didn't need to fly here just to put me in a crappy mood in person."

"Hailey."

That came from the brunette in the back with highlighted hair and a sharp jawline. While Tate took after their mom, Hailey and Charlie after their dad, and Holly, the older sister was a perfect blend of both. Hailey's blue eyes. Her mom's chocolatey hair, although by the looks of it, Holly's was professionally colored by an expert hand.

"Hey, sis," Hailey said, and she didn't move out of my arm or my hold while Holly came up and kissed her cheeks. Smiling, she flashed both of us a wink. "If it makes you feel better, I'm only here for the free food and drinks."

I chuckled, unable to hold it back and Holly grinned at me. "And personally, I'm not worried about my sister at all. We might be night and day with our life goals, but she has a good head on her shoulders, something all the men in our family should remember, and frankly, anyone is better than dickless Darrick."

"Holly," Hailey scolded her, but she was hiding her own laugh.

"You're my sister," Holly stated. "I know how smart you are."

"Thank you." Hailey leaned forward and squeezed her sister close to her with one arm, still not slipping her arm from me.

I wasn't about to let her go. Tate or Charlie would haul her off and give her a numbered list on reasons why I sucked. Probably in order of least important to most, to really seal the deal.

"Now that that's settled, let me go get all of us one of those free drinks. What would you like?"

"White wine," Hailey said.

"I'm good," I told her. With this family's eagle eyes on me, I wasn't drinking. Plus I was driving.

Further, why did I care? I'd prove them all right soon enough.

Charlie appeared, two fresh glasses of alcohol in his hand and scanned his entire family. "Did I miss the drama already?"

Tate rolled his eyes. "You are the drama."

Charlie pouted. Ken chuckled. Sue gave both of her boys a loving little shove and Hailey gave me a look that made a chill creep up the back of my neck.

She leaned toward me and whispered, "If I would have known they were here, I wouldn't have asked you to come. Sorry you have to deal with them."

Right. Why bother introducing me to the family or wanting me around them when we both knew I was leaving anyway.

God, this whole having feelings thing really sucked.

It was after the awkward introductions. After Hailey had a glass of wine and after her brothers lost their overprotective role and asked me about our upcoming season. Tate asked that one. Charlie asked me about my tattoos, and we spent several minutes going over some of the ones on my arm. His. Some of the ones he did himself when he was still learning, others he'd had done. Meredith and Hailey's friends swooped in, shoving most of us guys to the background while they oohed and aahed over all the women's dresses. Hailey stayed as close as she could, selling it to her family that we were good, we were comfortable with each other, but we were still new and weren't all over each other.

It sucked. Every time she shot me a smile, I wanted to kiss her. Every time she laughed, eyes shining on me, I wanted to cup the back of her neck and bring her as close to me as we could be in public. Every time her hand grazed mine, I wanted to pull her in tight against me.

"She's a good girl," Charlie said, catching me watching her laugh at whatever Meredith said. "We come on strong, I know, and I also know she hates being called our baby sister, but she is. Always will be, you know."

Yeah. I knew. "I have a sister," I told him.

"Dad mentioned her. Sounds like it's not the same thing, though."

I couldn't hide my sneer. "And how much did he tell you?"

"When it comes to the Parillos, we don't have secrets. At least not for long, so prepare."

"More worried about if I should be prepared for one of you to sell that shit."

"Damn." Charlie rocked back on his heels and frowned. "That sucks you think we'd do that. We wouldn't. Even if we didn't like you."

"You telling me this interrogation is because you like me?"

"No. I'm saying Hailey's had a shitty year and none of us saw it coming even if Tate and I never liked Darrick to begin with. But we were the ones who held her through that when she crumpled in her bridal suite after she realized he and Bianca were gone. We were the ones she leaned on. She loves Holly, but if she needs to talk, it's me she calls, then Tate. And we take our big brother roles seriously. I won't apologize for that."

He sipped his drink that looked like cranberry vodka.

If I wasn't planning on doing the exact thing Charlie was afraid of, I might like the man. Every woman deserved to have men like that in her life.

"We're new," I reminded him. "Can't tell you I won't hurt her, and I won't make promises I can't keep."

"Good. Then you're better than Darrick already. And speak of the devil, I might be gay, might like art more than sports, but I do work out. Want to help me kick his ass?" His gaze slid to the right, and he aimed his drink in the direction of a guy who looked like a living Ken doll.

The perfect match to Hailey.

He was polished. More fake than the implants and chin lifts Tate probably put into his patients.

"Hate that guy," Charlie said next to me. "And Bianca? She's always been a jealous bitch, always thought she hated Hailey and was just close to her because people liked her."

That tracked. The whole town seemed to love Hailey, and she didn't realize how deep that went.

"That's Darrick?" I asked. His name came out on a low growl.

"Yeah and based on the way your hand turned into a fist, I need to ask you, for Hailey's sake, not to punch his lights out, at least not publicly. Hailey wouldn't like it."

"Right." I flexed my hand and stretched out my fingers. As I was looking, trying not to stare, a woman who could have been one of Tate's most frequent flier patients pressed her chest to Darrick's arm, suctioned herself to him like an octopus. "That Bianca?"

"The one and only. I'm guessing she's fake. Could be cloned. Would explain a lot actually."

I laughed and grabbed a water bottle someone had brought for me from the table. "You're not so bad, Charlie."

"I'm awesome. You should also know he might not be looking now, but he has been, and most of the time he looks like he's trying to remember what my sister's ass looks like, hidden beneath that dress."

I choked on my water and covered my mouth with my fist. "Seriously?"

"Well, yeah, although now I'm thinking of my sister's ass, so I need another drink. Sure you don't want anything?"

"Get drunk and I might punch the prick."

"Right. Two drinks for you coming up."

He sauntered off, kissing Sloane and Misty's cheeks as he did, asked them if they needed anything and then was gone.

I went straight to Hailey, slipped my hand behind her neck and twisted her so her front was facing my side. "Dawson? What is it?"

"Darrick's watching," I murmured, and I dipped my chin, tilted my head, and kissed her.

CHAPTER 24
HAILEY

I HATED Dawson's kisses as much as I craved them. With every kiss, it became closer to my last kiss. It didn't stop me from pressing my hand to his chest, curling my hand into a fist around his suit coat lapels, and holding on for the ride.

He was going to bring attention to us, which I figured was his intention. He was staking his claim on me in front of Darrick, and I wasn't complaining, even if this was as fake as everything else.

Dawson pulled back, slipping his tongue along his bottom lip, and when I opened my eyes, he was peering down at me, a soft smile lifting the corner of his lips that brought tears to my eyes on sight.

Goddamn him for making me love him, giving me these looks.

"Best damn kiss I've ever had, Hailey. Every single one you've given me."

"Dawson." I clung to his biceps.

If that was true, why did he look so conflicted about the admission?

"Hate to break this up," Meredith said, bumping her hip into mine. "But Old Man Bonkers is pacing backstage, ready to get started so we might want to take our seats."

"Old Man Bonkers?" Dawson asked.

I smothered a laugh. "Manny Bonners. But he's old, and well, crazy. He's our mayor."

"Hence, Old Man Bonkers." Meredith swung her arm through mine and pulled me toward our table.

Dawson followed, now wearing an amused smirk.

She pressed her head against mine and whispered, "Later, when we're alone, you're going to tell me how that man can kiss you like that, and then you can both look so sad about it."

"Let's just say this isn't going to be one of your success stories."

"Psssh. There's always speed bumps."

I shook away the seed of hope she was trying to plant.

"Yeah, well, you were lost in him, but I took a glance at Darrick, and I have to tell you, he did not like that kiss one little bit more, Bianca definitely didn't like the way he was watching you, so at least that worked out well for all of us."

"I can't even believe she's here," I muttered and slipped into the chair Dawson held out for me. Once we were seated, his arm draped around the back of my chair.

Charlie was on my other side and nudged his elbow into mine. Next to him was Tate, then Holly. Mom and Dad were at the table across from us and then Sloane, Misty, Meredith and Tuevo rounded out the table sitting next to Dawson.

Tate and Holly were whispering, Tate's jaw clenched, still shooting the occasional daggers at Dawson while he and Tuevo talked about their upcoming seasons and off-season training. I only heard snippets, and none of it made much sense to me, so instead of joining or listening, I took a sip of my water and caught my mom's gaze.

"Proud of you," she mouthed to me and tipped her drink in my direction. "And I like him."

She and everyone else in the room most likely.

I blew her a kiss and settled back into my chair and Dawson's arm. His thumb drew lazy circles around my shoulder. It didn't matter one bit to me if it was for show, for Darrick or my family, I relished every last brush of his skin on mine for as long as I could have it.

I held the glass award with my company's name, my name, and Favorite Female Owned Retail Store etched into it on a gold-plated base in the air and leaned into the microphone, finishing my speech with, "Thank you so much, again, for all the love and support. Enjoy the rest of your night."

Applause rang through the country club's room, and as much as I tried to fight it, my gaze landed on Dawson.

He was standing, along with the rest of my family at the table, wearing a look that made me feel ten times larger and like this award was more like him winning the Super Bowl than it really was.

He dipped his chin and kept clapping. I seared the memory of that look of his into my memory. He wasn't faking that. He really was proud of me. Possibly more so than my own parents, and I wasn't quite sure what to do with it.

"Miss Parillo, congratulations."

I shook our mayor's hand. "Thank you, sir. Wonderful party tonight, isn't it?"

"Sure is. Make sure you and that man of yours get some more drinks and cut a rug on the dance floor later."

"Will do."

The backstage was darker, and while I could have taken the steps right off the stage down to my seat, I wanted a moment to process everything. The night. The fact I'd won. Maybe I had tried to downplay it, but when I'd found out I was even nominated, I'd cried happy tears for two days. What other woman at the age of twenty-four could look at their life and see all they'd accomplished in such a short time? My store had only been open for less than two years.

The backstage was dark and chilly. Goose bumps pebbled my arms, and I pushed through a door that would take me out to the back patio. I shivered from the sudden change in temperature.

Heat flooded me, and I took a deep breath. The back patio was lit, draped with lights, creating a cozy and warm space that'd been cleared of tables and chairs. Later, once the dancing and drinking began, the patio would be filled with people, mingling and laughing.

For now, the space was mine, nothing but the echo of the noise inside and the chirping of bugs, the occasional burst of light from lightning bugs.

Behind me, the whoosh of a door opening had me turning, but I already knew who it'd be. Dawson would never leave me alone for long. Especially not here.

But oh, how wrong I was.

Ice pricks danced down my spine as Darrick stepped toward me on the patio. My shoulders tightened, and I scanned for exits, but I'd have to go around him to get back inside.

"Congratulations." He said it with a smile. He slipped his hands into his pockets and rocked back on his heels.

Darrick was attractive. Everyone could see it. More, he knew it. With his sandy-blond hair swept to the side and his chiseled jaw, his rich-blue eyes, he had a smile that could melt cameras.

I'd always thought so. Until I'd had my hands on Dawson's tattoos and piercings and muscles and the rough feel of his beard as it scraped against my soft skin.

Looking at Darrick then didn't give me the butterflies I once would have had. Instead, it was disappointment that slipped through my veins, making me cold all over.

"What do you want?"

"Come on, Hailey. You can't still be mad at me."

I scoffed. He was the mad one here. "You drove through our wedding site to pick up a bridesmaid and took off without telling me you didn't want to actually marry me."

Doubtful he needed the reminder, but perhaps he'd hit his head while he and Bianca were busy enjoying what was supposed to have been our honeymoon.

"She's not the girl you marry, Hailey. She's the girl you date and have fun and sow your wild oats with."

"And I'm the woman you marry?"

"Exactly."

"So the woman you spend forever with, the woman you want to be your life partner is someone you've betrayed and disrespected and lied to? How does that equal a healthy marriage?"

"Well, if you forgive me, there would be no betrayal or disrespect. I just wanted more time. We have forever but I brought up delaying the wedding a couple of times and you didn't listen."

"Ahh...so this is my fault. Got it. I didn't take you seriously so you took my bridesmaid on our honeymoon. Makes perfect sense."

He scowled. "I'm not saying that."

"What are you saying then?" Dawson stepped around the corner and to my utter shock, there was Bianca. Tears streaming down her cheeks.

"I'm the girl you have fun with?" she asked. "What? The one good for fucking but not for building a family?"

"Bianca, you misheard what I said." Darrick took a step forward, quickly erasing the surprise on his face. Dawson threw an arm out, blocking his way to her.

"Not another step," he growled.

"No." She sniffed. "I didn't. I heard it perfectly. And I'm done listening to you tell me what I have heard or not or what I have understood or not. We're through." With tear-stained cheeks she faced me. "I'm sorry for hurting you. He said he loved me, and I thought he meant it, and well, I'm sorry for everything. Probably think I deserve this, huh?"

"No one deserves to be treated like an object." Karma, however, was my new friend, as shitty as this was. I wasn't exactly upset about the turn of events. Maybe someday I'd even be giddy over it.

"This is ridiculous." Darrick tugged on his suit coat. "You're both—"

"What?" Dawson grunted and stepped forward. "What exactly are they? Please, disrespect my woman again in front of my face. We'll see how that works for you."

"You won't hit me. You've already been fined and benched."

"Gotta a long season ahead. Worth it, this time, to take the bench for someone who means this much to me. So I'll give you one last chance, tell me exactly what your opinion of Hailey and Bianca is."

He scowled. Braver than I assumed because he wasn't pissing down his leg as Dawson towered over him, twice as wide and four times as strong.

"This is ridiculous." He glared at Bianca in a way that made my skin feel like it'd been covered in slime. How had I never seen how gross and nasty he was? "Find your own way home."

As soon as he was gone, Bianca glanced back up at me. "I'm sorry. I really am, for hurting you."

She grabbed the skirt of her dress and vanished behind the corner. Her steps echoed on the cement long after they should which told me she didn't head back inside at all.

Dawson's chest was heaving with deep heavy breaths and his knuckles were white in his curled fists. He was still glaring at the spot Darrick vacated like he was debating whether or not to run after him.

I was fighting back laughter. That was perfect. Absolutely one hundred percent, way too perfect.

"How much do I mean to you?"

He whipped his head in my direction and all that hair he'd combed back and styled flew out behind him. "What?"

"You said..."

"I know what I said."

"You said it'd be worth it to take the bench for someone who means this much to you. So I'm asking how much is that?"

His upper lip curled. Nostrils flared. His pupils were dilated entirely black from anger, but as I took another step toward him and he sucked in a breath, I figured it wasn't pure anger. Arousal was mixing in there, too.

We'd had a rough enough night. I could have gone easy on him. But this wasn't about our attraction to each other or the agreement we made.

This was about respect. I wouldn't keep giving myself to a man I was falling in love with who was still seeing me as some fake, temporary passage of time.

One last time. I'd give him one more chance. "Tell me I mean something to you, Dawson."

The words tripped out of my sore, scratchy throat, and pain followed in their wake as I swallowed.

Waited.

Moments passed. Far too many and he was still scowling, still breathing like a bull ready to charge.

I didn't need a forever kind of promise, I needed to know this was something real, something that wasn't based on whatever temporary arrangements we could get out of it.

"Right," I whispered because that wasn't going to come. I'd already put up with years of disrespect and lies. I was worth more. "Got it."

Like Bianca, I lifted the taffeta skirt of my black gown and waltzed around Dawson to head back inside. He didn't move a single inch to stop me.

Which might have hurt worse. He was totally okay with letting me walk away from him.

One of my siblings would take me home. All they needed to see was the look on my face and know I needed an escape.

CHAPTER 25
DAWSON

THERE WAS no doubt about it.

I fumbled the ball huge on a play that should have been an easy score. Since it took me far too long to pull my head out of my ass, I was too late in finding Hailey. She wasn't inside, but her brother Charlie was absent from where the family was still sitting.

Shit. I'd fucked that up huge.

Tell me I mean something to you.

She did. She meant more than something. She meant everything. And she had no idea how fucking terrifying that was for me.

"Fuck." I scrubbed my hand through my hair and slipped into my car. She was hurt. Upset. Probably throwing me and Darrick into the same pile of shitty ex-boyfriends who played with her body and her heart and her mind and tossed her aside.

The urge to chase her down screamed inside of me, but I wasn't right.

Wouldn't be right until I figured out what in the hell I did want from her.

Yeah, she meant something to me. Yeah, I cared about her. But she deserved a man who would willingly hand her the world.

Until I knew that man could be me, which meant I'd become a man

I'd never intended to be when it came to any woman, I needed to stay away.

She still owed me a date to Maggie's wedding. She could back out. Probably would. But that meant I had time to figure out my fucking head, get it on straight, and decide if I was willing to be the man Hailey needed.

A man who'd give her the world, a man who'd love her forever, a man who...

Holy shit.

I was in love with Hailey.

The thought slammed into me so fast I pulled off to the side of the road and hit the brakes.

"Fucking hell." My knuckles ached around my grip on the steering wheel. My heart thundered against my chest.

Sweat beaded at my temples.

This wasn't right.

Stabbing chest pain. Racing heart. Sweating. Chills. An ache growing in my gut.

I was experiencing all the symptoms of a heart attack.

Love shouldn't feel like this.

Should it?

There was only one person who I knew who would know the answer.

I jerked my car back onto the road, made a quick left and using my car's CarPlay, sent a quick text.

It was late on a Friday, but knowing what I knew of him, he'd be up.

And hopefully, able and willing to help.

Eden took one look at my face, the yanked-apart bow tie and my dress shirt I'd shoved up to my elbows and opened their front door.

"Cole's out back. Said you texted him?"

"Yeah." It was barely a grunt.

Eden's face was a mixture of concerned and amused.

I ignored the amused part. There was nothing fucking funny about any of this.

My phone, which had been pinging with notifications the entire forty-minute drive through Brentwood and Nashville up to Cole's house, was still in my car.

Fucking Meredith.

After I finally had Siri play Meredith's first text, an eloquent one-word message that said "dick," I turned off my ringer and disconnected the CarPlay feature from receiving any more. Cranking up the music hadn't helped. Rolling down the windows to get fresh air hadn't helped.

My heart was still jackhammering away inside my chest and my palms were so damn sweaty it was a wonder I could maneuver the steering wheel.

If this was love, I wasn't sure I wanted anything to do with it.

As soon as I slid open the back door to their deck, Bongo, Cole's golden retriever dog was at my feet. Jumping and sniffing, Bongo danced around me, ran in circles until I stopped moving and sank my fingers into his thick fur.

"I can put him inside," Cole called from where he was sitting on their outdoor couch. He had a wall-mounted television on beneath his covered patio. They'd renovated the backyard as soon as spring hit and installed an outdoor kitchen, massive sitting area that rivaled the size of his living room inside, and installed a pool.

"He's good." I gave Bongo more required scratches before I let him go and headed straight to Cole's outdoor fridge and helped myself to a beer.

If necessary, I'd crash in one of their three extra rooms, but getting blackout drunk would certainly help the heart attack symptoms.

"Are you?"

"Nope."

I twisted off the top of the bottle, flicked it onto the coffee table, and plopped my ass down into one of the couch cushions. "How's the game?"

Like me, when Cole wasn't playing football, he was watching hockey. Tennessee might have been kicked out right before the playoffs this year, but the Stanley Cup semi-finals were still going strong.

"Florida is surprising the hell out of everyone. Up two to nothing against Minnesota right now."

Minnesota kicked Tennessee out of the playoffs to win the last wild card spot. The fact they were still in it had everyone debating if they were going to have a mass implosion and completely fall apart or take it all. Carolina Ice Kings made it to the semi-finals and everyone had projected them to win it all originally, but Minnesota gave them a surprise four-game sweep to end up in the finals.

"That's not what brought you here tonight," Cole said. He took a pull of his own beer, one arm flung to the back of the couch.

He looked as casual as he always did, and he'd give me time. "You can though, you know."

"I can what?"

"Come over anytime to watch a game. Hang with Jasper. You don't need to have your life falling apart to need company."

Damn. Straight to the heart.

"My life isn't falling apart."

It so was.

"All right." Cole took another drink of his beer. "Nice suit you have on, by the way."

The smartass fucker.

I opened my mouth to come back with a sarcastic retort at the same time the slider door opened. Jasper flew out, Eden following with a gentle smile.

Jasper flung himself at Cole, completely ignoring me. "I wanted to come say good night."

Cole planted Jasper on the couch next to him, and wrapped an arm around his son, kissing the top of his head. "You brush your teeth and take your shower?"

"Yep. Eden made me do it."

"I'm such a monster," she playfully mumbled, standing close to me.

"Feeds you vegetables, takes you to school, makes you clean your room, she's horrible," Cole teased his son.

"She's the best." Jasper smiled before turning a pout toward his dad. "And it's not nice to call people names, Dad."

Cole ruffled his head and gave him a gentle shove. "I'll work on it. Get to bed. Love you."

"Love you too." He climbed off the couch and came to me. "Love you too, Mr. Butler."

I held out my fist. "You too, kid. Sweet dreams."

He ran inside, slamming the door behind him.

"Sorry about interrupting."

"Nothing to be sorry about, babe."

"Can I get you guys anything? Food? More drinks?"

Cole leaned back with a grin that I was pretty certain Eden saw a lot and liked even more. "I've got all I need, honey."

"All right." She gave him a wink, rested a hand on my shoulder as she passed me and once the door was closed, I turned to Cole.

"You're a lucky man."

"Fuck that. And you know it. You know the shit we went through, not only with each other but with Marley and Selma. I could have lost the best thing to ever happen to me in a snap. We're not lucky. We worked for what we have, still do."

"Not sure I have that in me."

"You do if you stop being a stubborn dumbass."

"It's not nice to call people names, Cole."

I smirked behind the mouth of my bottle and ended up with a pillow thrown at my face. I deflected it, barely, and tossed it back to the couch.

"Talk to me. You're here. You called. You drove all this way dressed all nice with a look on your face that says you're fucking miserable."

"Make a guy feel nice and welcome, why don't you."

"Tell me what happened and how you fucked it up with Hailey."

"It was temporary."

"If it was, then you wouldn't look like you kicked a dog while it was down."

"It was temporary, and then I wasn't sure I wanted to be that anymore, but when she asked me to tell her what she meant to me, I froze."

Cole pressed his lips together, nodding like he knew that was how I fucked up, and then sucked in a breath through his teeth.

"Walk me through it."

I did. I told him about the award, the event, how proud of her I was, how I'd already decided I was going to end it tonight before she got hurt and then I told him about Darrick fucking showing up, treating her and his new woman like trash. Although as hurt as Bianca was, the bitch had been flirting with me as soon as I got up to go to the bar, get Hailey and me drinks, so I didn't feel all that bad for her.

I told her about confronting Darrick, about what she said to me.

How she looked like I'd taken a knife and stabbed her straight through her gut right before she walked away.

"How are you going to fix it?"

"I'm still not sure I should. She can find better. Someone more ready for all these feelings and shit than me."

"Probably," Cole agreed, and my blood started boiling.

"Thanks, man. Lotta fucking help."

I shoved off the couch and went straight to the fridge for another beer. Normally, I would have grabbed two, but Cole could get his own damn beer in his own damn house after that.

When I turned around, Cole was glaring at me, leaning forward, forearms on his thighs.

"I'm not saying she should, I'm saying she could. And yet it sounds like she wants your pathetic, emotionally stunted self anyway. Why are you taking that choice from her?"

Possibly, because I was a full-grown adult with not only mommy and daddy issues, there were probably some abandonment issues as well. An inability to trust. Typical bullshit I'd never examined too much before because I'd never cared enough to.

"I knew the moment I saw Eden, all those years ago in high school, I was going to marry her. Seven years I lived without her. Got Jasper out of it, so I can't say it all sucked, but I can tell you that I didn't start living until Eden walked right back into it. Pissed, so damn pissed at her the first time I showed up to yell at her, and still, even that night, all I thought about was how much I'd missed her and wanted her. Scared, I was so damn scared she'd walk away again, but even with that fear, I made sure I gave her a reason to stay. You think you tell Hailey this, any of what's going on with you, she's not the kind of woman who would give you a reason to stay? Then she's not the one for you anyway."

"I'm glad you had that with Eden. I just don't know..."

"She's pregnant."

"What?"

"Eden. Found out a couple of weeks ago but she wants to wait until after Maggie and Davis's wedding to say anything. But yeah, she's pregnant."

A rush of something uncomfortable squeezed my chest. Hailey, swollen, hands on a large round stomach, filled with my child, hit me hard and fast.

Fuck.

"That look right there on your face, tells me all I need to know, Dawson. You are the man for her. Now you just have to be the man she needs."

"How?" I choked out.

"Deal with your shit. Figure out exactly what has always held you back from getting close to people and then figure out a way to change it."

Oh. "Easy then," I mumbled.

"Nothing worth having ever is."

He had a point there.

CHAPTER 26
HAILEY

"YOU NEED TO GO HOME."

Charlie rolled his eyes and went back to sanding a new china cabinet in the back alley. "I'm busy. Can't leave yet."

I stepped outside and squinted in the harsh sun. It was only mid-May, but we were in the middle of a hot run of weather that made the air thick and felt more like August. "I've loved your help this week, Charlie, but you don't need to stay in town to keep an eye on me. I'm fine."

He tugged down his face-covering mask to keep him protected from dust and the chemicals he was still sanding off the cabinet and dropped the orbital sander. "I know. You're Hailey. You're always fine. But it was only a few months ago you were supposed to be married, and now you look even sadder than you did after Darrick left. You're my baby sister. I'm staying until I feel better about leaving you."

I wouldn't win. Charlie hadn't left my side since he drove me home Friday night. He sat in my living room when Meredith, Sloane, and Misty showed up with champagne, orange juice, margarita mixes and got the front door when all the food they'd ordered was delivered.

Thank God for good friends and tequila, or maybe not the tequila.

I wasn't fully over that hangover until yesterday, three days later.

But today was day five without Dawson Butler wanting anything to do with me. Today was day five I woke up and cursed my stupid heart for being so damn gullible and thinking he really did feel something for me.

Today was day five of moving on...again.

I was fine. Damn it.

Charlie only left my side to handle the shop on Saturday along with Grace and then brought me to work on Sunday. He was my shadow, plying me with electrolytes and food, and on Monday did the same thing again except demanded I put him to work so I could have an easier week.

My brother was becoming a pain in my rear end, but he loved me, and he might have been more stubborn than I was.

So no, I wouldn't succeed in kicking him out.

"Well, as long as my heartbreak is all about you." I went for teasing. Failed. My voice cracked at the end, and I spun around so Charlie wouldn't glower at me again when my eyes grew wet.

Stupid.

So freaking stupid.

We'd spent a few weeks together. He gave me my first amazing orgasms even if we hadn't gone all the way. Even if he failed at his end of the bargain and agreement.

So what.

I didn't need him.

I needed a man who would respect me, who would fight for me. I needed a man who'd stand proudly at my side through every up and down of life and wouldn't be afraid to tell me he loved me or cared about me.

I needed a man who would be faithful and loving.

Frankly, I didn't think my standards were all that high but given my history, I was growing in uncertainty.

Five days, and I'd heard nothing from Dawson. No apology, not even a text making sure I'd gotten home okay.

The silence said it all.

Our agreement was done, and the only way to start moving on was to keep moving forward.

The brutal heat was keeping most weekday shoppers away, so the store was slow, giving me plenty of opportunity to work on smaller items in my workshop and rearranging the shelves to give the place a fresh look. It'd pick up in a few weeks, once school was out, but I wished it could have been the holiday season or something, anything to keep me busy and distracted. As it was, sanding and painting and staining in my workroom gave me too much time to think about Dawson.

Time to think about that piercing of his I'd never truly felt inside of me. Think of all the questions I'd wanted to ask about his tattoos but hadn't had the courage. It gave me too much time to think about the way he smiled at me, the way he'd so perfectly enacted some of the scenes of my books. That he'd stood tall in front of my dad, stood up for me, gave my dad all his baggage and had my dad respecting him and supporting him in a matter of moments.

Stupid freaking Dawson with his wicked smile, talented fingers and tongue, and dick piercing I never got to fully enjoy.

I tossed down my staining cloth and huffed, went to the bathroom, and washed my hands.

To my surprise, the store was no longer empty when I stepped out of the bathroom.

Isaac was there, Jelly the Cat on a leash at his side, Peanut Butter nowhere to be found. He was glancing down at a table of signs, stained, painted, and stenciled with a country finish on them. The sayings varied. From "Hey there sweet cheeks" for a bathroom to "Get Naked."

He'd bought a lot of items from me, but I doubted a country chic look was what he was going for in his upstairs apartment.

"Hey," I called to him.

Isaac's head rose, and he smiled in my direction. The smile quickly faded as he stepped toward me. "How are you?"

Oh. That was a very pity-filled question. "Tuevo told you?"

Mine was a statement more than a question. Considering when

Isaac found out I was with Dawson, he wasn't thrilled, him knowing we were now no longer together, didn't really thrill me.

Isaac shrugged. Answer enough, I supposed. "You doing all right?"

His concern was genuine, and it was my turn to shrug. "It was only a couple weeks."

I could play it off for others, but internally, my gut rolled. It had only been a few weeks, but I'd hoped for more. So much more.

Foolish, foolish me.

He scanned the store, and when his eyes met mine again, he rocked back on his heels. "This is probably too soon, but I feel like I need to be honest."

"Okay...."

"My mom died when I was seven, and I don't have a sister."

"What? That's horrible," was my first response, then I realized... "So, but...you're always in here buying things for them." Confusion knotted my rows together.

A half-smile popped on his face, and then he shoved his lips to one side. "Yeah. Except maybe I'm not shopping for them."

"I don't get it." I really, really didn't. "Why would you lie?"

"Because you were engaged to Darrick, and then I was giving you time to heal from that, and then Dawson showed up."

No. No way. He couldn't be saying...

"Isaac..."

"I've been coming into this store to buy things for people who don't exist so I could spend a few minutes with you, yeah."

Holy crap. I'd never thought. Never once suspected. Hell, up until two weeks ago, I didn't even realize he knew Meredith or Tuevo. Someone had to start giving me "how not to be oblivious" lessons.

Stat.

"I'm flattered, really, and I feel so bad I didn't notice earlier."

"Yeah, well, you didn't know I played with Tuevo either, so I'll cut you some slack on being aware of what's going on around you."

I chuckled, cheeks on fire. Isaac was attractive. Strange with his cats sometimes, but in another world, another day....

"I'm sorry," I finally said. I was, too. He was a great guy, and he'd gone to so much effort to get to know me. I could see it now, in hindsight. The questions he'd so casually ask about what restaurants I liked, what kind of flowers he'd buy his, now, nonexistent sister.

His lips pressed down into a frown, and he turned, studied a small, pink jewelry box I'd distressed because little girls would bang it up anyway and tilted his head in my direction. "Guess that's a 'not interested,' then, huh?"

"I think that my heart sort of recently ran away from me before I could stop it, and until I get my head on straight again, it's best I don't do anything to complicate it further."

At his feet, Jelly the Cat meowed, a sad sound while staring at me with her soul-sucking eyes. She was either feeling sorry for her owner or plotting my murder. Possibly both.

"Hey, Isaac!"

He nodded at my brother, coming in from the back, mask pulled down beneath his chin, sandiest all over his Slipknot T-shirt. "Hey, Charlie. You're still in town?"

"For a while, yeah. Wanna get a drink?"

"Love to." Charlie headed straight to the restroom and Isaac turned to me then. "We'll see you around?"

"Yeah." And for some stupid reason, my heart squeezed a bit inside. Almost like I was losing someone else important to me. "You know, you can come in and say hi sometime without being forced to buy things."

"Will do. Some time."

But probably not for a while.

"Can I ask you something?"

"Anything, Hailey."

"Well, um. You've lived here for a while now."

"And I've paid my rent on time every month like a good boy."

This guy. Funny. Sweet. Attractive. Was there something wrong with me? I always fell for the wrong guy. The emotionally unavailable one. The cheating one.

That was a question for a late-night session with alcohol and Charlie, perhaps.

"If you play professional hockey, why do you live here? In this apartment, I mean."

"You realize that's the first personal question you've ever asked me?"

"What? No. It can't be."

He chuckled and shook his head again. "That should have probably made things clear for me earlier, huh?"

"Isaac—"

He lifted a hand, palm out. "No worries. Honestly. I took a shot, and it went wide. It happens. And to answer your question, I live in your apartment because I like the town feel, like being around it when I'm in town. I bounced around a lot of teams for the AHL before finally getting my shot last year. A part of me still fears I'll lose it and get sent back. So...until I've proven myself, I'm here. If that's all right."

"Of course. As long as you bring Peanut Butter next time, too."

My phone pinged in my pocket, and Isaac heard. "I'll let you get back to work. Take care, Hailey."

"Thanks, Isaac."

"And Dawson's a dumb shit for letting you get away. I hope you know that."

My jaw dropped, and I was still gaping at him as he scooped Jelly the Cat off the floor when my phone pinged again.

I yanked it out, hating that small moment when there was a spark of hope it was Dawson.

The plummet came a heartbeat later when it wasn't.

Margo: Wine Wednesday. Your butt better be in one of my chairs tonight or I'm hunting you down.

Great. More commiserating and pity and drinking away my sorrows.

I'd stop this. Soon.

I texted her back saying I'd be there. Sent a text to Sloane and

Misty inviting them too. Misery loved company and all that. I was slipping my phone back into my pocket when a hand hit my shoulder.

I jumped with my hand to my chest and gasped. "Jesus, Charlie. You scared the shit out of me!"

"Sorry." He laughed.

Sorry, my ass.

"You were always so jumpy. Figured you'd grow out of that."

"Thanks," I muttered.

"Probably wouldn't be so jumpy if you were more aware of your surroundings."

"Yeah, I've been told."

"What?"

But really, all the men in my life had made some incredibly good points about that. Had it been the reason Darrick was able to cheat on me for so long? The fact I never saw my dad watch an actual football game in my life? Or Isaac's interest? Or Dawson...god...did I need to reexamine everything about the person I was?

"Nothing. Want to have dinner at Margo's with me when we're done here?"

Outside of going to work, I hadn't left my house in five days. Charlie had become my errand boy and Door Dash my best friend.

Charlie must have approved because his smile almost blinded me. "Absolutely, sis."

Sloane tipped the bottle of Montepulciano back and forth. Her frown grew. "Think Margo would give us another bottle of wine?"

The first was on her.

The second would not be.

"No." I took the empty bottle out of her hand. "And you're buying the next one. You still owe me."

Sloane stuck her tongue out at me but didn't argue. I started playing that manipulative petty card on Saturday. If I hadn't listened to them the night that started all of this, I wouldn't be so miserable now. Sure, I broke the rules and started liking my sex coach and all that, but it was their idea.

"Fine. Anything to eat?"

"Shrimp on ciabatta?" I asked Charlie. It was his favorite appetizer here and we'd already had one of mine.

"I'll go get both. You sit." He leaned in close to my ear. "And cut Sloane some slack. She feels bad enough."

I started to scoff but stopped when I saw the tightness around Sloane's eyes. The downward tilt of her lips. She glanced at me and changed to a sparkling smile in a second.

I shrunk to the size of a mouse.

Damn. Maybe I was being too mean to her.

"Love you, Charlie-Bear."

He stood off the stool and shoved me so hard I almost fell off mine.

All three of us laughed, and when he was gone, I apologized to Sloane. "Truly. I'll lay off. It's no one's fault, it just didn't work."

She squeezed my hand. "Love you. You'll bounce back in time."

"Yeah. I seem to be becoming a pro at that."

She chuckled, a sad commiserating laugh right along with me. "If you can bounce back after Darrick, if I can bounce back after Jakob, I think we'll both eventually be all right, sweetie."

I tipped her empty wineglass against hers. "Cheers. But do you think I should call him?"

Her brows arched in surprise. "You want to?"

I wanted to hear his voice more than I wanted to have another glass of wine. "I just...I sort of threw down an ultimatum out of the blue. What if he just needed more time?"

"Is that what you think he needs?"

Ugh. Sometimes Sloane made me feel like I was sitting on a therapist's couch. "I think that entire night was really weird and strange and maybe I overreacted to seeing Darrick and hearing all the awful things he had to say, and then Dawson was there, protecting me. He has to care, right?"

"Maybe. He probably does. I'll even give him that credit, but does he care enough? Are you important enough to him to know what he wants? I think you were right to walk away. Maybe you reacted to your shit with Darrick, but that doesn't mean you were wrong. You deserve a man who will chase you, honey. A man who will know he's letting a good thing slip away and go after it." She shrugged and gave me a sad look that told me everything she hadn't said but was about to. "And he hasn't. I think right now you need to give it more time. Let him figure it out, and if you hear from him again, then listen. Maybe. But only if you think it's healthy for you."

"Right." It wasn't what I wanted to hear. It was what I needed to hear though.

Charlie returned, grinning, uncorking the wine and glared at Sloane. "What'd you do to her? She was fine when I left."

I elbowed my brother in his ribs. "She didn't do anything. Men suck."

"Most of them, I agree with that."

He poured our glasses. Told us story after story about his dating life in Portland.

More food was delivered.

Margo stopped by when she could, and I spent the next couple of hours laughing, belly gut ripping open, hand slapping kind of laughing.

Until Charlie tossed me into the passenger seat of my car, drove me home, and I went to bed still smelling Dawson's cologne and masculine scent on my pillows.

I'd change those.

Soon.

Moving forward was the only thing to do.

CHAPTER 27
DAWSON

ONE WEEK.

One week without her smiles and her laughter. One week without Hailey's touches, without her soft lips exploring my body, gaining confidence in not only how to give pleasure, but how to ask for what she wanted and to receive it.

One week since I watched the best thing to ever happen to me walk away.

Seven days since I'd wanted to reach out and contact her, drive past her shop to see her smiling at customers, or wondering if she was safe at her home, living alone.

Seven long, excruciating days while I was trying to do what Cole suggested and ensure I was the man who could be the man she needed.

It took me three days to get a hold of my dad. Considering our last conversation and how we ended it and the fact I hadn't taken his call since, I wasn't sure if he'd even answer my phone call.

He had.

And any minute, he was going to show up at my door for us to talk. That was all I'd said. "I need to talk to you. In-person. Can you get a couple days off?"

He was a pilot for a private luxury line where he flew the richest of the rich all across the country and world. Or those who wished they were and went into massive debt pretending to be.

Regardless, I was dressed nice, knowing he would be. Harrison Butler had never been a jeans or athletic shorts and T-shirt kind of guy. He was button-down or collared shirts and belts and pressed pants at his most casual.

Even now, I wasn't sure what to say to the man. The man I'd idolized for years, the man who'd taught me to be strong. The man who'd supported me. The man who had eventually abandoned his children when life threw him a curveball.

I went to the fridge and grabbed a couple of waters. Beer or bourbon would be better, maybe take the edge off.

I debated, stood in front of my liquor cabinet, and jolted when a heavy knock rattled my door.

"Shit." He was there. A man I hadn't seen in five years, who rarely made it to one of my games and when he did, never bothered to let me know he was going to be there so I could give him one of my tickets or see him after.

Nope, he'd fly in, watch a game, leave, and send me a text a couple days later telling me he'd been there.

I left the water on the counter, the bourbon in the cabinet, and hurried to my front door.

My dad had always been leaner than me. Taller by an inch or two, and his profession required him to be clean-cut. I figured I knew what to expect when I opened the door to see him. Dark hair like me, styled short and swept to the side, held in place with gel. Maybe a few wrinkles, slight graying of hair at the temples or some shit.

Instead, the man looked like he hadn't aged a day since I was eighteen, and he'd been in town for my high school graduation. He was dressed as I predicted, a gray athletic polo tucked into black dress pants, recently pressed and perfectly creased with a black belt and shining gold buckle he probably polished himself. He wore black leather slip-on shoes, and there wasn't a wrinkle or age spot that placed him any older than the last time I saw him years ago. He was edging close to being sixty years old and didn't look a day over forty.

Both of us stared at each other, and the words I wanted to say to him stuck in my throat, leaving me speechless, nervous as that eight-year-old little boy I was when he left me in charge and told me to take care of them, make sure the girls in our lives stayed out of trouble.

Shit. Maybe I shouldn't have done this.

"Hey, Dawson." He broke first, but I was certain the nervous look on his face mirrored mine.

I opened the door and stepped back. "Come on in."

His gaze roamed the space, my house. He took in everything, and I caught a flash of amusement when he spied my putting green out back behind the pool. The yellow flag attached to the pin in the hole gave it away.

"Nice neighborhood. You golf?"

"Poorly," I admitted. I picked it up years ago, because it was what athletes did in their off-season, but I'd never mastered the patience of it. Catching a ball flying through the air was so much easier than hitting a tiny ball into a hole you couldn't exactly see from two hundred yards away, or sometimes, ten.

"Was always something I wished I had time for."

He'd had the time. I'd realized that recently. There'd been time for him to be home more, or in the twenty years since. He hadn't always had to be the pilot that took the week-long flight to Japan or Southern Asia or Australia. He could have worked less. Been around more. Maybe not when we were little, but he definitely could have done it since.

My anger with him pulsed, and I fought to lock it down.

"Want anything to drink?"

"I'm good. You needed to talk to me?"

"Yeah." Except now that he was here, the beginning was difficult to find.

"Everything's okay, right? With you? Or your sister?"

My jaw clenched. "Would you care if there was something wrong with her?"

My dad's eyes widened, and then he twisted his neck and stared out my back windows. "I probably deserve for you to think that I don't, but I do."

Hmm. Right.

"I haven't heard from Crystal since the winter when I told her if she showed up here again, I was having her arrested for trespassing. She seemed to have gotten the message this time."

I wouldn't hold my breath, but she was done coming to me for money and attention. I'd made it clear if she ever wanted a relationship with me that was healthy, I'd be here for that. It'd only been five months, so I wasn't surprised I hadn't heard from her at all. Six to nine months was the average time she went before upending my life with her drama.

"So, what is then? Because it sounded important."

"Why'd you bail on us?"

"What? I didn't—"

"You did." Enough of this. I was a thirty-year-old man who hadn't been able to trust women since I was fourteen because as soon as my mom had an affair, I lost my entire family. Maybe that was fucked up to hold on to it for so long, but there we were. Me finally confronting the man I'd idolized, who'd, at minimum, manipulated that but then when I needed him, left. "Soon as you could, you went back to work, just let Mom have us, and she bounced us around house after house for fucking years. The the only time we saw you was on birthdays or graduations and then...nothing. Not since college."

"I've always been there." He looked shocked. Actually fucking shocked.

"The fuck you were." My blood was boiling, and I shook out my arms to relieve some of the tension before I punched him in the face.

"I was there, Dawson." He stepped toward me, and I braced. "I was at every game. Every ceremony. I've always been there, even when you didn't know it."

He was lying. He had to be lying. "Why? Why would you do that?"

"Shit." He stopped, swiped a hand over his forehead, and squeezed his eyes closed. "Fucking Cecilia."

"Mom?"

"When's the last time you talked to her?"

"Day I was drafted. She called and asked for her cut of my first signing bonus because she said she'd paid for my football all those years."

"She never fucking paid a dime. I did that."

"What? With child support or some shit? Or alimony?" My head was spinning. Of all the things he'd said.

"In addition to the sixty grand a year I gave your mom for all of that, yeah. I paid for every goddamn penny of anything you needed."

"So that excuses you not being there? Blaming me for Mom's affair in the first place? Taking off?"

"Blaming you—what the hell are you talking about?"

His face paled. Actually paled to the color of his gray shirt. "Dawson..."

"You did," I seethed. "You fucking did. Day you caught Mom, you said, 'I thought I always told you to keep our girls out of trouble.' And then you left."

His eyes closed, chest heaved. "Dawson. I am so sorry." He opened them again, and the pain in his eyes was damn deep. I felt it like a punch to the gut. "I don't remember that, son, but I swear, I didn't blame you for it. I was pissed, not thinking straight. Your mom's shit was her own."

Bullshit. So much fucking bullshit.

"Still doesn't explain why you stopped calling. Didn't even fight for custody."

"I fought. I fought as hard as I fucking could. Your mom hired lawyers, tons of them, paid for by the new guy she was already living with. I fought for custody for three years until you were seventeen, and I was prevented from seeing you every step of the way. And I called.

You ever wonder why your mom kept changing the home telephone number? Making it private?"

"I don't understand."

And I didn't. For the first time, I understood absolutely nothing about what was going on, what had happened. But there was no denying how absolutely wrecked my dad looked like, facing me, telling me this shit.

"She painted me as an absentee father, said I'd never been home. Told the judges you kids didn't want to spend time with me at all, and since you were old enough, you got to say where you lived. She had signed documents with your and Crystal's signatures, stating the same thing."

No. No way. "She wouldn't have done that."

"She wouldn't have?" His head tilted to the side. He was more contemplative than dismissive. "I was there. For every game of yours in high school. I was there the night you broke your wrist, and I was in the waiting room at urgent care until I heard you were okay. I was there on your collegiate signing day, and I was there when you first took the field at Michigan against Ohio State. The day you were awarded Offensive Player of the Year, I was there, when you wore that dark red or maroon suit."

Shit. He couldn't...most of that shit wasn't televised. Never promoted on social media because it wasn't as big fifteen years ago as it was now... "Dad..."

"I've been there, Dawson. As much as I possibly could, cheering you on proudly but thinking you and Crystal didn't want me anywhere near you, so I stayed back, only showing up when I thought you'd allow it. And every year, I sent Cecilia the money for new football equipment, for your sports registration in high school. I paid for Crystal's dance lessons and uniforms. And when you were living with your mom and Daniel, that CEO of whatever, I was the one who sent her an extra twenty-five grand to get you a car. Did the same for Crystal, too."

"Daniel said it was from him." One of the few decent men my mom had hooked herself too in a short few years, Daniel had always bought us everything. At least...no. Fuck. "Mom said Daniel bought it."

My throat clogged, and an irritation pulsed behind my eyes. All this time...

"I always thought you were pissed at me about the affair, and that was why you didn't want to be around me."

"Never." There was venom in his tone, pure seething fury that seeped from his pores and filled the air in the room with his anger. With his honesty.

I hung my head and stared at the floor beneath my bare feet until my vision blurred. "Mom said you told her she could have us because you traveled so much it didn't make sense for you to have a home where we could stay with you."

"For ten years, until you were out of college and stopped going back to be with your mom in the summers, I had a three-bedroom apartment no more than ten minutes away from wherever your mom moved to so I'd be close in case you guys ever reached out. In case you changed your mind about seeing me."

Ten years. Ten goddamn years.

"Fuck." My chest rattled and heaved and fucking salty drops fell from my eyes. I'd never cried. Couldn't remember ever doing it, but right then, seeing how serious my dad was, how much he meant it, and how fucking wrong I'd been...

A warm, firm hand landed on my shoulder, and my dad gave me a quick shake. "I'm sorry. I'm sorry your mom was never honest with you, and I'm sorry Crystal never told you. She said you knew and didn't care."

"Crystal?" My head snapped up, and I stared into eyes that were identical to mine, complete with the wet sheen of tears. "She knew? For how long?"

Dad removed his hand from my shoulder only to wipe it down his face. With a shrug, he crossed his arms. "It was one of the last times she and I talked."

Years. That was years ago. At least five when he finally gave up on her and told her not to call him anymore.

"I need a drink." I walked around my dad, felt the way he turned to watch me, and after I pulled out a bottle of bourbon from my liquor cabinet, twisted. "Want one?"

"Yes. Absolutely yes, I would love to finally sit down and have a drink with you."

Damn. That burn in my throat started again and crawled right up to the back of my tongue, but this time, I swallowed it down.

I made our drinks and took them to the living room.

We had more to talk about. There was still a reason I didn't trust women, and he'd only confirmed why to me. My mom was a liar. Crystal too. Both of them played me so hard and used me. It was no wonder I couldn't trust anyone. Add on to the fact I just figured my dad essentially abandoned me, outside a couple of phone calls a year, well, who wouldn't be fucked up.

We sipped our drinks. The quiet was tense, and finally, my dad leaned forward and looked me right in the eye. "I shouldn't have ever told you to focus on your football career and not find a woman. That was my baggage getting in the way of your happiness. I was trying to look out for you, but now knowing especially what Cecilia did, it definitely wasn't right."

Fucking hell.

How had a man I barely had a relationship with read me so well?

"Her name's Hailey," I told him, and then for some damn reason, I opened my mouth, and all my bullshit spewed out of it.

CHAPTER 28
HAILEY

"I'M EXHAUSTED, Meredith. Can we do this another night?"

My store was a mess. My hair hadn't been washed in days. I still hadn't been able to bring myself to change my sheets to erase the scent of Dawson even though it was most likely only remained in my head and memories.

I'd worn cutoff denim shorts and an old T-shirt I'd ripped and cut into a crop top. Both items of clothing had stains and paint on them, along with the tops of my toes and my Birkenstock sandals because I'd made an absolute mess working on projects that day.

"Any other day, I'd say yes," she said through the phone. "But not tonight. One drink at Margo's and if you're still in a funky funk, I'll take you home."

I adored my friends. Loved them dearly.

Occasionally, I wanted to punch them in the throat.

"Please?" she begged, and I pulled my phone away to check the caller really was Meredith. She never begged.

"What's going on?"

"Nothing."

She said it quickly. Too quickly.

"Just come. As soon as you can close down. Thirty minutes, one drink, max. I promise. And don't roll your eyes at me."

I chuckled and stopped my mid eye roll. Crazy how well she knew me. I finally sighed into the phone. "I'll be there in fifteen minutes, but don't expect much."

"Great. See you soon, chickadee!"

I frowned at my phone's screen, the timer flashing as the call ended. "Chickadee?"

She'd never used a nickname on me. Something was definitely going on, and I wasn't showing up looking like a deformed rat who'd been put through a blender so after I flipped the sign on my door to Closed, locked it, and shut off the main lights, I headed to the bathroom.

In the locked cabinet where I kept cleaning supplies, I also kept an emergency stash of makeup and hair products. This wasn't the first time I'd been yanked out for a night on the town and after the first, I refused to find myself unprepared again.

I couldn't do anything about my current outfit, but I scrubbed paint splotches off my cheekbones, washed my makeup-free face, and applied a bit of concealer, blush, and mascara. I tore my hair out of the braided bun I'd put it in that morning, sprayed on some dry shampoo, and scrubbed the worst of the oily mess out of it. With a few quick flips of my hair, it was styled back in a clip, still messy but not embarrassingly so and after a spritz of fresh perfume, a couple swipes of deodorant, I was as good as I was going to get without a complete overhaul.

It took only a few more minutes to finish closing down, grab my purse from the back room where I applied a fresh coat of lip gloss, and then lock the back door to the alley.

Almost fifteen minutes later, I was walking toward Margo's, getting closer and growing nervous at the size of the crowd standing outside. The street was a narrow two-lane road with minimal street parking, but the entire street was packed with people. Some had their hands cupped around the sides of their faces, peering into her restaurant.

It was Saturday, and yeah, the shops and town had been busy, and Margo's generally had a small wait on weekend nights, but to this extent?

I'd never seen anything like this.

I headed into the fray, slipping through gaps in the crowd and as I approached the front door, Bill, Margo's husband, opened the door.

"Get in here and quick before they follow."

"What is going on?" I asked, laughing up at him.

He nodded his head toward the back of the restaurant. "That."

"What–"

Oh my god. Blood rushed from my face, my fingers grew cold, and my feet were firmly glued to her restaurant's floor.

Everyone I knew stood in a semi-circle, completely blocking the bar from me. Front and center in front of my mom, dad, Charlie, and Meredith and Tuevo, and Sloane and Misty and even my coworker Gabby was the most surprising guest of all.

Dawson.

My knees wobbled, and I reached out and grabbed hold of Bill to steady myself.

"What is this?" I asked him quietly. His hand settled on my lower back and gently pushed me forward.

"Hear him out. He's stood tall in front of everyone who loves you and planned this whole night."

This explained the crowd. Especially if word had gotten out Dawson Butler was there. Tuevo too.

I shook my head and forced my feet to move as Bill kept pushing until I was in front of Dawson, far enough away I couldn't touch him, close enough I took in the darkness rimming his lower eyes and the small twitch in his cheek.

"What are you doing here?"

"I hurt you a week ago, and I want to fix it."

He rocked back on his heels while I swayed on my legs again.

Was it possible he was even more attractive? His hair was down, that sexy curl to it that came from letting it air dry naturally. He filled out his black T-shirt perfectly and the jeans he wore might as well have been painted onto his legs, especially his thick thighs. His arms were behind his back, hands must have been clasped together.

My throat grew warm, and my hands turned sweaty with nerves. "I don't understand."

Because I didn't. He wanted to walk away with my blessing? With making sure I wasn't hurt?

I scanned the crowd, brows tugging in. Everyone stood exactly like he did, except Misty was grinning, shifting her weight from foot to foot like she was about ready to jump in the air but trying to contain herself.

"Last Friday, you wanted me to tell you that you meant something to me. Wanted me to show you that I care about you, and I froze, couldn't do it because I wasn't sure I was the man you should take a chance on. Wasn't sure I could be that guy you needed."

Butterflies swarmed in my stomach, and my heart squeezed painfully inside my chest. "Dawson."

"Did some thinking this week, talked to some people who helped me get my head on straight." He gestured with a tip of his head, and Eden and Cole were both at his back, grinning broadly. A man I didn't know but who had Dawson's exact hair color and eyes stood next to Cole.

His dad? I flicked my gaze back to Dawson.

"I'll explain my dad being here later, but right now, there are more important things to say to you."

"Okay...." My head was still spinning.

He stepped toward me slowly, giving me time to back up. Little did he know, if I moved, I'd probably collapse.

"What are you doing?" I asked when he stood at my side, both of us, together, now facing the crowd in front of us.

"Meredith," Dawson said.

She came forward, blew me a kiss and then pulled out a sign she'd been hiding and holding behind her back.

Every time you laugh, I feel a joy I've never known.

"Oh my god," I whispered.

"There's more. Sloane?"

She stood next to Meredith, did a quick little curtsy, and brought another sign out from behind her back. *Your smile reminds me of sunshine and warm summer days.*

I swallowed a thick lump of cotton in my throat and settled a hand to my chest to slow my racing heart.

"Misty," Dawson said.

And another sign.

He went through them all. Every single person held a sign...for me, and without having to say a word or explain all the things Dawson liked about me.

The way other people smile when you talk to them, and you don't notice it. You make everyone you meet feel like their best friend.

The way you downplay your awards and success but talk up everyone elses makes me see how humble you are.

You're incredibly talented with your job, and your passion inspires me.

I like that you love to read...especially love what you read... ;-)

Winky face and all. I barked out a laugh, wiped tears from my eyes until twelve signs were being held by the people I loved most, all given to them by the man I now knew I loved beyond reason.

"One more." Dawson gently placed his hand at my lower back, testing, and I grinned up at him. "It's enough."

"Don't move. Dad?"

He walked toward his dad, and he handed Dawson not one but a small stack of cards. He then put his back to my family and friends and one by one, slowly showed me everything that was on his own stack of signs.

I hurt you last week and I'm sorry

I've spent a week without you and now know...

I never want to spend another day without you.

You deserve the best

I was afraid that wasn't me, that I wasn't capable of it

But good men proved me wrong and told me not to lose...

The best thing that had ever happened to me.

I love you, Hailey.

The sign fluttered to the floor, and I gasped, watching his words in writing fall, stuck on them.

Love?

"Dawson," I croaked, eyes so blurry from tears I could barely read the next card.

He grinned at me, a crooked, teasing grin that had me chuckling. "Few more."

I will spend the rest of my days making up for my mistakes

Trying to never hurt you again or make you sad

I will spend every day from here on out, loving you as you love others

Selflessly

Powerfully

Unconditionally

Resolutely

I love you. Forgive me?

"Yes." My entire body trembled, and I ran to Dawson, but he caught me first.

His hands, warm and strong and steady, cupped my cheeks. "I'm sorry, Hails. So sorry."

"I forgive you. Just kiss me."

He laughed, pressed his lips to mine, and a round of claps and whoops erupted behind us. When Dawson pulled back from the kiss, my body was burning hot, my sex needy and already wet and my eyes were still shimmering from all the tears.

"I missed you," I admitted quietly, for only him to hear.

"You'll never have to miss me again. I promise. I'm yours for as long as you'll have me."

Another kiss, and then he turned us, held me in his arm at his side while my family and our friends rushed to give us hugs.

"He planned the whole thing," Meredith whispered in my ear. "Called me this morning, said he couldn't wait another second to talk to you."

I leaned against Dawson, and his lips pressed to my temple.

"Good man you have there," my dad said. He kissed my cheek and gave Dawson a one-armed side hug since Dawson's arm was wrapped around me and he was making it pretty clear he wasn't going to let me go.

"Proud of you, Dawson. Real proud of you."

"Thanks, Ken."

We were surrounded and wrapped in hugs and then Margo and Bill were there, bringing out glasses and wine bottles and trays of all my favorite foods.

Bless my friends, Bill for being the bouncer and guard at the door, Margo for knowing all the things I loved, and the rest of them who knew Dawson had hurt me, but still came to throw their support behind him in getting me back.

When we had a break, glasses topped with wine, some beer for the occasion, one in Dawson's hand, I rolled to my toes and whispered, "When do you think we can sneak out of here?"

"Promised Meredith I'd make you stay for thirty minutes."

Ahhh. So she'd really meant that. "How much time do we have left?"

He twisted his left wrist and smirked. "Ten."

"I suppose we can wait."

He kissed me then, slow and sweet without tongue but it didn't matter how Dawson kissed me, I loved every single one of them. "I want you to meet my dad."

"Yeah. You're going to need to give me the story on that."

"I will. There's a lot we still have to talk 'bout."

"Later." Because tonight, I was hoping once we left, there'd be very little talking going on for either of us. And a whole lot more of something else.

A throat cleared behind me, and Dawson pulled back, still grinning down at me.

"Dad," he said and turned me toward the man with Dawson's matching eyes and hair color.

He wasn't as tall, leaner, but it was still very clear he was a man who took care of his health and his body.

"Dad. I'd like you to meet Hailey."

"Call me Harrison." He held out his hand for me to shake. Dawson's hand was at my lower back, fingers pressing in. Warm. Loving. I took a risk and instead of shaking his hand, I stepped forward and gave him a quick hug.

He froze at my touch, whether it was surprise or being unwanted, and then lighting hugged me back. "It's great to meet you. Thanks for being here."

"I wouldn't have missed it for anything." Harrison stepped back. There was uncertainty on his features, but calmness too.

Dawson and I would definitely be talking about what happened with him and his dad in the last week.

"I'm going to head back to my hotel," Harrison said. "Any chance the three of us could have lunch or dinner before I need to fly out?"

"I'll talk to Hailey, and we'll figure it out."

"Good." He turned to me and grinned. "Lovely to meet you. Thanks for giving my son a second chance." He slapped Dawson's shoulder and gave him a quick squeeze. "I'll see you soon, then."

"Good night, Dad."

Harrison turned, went straight to my parents, and shook both of their hands. I leaned in close to Dawson as we both watched our friends, families, together.

"Want to know a secret that only I know?"

"Absolutely," I told him.

"See what Eden's drinking?"

I found her next to Cole, talking to Sloane and Misty.

"Water," I whispered and then gasped, covering my mouth with my hand. "Is she...?"

"Pregnant. Cole told me last week."

"That's wonderful! Why is she keeping it a secret?"

"Doesn't want to take any fun away from Maggie and Davis or their wedding next week. Although if she's not drinking at the reception, I figure that'll give it away."

"That's awesome." She'd told me about her and Cole's past, the sadness of it, the difficulty in trusting anything good could happen to her again. Life was wild, and she'd had a hell of a ride to find her happiness. "I'm happy for them."

"I want that," Dawson murmured. "Want what they have. A home. A family, and I can say before I met you, before I let you walk away, I'd never once considered it. But with you, I can't not think about it."

Tears burned my eyes, and I spun and pressed my hand to his cheek, the coarseness of his stubble scratched against my palm. "I really think that's all the talking we need to do."

"Good. Then we have about three minutes left of our required time, and that'll be done by the time we say our goodbyes, so how about we get on that."

We were out the door three minutes later, exactly, the fastest I'd ever been able to say goodbye to my friends and Dawson.

But I had better things to do.

And hopefully, Dawson was thinking the same exact thing as me.

CHAPTER 29
DAWSON

I KNEW I wanted to be a professional football player since I was nine. I worked at it. Earned every accomplishment through high school, worked my ass off in college every week in practice, drills, and every Saturday, we took the field. When I went up for the draft, I knew my worth, knew exactly the kind of effort and results I'd put up for any team who took me. The night of the draft, I wasn't worried. Wasn't nervous. I sat in my chair and went halfway through the first round exactly like everyone had predicted.

The day I took the field for my very first official NFL practice, I was solid as steel.

Nerves and worry had never once had a place in my life.

Until Hailey. Until it came time to not fuck her over or be an ass. Until it came down to this moment, where she was holding my hand, unlocking her front door and leading us both inside, where we knew exactly how the night was going to end up.

God, I hoped like hell I made it good for her. Hoped like hell I was worth what she was about to give me. Hoped like hell she didn't regret it.

I shut the door behind me. Locked it. The flick of the lock echoed like a gunshot through her darkened house. The only light on was above her kitchen island, two hanging pendant lights put off a light, warm glow.

Hailey's eyes were on me. I could feel them staring. Watching. Waiting to see what I'd do next and over the last week, I'd determined to be the man she needed.

And right then, the man she needed was someone who was honest.

"I'm worried I'm either going to hurt you, or you'll regret this someday."

I expected a soft smile. Understanding.

What I got was Hailey, a grin stretching wide, amusement flaring in her blue eyes right before she busted out laughing.

"Dawson," she finally managed in between laughs. "I've been waiting for this, not for twenty-four years, but ever since I sat across from you at that restaurant. Tonight, you proved with one hundred percent effort that I will never regret a single moment with you. And as far as hurting me, I've loved and enjoyed every single thing you've already done to me. How could you think this would be different?"

By the time she was done, she was in front of me. Hands pressed to my pecs. Her body was so close I could see nothing but her confidence and joy, and most of all, her trust. Her scent invaded me, straight to my marrow, that light, floral and citrus scent of hers I'd been smelling on my damn sheets and all over my house for the last week.

My hands settled at her hips, brushed up the sides of her body and back down until I laced my fingers together behind her lower back. I bent down slowly. We would take our time with this, give her all the time she needed to make this as good as it could possibly be for her.

She inhaled a quick, sharp breath as I brushed my lips over hers, moved to her jaw. She tilted her head perfectly while I ran my lips over the hinge of her jaw, back to her ear, down the column of her throat.

"So damn sweet," I whispered and elicited a shiver that ran through her body. "I've missed you."

Her fingers at my chest dug in. "Me too."

Her lips pressed against my collarbone, and I pulled her closer, wrapped my arms around her and held her close, taking a moment to breathe her in, to feel her body against mine. She slipped her hands from between our bodies and held me back.

This. I could have this forever.

"If you don't kiss me and take me to my bed soon," Hailey whispered, a teasing tone in her voice, "I'm going to think you've changed your mind." Her hips rolled, pressed against my crotch.

"Already wet for me?"

"From the moment I saw you."

I slammed my mouth to hers. This time there was no holding back. I pushed my tongue inside her mouth and invaded her, slipped my hands from her back to her ass and with one quick move, was holding her and heading toward her bedroom. As soon as I entered, I flicked on her bedroom light, kicked the door closed with my foot, and didn't stop moving until I was on my knees on her bed, lowering her down to the bed.

She was already going wild, grinding against me, whimpering her need, and with as much patience as I could muster, I flicked open the button of her denim shorts and tugged them down her legs. I followed, staying close, kissing every inch of her exposed body as I could and ran my nose over her red, lacy thong-covered sex. I shoved my tongue inside of her, knowing she loved the way the lace abraded her clit.

I teased her for a moment, and then two, until she was arching her back and whispering please and more and hurry.

"Patience," I told her and tugged down her soaked wet scrap of lace. I tossed both shorts and thong to the floor, stood, tore off my shirt, and shoved down my own pants. I stepped out of socks and shoes and by the time I returned to the bed, she'd removed her T-shirt and her bra, and there she was.

My goddess. My virgin.

My greatest weakness and largest, most important part of my life.

Her feet were planted on the mattress, knees bent, legs spread wide, exposing every beautiful single pure inch of her.

"Fuck." I took my hard dick in my hand. "I want you so damn bad."

She spread her arms wide on the mattress and gave me a wickedly enticing smile. "Then come do what you want with me."

Game. On.

I climbed onto the bed and slid my hands up on her legs, pausing to kiss her ankle, her calf, and the back of her knee. Trailing my lips up her inner thigh, I skipped over the wet, glistening pussy and kissed her other thigh, moved my hands up to her hips, her stomach, cupped both of her breasts and pinched her nipples the way she liked it. Hard, firm, with a tug that created an even more beautiful stab of pain and pleasure.

"Ohh...yes." Her hips bucked off the bed, seeking me. Craving it, but I kept playing with her nipples.

The sounds she made drove me wild as I kissed her belly button. Her stomach. I could play with her tits and nipples for days and never grow tired of the way Hailey responded.

Someday, I'd talk to her about getting them pierced, maybe buy some clamps.

As I moved up her body, I couldn't get the thought out of my mind, how fucking sexy she'd look, all sweet and cute to the outside, but pierced for our pleasure hidden beneath her clothes.

I took one of her nipples into my mouth, slid my hand down to her cunt, and as I drew circles around her clit with my thumb, pressed two fingers against her opening.

"Yes. Please. Dawson, I need you."

Every time she arched into me, I moved back.

I bit her nipple, and my dick jumped at her cry.

"You drive me crazy," I told her, licking around her nipple.

"You're driving me crazy," she rasped.

Her eyes were glassy with desire.

"Someday, I want your nipples pierced. What do you think about that?"

As I asked, I shoved my fingers deep inside of her. Hard. Fast. No warming up because she was already ready and everything I learned about Hailey told me she enjoyed a bit of roughness.

"Yes," she cried out as I began fucking her with my fingers. My thumb pressed against her clit and her core pulsed around me.

I removed my fingers from her.

"Dawson!" she screamed, grabbed the back of my neck, and slid her fingers into my hair.

She tugged hard, and when I grinned at her, she growled.

"I was almost ready to come."

"I know." I smirked and pushed up farther so I could slam my mouth against hers.

We kissed, hard, wet, and I swallowed the sounds she made while giving me my own. My dick, hard and red and throbbing, slid through her wetness, my piercing hitting her clit.

There was no more slow. She was ready, and I was too desperate.

"I have condoms," I told her, because I'd hoped like hell she'd forgive me tonight and would want this night to end exactly how it was going to.

"I'm on the pill."

I knew that. She'd already told me. I'd shown her my test results weeks ago before I ever made her orgasm with my fingers so she'd know the guy she was giving herself to then.

"Are you sure?" I asked, because fuck. Going in bare with Hailey? Never having that barrier between us?

Divine. My dick, hard as steel and so damn ready to sink in to her, almost wept with excitement. But her comfort was my priority. Always.

She snaked her hand in between us, wrapped her hand around my shaft, and I almost came in her hand when her thumb swept over my piercing. "Fuck me, Dawson. Like you mean it."

Shit.

I settled my forehead against hers. Our gazes held as I told her, "Then put me inside of you, honey."

She bit her lower lip but listened, and right as her warm, wet cunt began strangling the tip of my dick, I was the one biting down a groan.

"Goddamn heaven," I groaned against her mouth. Her mouth parted on a rasp, and she moved her hand to my hip. "If this hurts—"

She kissed me, pressed her lips to mine, and kissed away my warnings and my promises as I sank inside of her. Slowly. Inch by fucking inch, it took forever and was over way too soon before I was seated fully inside her.

Her fingers gripped my ass, one held on at the back of my head.

"A minute," she whispered. "I feel so full. I..."

"Hurt?"

"No. Not at all, but oh...pull out a bit."

I rolled my hips back, pressed back in, giving a little thrust at the end.

"Oh god," she moaned. "I am going to love sex."

I laughed against her mouth, pulled out, pressed back in again. Every time I hit the end of her, she groaned. And soon, we were working as one. She'd obviously had a healthy and vivid fantasy life. She'd always been confident regardless of what he'd done. It didn't long at all for her body to be trembling, for her to be fucking me, yanking my hips harder against her. I let Hailey set the pace, figure out what she liked the most, exactly where I needed to hit her inside to create the most pleasure.

And then I took over. I pushed off her, bent her leg. Holding one of her thighs out wide, knee bent, I could reach even deeper and once I added my fingers to her swollen, needy clit, I moved.

My hips slammed against hers, her pussy strangled my dick, and soon, all too soon, and not nearly soon enough, she was crying out my name, digging fingernails into my thighs as she came, clamping down at my dick, I forced my eyes to stay open, and I soaked in every beautiful second of her orgasm. The way her eyes clamped close, a flush rushed to her checks, mouth opened, her entire body shook with the force of her orgasm, and I rode her through it, kept going hard until right as she started to slow, I pulled out, wrapped my hand around my dick, and shot my release all over her stomach.

"I wanted you to finish in me."

"Next time," I told her, and I slid down the bed, put my mouth to her, and I ate her until she was pulling my hair as she came again.

Sated, two orgasms for her. When we were finished and I'd cleaned her up, I laid down on the bed next to her and pulled her to my side.

"You good?"

"I knew it would be good. That you'd make it incredible, but I wasn't sure it'd be that amazing."

I chuckled and gave her a kiss. "I'll have to work hard to make sure I can top that, then."

"Now?" She said it with such hope I laughed, but she wasn't joking. Her hips were pressed against me, already rolling.

"I'm going to need about a ten-minute recovery." I kissed her though, and when she pouted her displeasure, I slipped my hand between us, took care of her with my fingers.

Ten minutes later, when I could have easily gone again, she was naked, wrapped around me, one of her legs thrown over mine, sleeping peacefully.

CHAPTER 30
HAILEY

"FUCK YES, JUST LIKE THAT, HAILEY."

I smiled down at Dawson. Straddling him, my hands at his chest, I'd woken him up with my mouth around his dick, my hand at his balls, and as soon as he'd grunted, he'd hauled me up and slammed me down onto his massive, thick dick, that made my eyes roll back into my head every time he did it.

A week since we'd been having sex, and it kept getting better. More amazing. We'd barely come up for air last weekend, and I'd almost cried when he'd needed to head home and go work out for practice.

We hadn't spent a moment apart when I was done with work, and every morning, he ate me out until I came, and then he made love to me slowly, or took me hard, usually bent over in front of him in the shower.

I wasn't quite sure what my favorite position was, but it was hard to choose when every single thing Dawson did to me left me screaming his name and my limbs feeling like jelly afterward.

I was shaking, the pleasurable burn starting at my sex and working its way outward.

"I'm going to come," I warned him.

"Do it." He grabbed my hips, slammed me down on his dick, and lifted me up. Sometimes we had sex slowly.

Sometimes it was rough. He'd yank my nipples and slap my clit and smack my ass until I was a trembling mess, so much like now.

One time, while I was reading a book, he made me read the next scene out loud. He'd thrown my body to the floor and taken me right there in my living room exactly how the book had done it...but I was pretty certain, even as good as the writing was, my orgasm was still better than that heroine's.

God, I freaking loved sex.

"Dawson..." I licked my lips, my hips shook, and as I started to come, my orgasms blasting through me, he snaked his hand into my hair, tugged me down, and slammed his mouth to mine.

The change in position hit my clit in the exact right place, and I cried out my orgasm into his mouth while he kept thrusting into me, hard, fast thrusts that made me feel his piercing deep inside of me.

One orgasm rolled straight into a second and then he shoved my hips against his, seated himself so deeply inside of me I was pretty sure he went straight to my soul and grained out his own orgasm as his dick pulsed and he came inside me.

He was so large, I was stuffed full, and sometimes, the throbbing of his dick drove me even more wild even when I would think it wasn't possible for me to come again.

He slowly tore his mouth off mine, pressed his lips to my neck, and wrapped me in a bear hug that made me feel small and safe and taken care of and treasured all at the same time.

"How much time do we have until we need to leave?"

He must have looked at the clock, because his head turned and then he was kissing my shoulder. "Almost two hours."

"I should shower." Once I could remember how to use my legs.

"I'll get you a cloth."

He slipped out of me and rolled me to my side.

I unashamedly watched his muscles flex and his dick, still half-hard, sway as he moved to his bedroom.

It was Maggie and Davis's wedding today, and while only her sister and younger siblings were standing up with her, Eden and I, along with her best friend Belle, were all going to be there early while she was getting ready.

Dawson came back, cleaned me up in a way that was so gentle and so slow, taking extra time to run the cloth over my clit. My hips arched into him.

"Fucking hell, Hailey. You ready again already?"

He wasn't complaining. Dawson rarely needed the ten minutes he told he'd needed that first night. Maybe after our second round of sex, he'd need the recovery time, but never the first.

"I can take care of it myself," I told him and pushed the cloth out of my way and settled my fingers where it'd been.

He glared at me, but his dark eyes flared with desire as I spread my legs and bent my knees wide for him to see it all.

His dick hardened while I worked myself and he bent down over me, his hands stilling my hips with a firm, demanding grip. "Shower."

Those hands at my hips grabbed me, lifted, and he did. I wrapped my legs around his hips, gripping his hard shaft with one hand before impaling myself on his dick.

"Fuck." He stopped moving for a moment, and I bit down on his shoulder from the quick burst of pain from the angle and depth. "You're a sex monster."

"We can stop at any time."

"Never."

By the time the shower water was warmed up, I was still in his arms, rocking against his dick in short, hard movements, and coming for the third time that morning.

Which meant by the time our shower was done, he'd ensured I came again while he came all over my back.

"So it's not dripping out of you at the wedding."

Dawson had been worried he wouldn't be good for me, wouldn't be a guy that could be good enough for me, but as crass as that was, it was only one of the many reasons I loved him.

He was always taking care of me, in the big things and the small things in a way I knew that'd never change.

The wedding was over. Maggie was now officially Mrs. Hall, and when she and Davis kissed at the altar, tears had dripped down my cheeks. They were adorable together, Davis somehow managing to dip her backward and curling his body over hers even with that massive belly in the way. Maggie hadn't gone for some large, flowing dress to hide the massive pumpkin growing inside of her, who I learned earlier would be named Luella. Her dress was white, stretchy, hit at her calves in the front in a mid-length but left a lightweight flow train behind her. That sucker had been molded to every single inch of her tiny little frame sporting the massive stomach.

Like everything else I'd learned about Maggie so far, it was as adorable as the rest of her.

The ceremony was held in Cole's parents' backyard and once it was over, everyone had been invited inside and to the deck, where most of the men immediately went into action, whisking away the chairs, resetting them around tables and a modular dance floor was put in place. An entertainment company came, set up music. Lights were restrung. Cole's family should have gone into event planning.

Forty-five minutes after "I do's" were spoken, the backyard had transformed into a romantic dance floor and reception area.

Drinks were had, and I noticed Eden carried around a glass of champagne, but never actually drank from it.

The first dances were done. I'd eaten my weight in seafood and steak and a variety of veggies and dips and hummus and crackers and cheese and desserts. I was sitting with Dawson at one of the tables, leaning against his shoulder while his arm was draped over mine. His thumb was drawing lazy circles at my exposed shoulder and every so often, he leaned against me, kissed my temple, and gave a contented sigh that only further reinforced why it was such an easy thing to forgive him last week.

This was it.

He was it for me.

We were watching Maggie's younger sisters dance and flail their little bodies around the dance floor while Cole and Eden spun them around. Davis joined them, Maggie content to watch from the sidelines with a hand at the bottom of her round stomach and her eyes shimmering with happiness.

"You want kids?"

That came from Dawson, his voice a low rumble in my ear that made me stiffen with surprise. We'd talked a lot over the last week. He told me all about the conversation with his dad, how he'd blocked his sister's number and swore he was never going to see her again. And how he and his dad were now talking. Not daily. But texts were sent. I'd been angry for him once I learned what his dad had said. And mostly hurt. It was no wonder why he wasn't willing to trust me so easily and why he'd put a brick wall between him and others. He'd thought the man he idolized had abandoned him, but it was women in his life who had manipulated and lied to him.

But kids? We hadn't talked about that. Or marriage. Or anything long-term and permanent outside Dawsons saying he wanted me for as long as I'd take him.

Forever. That's how long I'd take him.

"Kids?" I asked, and the word sort of stuck in my throat.

"Yeah. Kids. You want them?"

I'd always wanted kids. Growing up the youngest of four had meant my house was loud and bursting at the seams even though my siblings had been older. Did I want that many? I couldn't picture it then, not at my age, but maybe someday?

"Someday," I said.

"How many?"

"You want kids?" I turned to face him. I'd assume he wouldn't.

"Never thought about it until right now, but Davis and Cole look like they're having fun."

I chuckled and kissed him as I laughed. "You'd be a great dad."

"You think?"

"Absolutely."

"How many are you going to give me then?"

The number no longer mattered. Dawson said he'd bust his back to give me anything I wanted, and I'd do the same for him. "As many as you want."

A shriek of happiness rang through the air, and I jolted away from Dawson's lips on mine, the look in his eyes to see Maggie throwing her arms around Eden, swaying her back and forth so hard it was a wonder she didn't break her back.

"You're pregnant!?" she shouted, and Eden flinched from the loud noise in her ear. "That's amazing!"

Eden laughed. "I was trying to wait until after your day, Maggie."

"No way! We need to celebrate this! Davis! Did you hear?"

Davis grinned at his wife, holding Martha on his hip and Leah's hand in his at his side. "Think the state of Tennessee heard you, honey."

She stuck her tongue out at him and grabbed Eden's hands, yanked her to the dance floor. "Let's dance! Everybody!"

Dawson's chair scraped back, and he had my hand in his.

As soon as we were on the dance floor, fast, loud, clubbing music going on, Dawson hauled me against his chest and forced us to move slowly. His hand was at my lower back, his other hand holding mine, and his lips were at my ear. "I want all of this with you someday, Hailey Parillo. A home. A family. A wedding and a honeymoon where we'll spend all week acting out all your favorite sexy scenes."

I laughed and kissed the dip in his throat. "Whenever you're ready for it, I'm right there with you."

EPILOGUE

HAILEY

FOOTBALL WAS AWESOME. I barely knew the rules, but every time I'd been fortunate to see Dawson take the field so far, I was absolutely blown away with how incredible he was. How talented everyone was. And mostly, how insanely loud the stadium would get after a great play or a touchdown.

Misty was at my right, Meredith at my left, and both of them were holding on to my arms like I was their lifeline. The screams coming from our throats would leave me unable to talk correctly until Wednesday.

"That's my man!" I shouted, throwing my head back to the vibrant blue Sunday afternoon sky.

"He's incredible!" Misty yelled back at me.

In front of us, Harrison Butler turned around and slapped both of his hands against mine. "One more TD for the books!"

Next to him, Sloane was just as happy.

We weren't sitting in Dawson's seats for this game. I hadn't missed a home game yet and didn't plan to miss any. Dawson had two seats for every home game so I could always go with someone, but today was the first time his dad could be in the stadium with us. Tuevo was on an away stretch to start their season and Meredith didn't want to sit home alone, so we'd purchased tickets for the five of us to all hang out together.

Harrison was a quiet man, and I often caught him looking at Dawson with lingering regret and sadness in his eyes. He came to visit as much as he possibly could and when I moved in with Dawson in July, he was instrumental in helping work with contractors to build me a workshop. He'd taken a two-week vacation to come help frame it himself. I loved my new space right off Dawson's four-car garage. One of the doors opened garage-door style for ventilation, but it was also a clear glass that allowed me to see the pool and acres beyond. It was also easier to load items into my new pickup truck or on a trailer than it was to work in the small room at my store that was now mostly used for storage.

My shop that went wild with customers after word got out Dawson and I were dating. That hadn't pleased me, and for a few weeks, my dad had insisted on either being in my store with me or having some of his retired police officer friends stay close. Considering my new customer base was women in their midtwenties, I wasn't all that threatened, but Dawson had agreed with my dad.

"Never know when a fan can go crazy, and I don't want you there unprotected if necessary," he'd said.

To say he was protective was mild, but I tolerated it because I loved my dad, and his friends always bought my lunch.

Life was wild, with a whole new family including Eden and Maggie and other team wives. I had no idea a football team would be so social, but Dawson was truly surrounded by brothers. Once Dawson started showing up more to parties or events, he realized life with a brotherhood at his back was pretty damn special.

Today, those were the most special because I was surrounded by all my favorite people, watching my man score a touchdown on a pass from Cole to secure their lead with only two minutes left in the game.

Plus, it was my twenty-fifth birthday, and I had a secret of my own to share with Dawson once we got to him later.

I'd decided to throw away my birth control pills.

Ever since Davis and Maggie's wedding, Dawson kept asking if I wanted babies. He'd somehow gotten the idea in his head that we had to move at warp speed to start our forever together. A week after their wedding, he thought we should go elope.

I'd held him off on that, instead asking for a date in public since we'd mostly stuck to spots near my shop in Friendswood.

He'd agreed.

A week later, he took me to a steakhouse on the top floor of a building where Maggie used to work, and in the middle of the room where everyone could see us, slid a house key across the table and asked me to move in.

That one had been tricky. I loved my little bungalow home, and I was proud I could own my own home at a young age and have a successful business. I'd held him off until the Fourth of July weekend when I'd shown up with my car packed with all my boxes of books and told him I wanted to start moving in.

The wedding or eloping had gotten pushed to the side shortly after that and it was then Dawson started pointing out babies and kids.

"We should get that stroller when we have kids," he said when we were walking through a park.

"That'd be a safe car to drive." He pointed to an enormous SUV when we were out to dinner.

"Cole said Eden is really enjoying her second trimester," he'd said one night when he got home from practice and thrown me over his shoulder. "I wonder how much more you'll want it when you got our kid in you."

The man had gone insane, from terrified of dating to wanting it all right away. I wasn't sure if a baby before marriage was the right move to make, but he wanted it. I'd give it to him. The wedding would happen at some point when it was right.

Life with Dawson was as simple as that. I wanted something. He bent his back to give it to me.

He wanted something—I gave it to him.

Right then, with the clock ticking down and it looking like our defense wasn't going to let Indianapolis get anywhere close to scoring, Misty and Meredith's hands holding on to mine, I wanted to get Dawson.

Throw my arms around him and congratulate him.

Take him home and do some things to him I'd read about in a recent book, where it'd start with me on my knees in front of him as soon as we walked in the door to our home and end with me bent over the kitchen table or couch.

Yeah, life with Dawson was pretty damn perfect.

We were in the team's hangout room outside their locker room. The room was set up with multiple leather couches, massive television screens and video game consoles. There were trays of food on tables and bottles of water and sports drinks. Arcade games and a few exercise bikes along one wall. This was where the team relaxed before games, hung out after. It was also where family members could wait for the players after the game if they didn't want to stay in the halls or if they didn't have small children in the connected family daycare area.

Currently, Maggie was holding Luella. At three months old, Maggie had started bringing her to the games, but left her in the daycare room so the noise wouldn't scare her. Her little sisters were running around, wild and sweet like they always were, and Davis bent over Maggie's shoulder to give Lu-lu, as he liked to call her, a kiss on her sleeping forehead.

Cole and Eden were there, talking, Eden's seven month pregnant belly round and firm in front of her. Cole's Nashville Steel jersey stretched tightly around her growing midsection. He bent down, tucked a chunk of hair behind her hair and whispered something in her ear that made her cheeks burn hot pink.

I looked away, waiting for Dawson to come out of the press room he'd been hauled to. Even though the coach had told him he didn't care much about what management wanted him to do, and since he'd definitely settled down with me, he didn't have to do them, but he said he'd play management's game. No way was he risking being traded now that he'd found me. I was thankful. I was born and bred in the Nashville area, and it would have killed me to have to leave.

The door opened from the locker room and Dawson strolled in. He scanned the room, nodded toward his dad and got a strange look on his face when he saw my friends. Meredith winked at him before he dropped his bag and headed straight toward me with that strange, tense look on his face. As he moved toward me, everyone seemed to sense the same thing and circled behind him.

"What's wrong?" I asked when he was in front of me.

Behind him, our friends stood, watching.

Misty's face broke out into a huge smile, and I glanced back to Dawson.

"Dawson..."

He wouldn't. He wasn't going to....

He dropped to a knee in front of me. "You didn't want to elope, and it was hell talking you into moving in with me, but I've waited as long as I can, Hailey Parillo. I want our life together, a home with babies and friends and family. I want it all with you, and I swear to you if you don't agree to marry me today, I'm going to lose my damn mind."

I busted out a laugh. Only Dawson could sound so frustrated about a marriage proposal.

"Dawson." I laughed. Started to cry.

He reached into his pocket and held open a box. "Marry me, Hailey. Let me love you forever with you being my wife and not just my girlfriend and give me all the dreams I started having the day I met you and the chance to create and conquer more dreams together."

"I love you," I rasped. His face was blurry in front of me, and then a cold metal ring slid onto my finger.

He scowled at me. Then smiled and shook my hand. "You haven't said yes yet."

I crouched down, settled my hands at scruffy cheeks and pushed them back through his long, still-damp hair. "Yes, I'll marry you, and I already threw out my birth control pills."

His eyes flared with surprise. Turned straight to molten with desire. "You fucking serious?"

"Let me give you that family you want so badly."

He stood, wrapped his arms around my lower back and bent down to kiss me as cheers and hollers for our happiness rang through the cement-walled room. "Wedding first. Then babies. Both as soon as fucking possible."

"How does Christmas sound?" I asked.

He slammed his mouth to mine, kissed me like we were alone and didn't give a shit we weren't.

And then he spent the rest of the night not just making my dreams come true but reenacting a favorite scene of mine.

Except it didn't start with me on my knees.

It started with Dawson on his and me on the floor of the living room before we could make it upstairs.

Second round was in the kitchen.

Third in the shower.

The fourth through sixth ended up in bed, proving once again Dawson never needed that ten-minute recovery period...

And that he was the man I'd always dreamed of in a way I knew he'd never stop being that for me and our future family.

Thank you for continuing to love the men of Nashville Steel! Risky Game, book four, will release on October 17th! Pre-Order it here: https://geni.us/Ay5Qeti

Want to be notified of all my releases and sales? Join my newsletter today: https://bit.ly/3nC4exd

THANK YOU

HUGE thank you to Nina and all the incredible women at Valentine PR for throwing your full enthusiasm and support behind me and these books. I've loved working with you and can't wait to see what the future brings us.

Ellie and Virginia, as always, thanks for putting up with my mess and spit-shining each manuscript until it sparkles. Thank you especially during this crazy time in our world for your flexibility and your extra hard work.

Shannon, you're the best. Always. Forever. Your talent is astounding and I'm thankful I can call you a friend.

To my Sweeties! I love you ladies and your excitement for my books!

To all the bloggers who devote their time and passion into reading books, book tours, release events, leaving reviews, promoting and pimping – you are all rockstars! Thank you for all the love over the years.

My family— I love you all to the moon and back. I don't know what I would do without you in my corner, cheering me on every step of the way. Your support is everything to me and I love you all with all of my heart.

To my girl crew— Tamara, Lauren, Niccole, Cassy, and Bree. What would I do without you ladies? Thank you for blessing me with your friendships. My life is a hundred times better with y'all in it, and a gazillion times more entertaining! To the SteelP! May we forever reign.

And last but definitely not least – to you, the reader. I'm blown away with every release how much you adore my books. You have made my dream a reality and I hope I can cheer you on with yours. Please don't forget to leave reviews on Goodreads or whichever retailer you've purchased this copy from. It helps us so much!

ABOUT THE AUTHOR

Stacey Lynn likes her coffee with a dash of sugar, her heroes with a side of bossy, and her wine a deep shade of red.

The author of over fifty romance novels, many of which have been best-selling titles, she loves being able to turn her vivid imagination into a career that brings entertainment and joy to her readers. Focused on sports romance and emotional, small-town romance, she also loves stretching herself in different genres.

Born in Texas and raised in the Midwest, she now makes her home in North Carolina and loves all things Southern. Together with her ultimate tall, dark, and handsome hero, she has four children. Her life is a loving, chaotic mess, and she wouldn't have it any other way.

Subscribe to her newsletter so you can stay up to date on all her new releases. www.staceylynnbooks.com

OTHER BOOKS BY STACEY LYNN

Nashville Steel ~ football romance

Sneak Attack

Time Out

Tight Spot

Risky Game – releasing October 2023

Las Vegas Vipers ~hockey romance

Final Shot (free on all retailers)

Game Changer

Dream Maker

Rule Breaker

Shot Taker

Goal Chaser

Secret Keeper

Ice Kings Series ~hockey romance

Playing With Fire (free on all retailers)

Playing To Win

Scoring Off The Ice

Hooked One Her

Hard Checked

Fighting Dirty

The Rough Riders Series ~football romance

Dirty Player

Filthy Player

Wicked Player

Cocky Player

Love and Lies Duet ~angsty slow burn, romance

All the Ugly Things

All the Beautiful Things

Love and Honor Duet ~angsty, romantic suspense

Twisted Hearts

Unraveled Love

Love In The Heartland ~small town romance

Captivated By You

This Time Around

Long Road Home

Before We Fell

Crazy Love Series ~small town romance

Fake Wife

Knocked Up

28 Dates

Weekend Fling

The Fireside Series ~small town romance

His to Love

His to Protect

His to Cherish

His to Seduce

Tangled Love Series ~erotic romance

Entice

Embrace

Enflame

The Luminous Series ~BDSM romance

Dominate Me

Crave Me

Long For Me

Just One Series ~rockstar romance

Just One Song

Just One Week

Just One Regret

Just One Moment

The Nordic Lords Series ~MC romance

Point of Return

Point of Redemption

Point of Freedom

Point of Surrender

Standalones

Remembering Us

Don't Lie To Me – billionaire romance

Try Me – A Don't Lie To Me Novella

www.ingramcontent.com/pod-product-compliance
Lightning Source LLC
Chambersburg PA
CBHW020012121225
36702CB00048B/896

* 9 7 9 8 9 8 9 2 1 6 8 0 2 *